THE ADVENTURES OF JACK THE CAT

- The Sewer Murders -

Book II

Sven Rodrigues-Wagner

The Adventures of Jack the Cat by Sven Rodrigues - Wagner

Published by Sven Rodrigues-Wagner

Copyright © 2022 Sven Rodrigues-Wagner

Sven Rodrigues-Wagner has asserted his right under the Copyright, Designs and Patents Act 1988 to be identified as the author of this work.

This book is a work of fiction. Any resemblance between these fictional characters and actual persons, living or dead, is purely coincidental.

No part of this book may be used, edited, transmitted in any form or by any means (electronic, mechanical, photocopying, recording or otherwise), or reproduced in any manner without permission except in the case of brief quotation embodied in reviews or articles. It may not be lent, resold, hired out or otherwise circulated without the Publisher's permission.

www.SvenRodriguesWagner.com

Copyright © 2012 Sven Rodrigues-Wagner

ISBN 9798357089915

All rights reserved.

**To all the Fans of Jack the Cat!
You made a dream come true!**

Prologue

It is a late night, and a black cat tumbles through The Five Streets. A disgrace for the ones who are still up and seeing him. Its head hangs low, and its black fur is full of leaves and dirt from sleeping rough. The cat sways from side to side while strolling down the street. It lifts his head, checking where it is. Shacking its head as if to clear its mind, the light of a nearby streetlamp reflects the green of its eyes. Its sharp eyes stare into the night. He needs to find his way home; it has been too long since he has slept in his own box.

He knows he spent the week indulging in his food addiction. His fellow cats bore his mind with the mundane tasks given to him. He's bored with being a leader, bored with fixing the simple issues of the many who ask for his help. He solved their mysteries, all of them. Nothing has challenged his mind lately. That is how he got himself caught up in a week full of gluttony. Clearing all his food places, eating, passing out, eating again, and passing out again. He did not care what anyone thought. He went as far as lining up at the food distribution, looking ragged and ashamed of himself.

It got worse when he felt Churchill watching him from afar with his one good eye, full of sadness, but he could not help it. He needed to shut down his mind for a while. What seemed like a blessing to solve his first mystery involving the fox and Thumbs soon became a curse. His mind is always asking for something new, something exciting—an excellent case to solve, a new challenge to conquer.

The only remedy to these thoughts he could think of was knocking himself out and giving in to his demon.

Food is a necessary thing for many, but a dangerous addiction for him. He spent days and nights eating, then just lying around asleep, passed out. As soon as he woke up, he would move to the next potential spot for more food. His black fur is ragged and dirty. He looks like a beggar working on the streets.

Many see him like this and wonder what he is up to. But no one dares to interfere. He is Jack, leader of 1st Street and the famous fox catcher, the one cat who saved The Five Streets from Thumbs and her plan to throw them all into war against each other. After that day, many used his new skills to find lost things, lost family members or whatever. But nothing came along that Jack could not solve in a matter of hours. Often, he did not even need to leave his box or Gina's house to solve his cases.

Jack shakes his little head; Gina will not like it if she hears about Jack and his recent escapades. He is sure Gina will give him a good earful the next time he sets a paw into her home.

They all are so impressed with him. So full of praise. They know little about his mind, but demand more and more every time. One case closed is just one more to file and every day, his mind asks for something else. Something better, harder to crack, a real mystery. Something his mind can dig its teeth into and hopefully, the bite will be too big to swallow. The bigger, the better for Jack. But no, for now he has to follow the demon to keep his mind quiet, at least for a little while.

"I need to get back!" Jack thinks. His brain is a mess, but a foggy mind is better than a never stopping and demanding mind. All he did over the last few days was to stop his mind from catching a clear thought. Jack knows he needs to stop right now with his devastating food addiction marathon, or he will get lost in it forever.

He stumbles around and looks up, unsure where he is now. The last days are one big blur in his head. His mind is silent if he keeps the delirious status up by consuming extensive amounts of food, eating until he knocks himself out. Jack's body feels awful after all that food, but his mind has no way to complain. It only complains in his sleep. His intestines are close to bursting, his fur is disgusting, and his eyes are watering constantly like a green-coloured waterfall. He took it too far this time. This week has cost him a lot. He needed to get out of his mind or lose it. His body had to pay the price.

Jack walks on, his paws dragging over the street, his claws scraping off the pavement making a scratching with each step. Jack neglected his whole cleaning routine for a week. Claws, fur, eyes, and tail are a mess.

The moon is up and shines its light on the small, black cat slogging its way along the empty street. No one would suggest this is the proudest achievement of The Five Streets that ever walked these streets. Right now, Jack is a mess, and it is all because of the lack of a proper challenge for his mind. His mind has become dangerous over the last few weeks. He is close to insanity or close to overeating himself to death.

Jack walks on. It feels like hours for him. Slow, tiny steps. One after the other. His instincts guiding him, Jack is not sure where his instincts will lead him. Could be to more food or finally home. His mind is slow: his body is slow. All he does is take one step after the other. Slugging on the street, he feels the rough pavement under his paws. The moon shines its silent light on Jack, and Jack walks the walk of shame. His unstoppable desire for food is only matched by his intelligence. But Jack has not broken the circle yet. Today, or last week, or whenever he chose the easy way and gave in, he found it more attractive to ride his demon to the limit and eat, eat, eat.

One more slow step, one more claw scratching over the pavement. Jack takes one more desperate look at the moon, his green eyes full of a silent plea to stop his mind from waking up ever again. A silent plea for a quick ending. No one is listening to his plea. Jack knows it. His mind, slowly but still intact, starts stirring in the back of his head. The food and drowsiness are wearing off, faster each time. Harder each time to reach the point of no return.

"Come on, you idiot! What are you going to do? Brave enough for another push to finish it all?" Jack mutters to himself and the moon.

Of course, Jack is not ready to take the last step. The Five Streets still need him. Jack's mind wiggles itself back into his brain. His mind taking over now, his steps get faster, following the streets, knowing where he should go now. He hurt himself physically, but now his mind has had enough of playing games and steps in, taking control of where Jack has lost it. His steps lead him back to his box, his home.

"Finally, home!" Jack whispers and slides through the small piece of fabric that serves as a door to keep the cold and wet out. His head brushes the fabric aside, and he enters the welcoming warmth and comfort of his box. He is back, and all he needs now is sleep after the tiring chase of his demon.

Just a few streets away, a small kitten is waking in the early morning hours. Jimmy is excited as today he will watch his favourite cat in the universe. Buddy, the big black and silent cat, was on guard duty last night and Jimmy will not miss the change of guards this morning. His parents did not let him stay up late to watch Buddy take on his shift, but no one can stop him from getting up early to see the guardian cats.

Jimmy dreams of being a guard cat, watching over the food supply at the bin storage. He will be a splendid guard, like a knight in shining armour, but better, with shining fur. Buddy is his favourite. He is strong and unusually big, and his fur is so fluffy. Jimmy adores Buddy. He takes every chance he can to see Buddy and follow him around. Buddy never chases him away or tells him to get lost. The others do. He is always tiny Jimmy, skinny and small, too small for his age. But Jimmy doesn't mind; he can dream big!

Jimmy sneaks out of his parents' home and runs over to the car park. He hopes he will make it in time to see the change of guards. He might tail Buddy a bit, ask him many questions. Not that Buddy ever answers Jimmy's questions, but Jimmy enjoys talking to him, regardless. His little paws fly over the cold tarmac of the street. The night is still more present than the morning. It feels cold and damp. The last few days, the weather has changed. It is getting colder now.

Jimmy looks up. The moon is still up, but the sun will soon be joining. It is the only time of the night or day where both can meet. Just for a few second the moon can look at the sun.

Jimmy knows the story about the two cursed lovers, never getting together again. Gina told him all about it.

Jimmy picks up his speed. His young legs carry him with ease to the parking lot, and he arrives on time. Buddy is still sitting next to the storage room. His chest is all puffed up, but Jimmy can see the tiredness in Buddy; it was a long, chilly night for Buddy. Jimmy looks around. It feels like it is only him and the guards. They would not mind him at this hour of the morning. They will be eager to change the guard and go home for some well-earned sleep.

Jimmy stops. There is another cat laying right in the middle of the car park. It looks like it is sleeping. Jimmy is surprised that the guards did not chase this one away. Normally, everyone should be home or be in the shelter if you have no home. No one is allowed to linger around the car park at night. Jimmy finds it strange and wonders if the guards have not seen the other cat. But it lays very flat on the side, not moving at all. Jimmy gets excited now. Maybe it is a spy and Jimmy was lucky to sneak up on it. Looks like it is Jimmy's lucky day. Not only will he be able to watch the change of guards, but he also caught a spy in action. What a morning!

Jimmy lowers himself to the ground. His little belly touches the rough street, his legs are all tucked in, and he sneaks forwards. He moves slowly, making no noise. He smiles to himself while sneaking. Azrael will be upset if he finds out little Jimmy caught one of his spies. Jimmy creeps closer. He can now see the cat's fur. It is brown and white. There is no way the guards could have missed that. Jimmy stops and looks closer. The cat is not moving at all. It just lays there. Jimmy gets up and sits on his hind legs. Something is not right here; even tiny Jimmy can feel it now.

He gets up and walks over to the cat, not trying to sneak any more. The cat still does not move.

Jimmy is now right next to it and his paws step into something wet. Jimmy stops and shakes his wet paw. The water splashes all over him. Jimmy lifts his paw to clean it but stops with his paw right in front of his face. The water is thick and drops from his paws. It does not look like water at all. Jimmy lifts his paws closer to his face. The water looks red. Jimmy sniffs the water and recoils from the smell. No, this is no water after all. It's blood. Jimmy screams as loud as he can. His little heart jumps up and down in his chest. Jimmy just found a dead cat in the middle of the car park.

The guards jump towards the scream. Well-trained cats, ready for trouble, they do not lose a second to think. Buddy pushes little Jimmy to the ground, his enormous paws pinning the little cat to the ground. A second cat jumps towards the dead cat on the ground, but he stops his paw from touching it. Its paw stops above the body of the cat and the guard looks up at the others. The cat uses his paw to touch the other cat gently on the head, notching it as to say, get up. The cat on the ground does not move.

"Something is not right here! We should get help!" the cat says and shows his drenched paw to the others. The cat's paw was wet with blood from where he touched the body.

Buddy nods and the other cat pushes the dead cat with his paw. Jimmy sees the head rolling to the side and the dead eyes of the cat staring right at him. Jimmy loses it and screams until Buddy puts his paw on the little cat's mouth. Buddy shakes his head.

"Be quiet!" hisses the other guard cat.

"Buddy, you stay here! I am getting Churchill; he will know what to do!" says the guard cat as he jumps away from the dead cat and into the night to get some help.

Buddy lifts his paws off tiny Jimmy and winks at the small cat—his way of saying he is sorry for the attack. Jimmy understands. Only your instincts keep you alive in the street. Jimmy clearly had none, as he never saw Buddy coming. He is only lucky it is Buddy next to him. It nearly makes the discovery worth it.

"What are we doing now, Buddy?" Jimmy asks the big silent cat.

Buddy shakes his head. He doesn't know. All they can do is wait for Churchill to arrive and tell them what to do.

Jack wakes up all snuggled up in his box. No place feels better than his tiny box inherited from Old Boy. He pokes his head out of the small flap door to check on the weather. The sun is already high up, and Jack is sure it will be another scorching hot summer day. Life in the streets has changed since Thumbs attempted to take over the streets for herself, but the seasons are still the seasons. For Jack, summer has always been his favourite. Long days and short nights, the light keeps the darkness limited. He wished this would be the case for the cats in The Five Streets and for the weather.

It has been over a year since the big incident that changed the streets. Thumbs is long gone but not forgotten. She shaped the streets, different from what her idea was, but she changed them all the same. Thumbs left the streets with no big drama. Since then, no one has ever heard from or seen her.

The same goes for her partner in crime, the fox. He went back to his woods and has avoided the city. Jack went to see the fox a few times. The fox was the only link Jack had between Thumbs, the fox and the mysterious Grey. The Grey has not made an appearance either. Only Thumbs mentioned him in her last words. A warning to them all, but so far, nothing has happened. The others hope it was only an empty threat from a desperate cat to save her own fur.

"He will come for you all! Be aware, very aware! You beat me, but you will never beat him!" Thumbs' last words ring in Jack's mind. He replays them over and over, trying to find an angle or a clue. Thumbs has not given away the identity of The Grey.

Jack spends many hours with Azrael. Azrael was now the official leader of 5th Street. 3rd Street got demolished a few months back. The humans decided it was time to rebuild the road between the houses and to build an underground parking space. They dug 3rd Street open in the middle of the road and left a big hole. Work progressed slowly as soon as the workers discovered the old sewer system underneath the street. This event resulted in the evacuation of the cats from 3rd street. The best idea was to merge them with 5th street, and it was the only a logical decision to have Azrael lead the new 5th street. Now he managed the spy network openly and officially, an endless resource of knowledge and rumour.

Both Jack and Azrael have spent hours trying to figure out who The Grey is and what his next steps might be. The conspiracy experts have developed theories. All from a human being The Grey to The Grey, never existing other than in Thumb's head.

It was a danger to the streets that needed investigation. Azrael put his best paws on the case, gathering information from all around the city. Nothing came up. No one had heard about this character called The Grey. The Grey is a ghost. No one ever heard of him or her in The Five Streets or The Big City.

Jack went to visit the fox a few times in the woods over the last few months. He is the only other lead or connection to The Grey. The fox lives secluded from all now. His experience with Thumbs broke him, but what changed him was Nina. Nina saved his life and forgave him. For the fox, this was the worst thing that could have happened to him. He was ready to die this day. His life had lost all purpose the moment he got caught. Thumbs gave him up and sacrificed him for the greater plan. The fox lost his will after Thumbs left him alone; he felt betrayed again.

After Nina let him go, he had to live with his choices. Now he spends hours in his den, thinking and talking to himself. Looking for salvation for what he did all those years. His bloodlust was gone, another friend that had abandoned him. He was a broken mess, but he was the only source Jack had. They spend hours talking, mainly the fox talks and Jack listens. The fox talks a lot about his past. It seems to Jack as he needed to tell what he did, who he was all these years. All the anger and nastiness had vanished from the fox, only sadness and regret left behind. The fox had no more information about The Grey or his whereabouts or identity, but Jack felt responsible for the fox. So, he came back again and again, often just to check on the fox and to listen to him. It felt right.

Jack is very emotional this morning. His mind is full of the memories of the fox, Thumbs, and Nina. Full of the ones gone now. Nina left them a few weeks after Thumbs. It was her time.

Cecile stayed with her until the end. She made sure Nina could go in her own time. Now Cecile runs Nina's Street. It was Nina's dying wish for Cecile to take over. No one disagreed with that. It seemed logical. Cecile is a born leader. She is calm and wise. The weeks she spent with Nina has been a good learning experience for her. Now Cecile is one of the most powerful leaders. She is a leader, and, like Gina, she has the knowledge of the healing purr—a mystical ancient ritual, long forgotten and discovered by chance. Now a well-kept secret between Gina and her few selected healers, Cecile works close with Gina; their friendship has grown and both work on making life on the streets easier. Food distribution and healing is the primary focus of the two.

Churchill, old Churchill, he is still with Gina, more than ever. Both admitted to their love openly now. Churchill, Gina's knight in shiny fur, has taken overlooking after the shadow cats—the small army Thumbs created. They are still here in the streets, functioning as the last protection between the city and the streets, in the same way as Azrael and his spies. They all work for the greater good of the streets.

Jack spent the last few months working on his new skills. The word was spreading fast in the streets about this new talent and calling. He spends hours solving cases brought to him by random cats. Mostly, the cases are about missing family members, daughter or sons, husbands and sometimes wives. The cases had all been straightforward and no challenge for Jack or his new mind.

He could always find sons and daughters in the Big City, runaways from home, following a dream of a better life or lured away by the apparent love of their life. As for the husbands and wives? It often came down to affairs and lies.

Jack enjoyed working on the cases, but his mind was asking for more and more every time he solves one. The mundane task of solving mysteries with a reoccurring theme bore him.

Jack remembers the last one that surprised him, woke him up for a bit, even proved a bit of a challenge. The disappearance of a daughter. The case differed from the beginning. It was the first time Jack got approached by some other animal of the streets, not the usual cats. Instead, a couple of mice seeking his help. The daughter had disappeared overnight and not turned up after days. The difference fascinated Jack and made him accept the case. He had to find a new way to investigate, new behaviours to be studied and understood.

Jack immersed himself in the underground life of the streets. He spent hours down in the darker world of his own streets—a completely new world to him. Full of dark sideways and dark spaces. Mice were the main population in these dark corners, keeping mainly to themselves, but he also found cats in the underground. Some working for the spy network as Jack soon found out, but others were part of an even darker secret of the streets. Life here was different. The mice showed Jack their home, the place the daughter used as her own room. He talked to many other mice to get a feel for them. In the end, Jack established that a mouse and a cat have more in common than one might think. Their lives are all about putting food on the table and surviving the day.

Jack found the daughter, of course. The story, in a nutshell, is that the daughter fell in love with a boy from the neighbouring clan and both wanted to give their love a chance away from the ever-fighting clans. They did not make it very far and stayed around the corner in one of the abandoned houses. Already getting on each other's nerves, neither of the two had any idea how to live on their own or be responsible for someone else.

Too young, too soon. Jack found the two arguing. They drew him towards them with their loud voices, close to shouting and forgetting about where they were and that they were trying to hide.

Jack welcomed the change in cases, but again, it was because of his intellect that he solved the case. It was a bit of luck and the inexperience of the runaways. Jack still learned lots from this case, especially about the world underneath his own paws. A fascinating world, one Jack still visits now and then.

Jack sits in his box and enjoys the moment of memories. His life had changed the moment he tried to find the food thief. His green eyes lit up at the memory of his first mystery. Since the fox, life in the street has changed, not only for him. The last few months showed Jack that there is a different world next to the one he knew all his life. A somewhat darker place, a kind of grey area. A place someone goes and finds out his worst nightmare. Some will run away from it as fast as they can when they discover it, but others embrace this different world. This new world fascinates Jack. Not that his own motives had changed to the worst, not by all means.

This new world, the dark place, as Jack calls it, showed him the diversity of the surrounding animals. How quick they can change if exposed to the wrong influence. Before the fox, Jack did not know about the hidden evil around The Five Streets. It had always been there, in hiding, but now Jack saw and felt it for himself, and he cannot forget about it. It is here, and it wants to come out and be part of the lives of as many as possible. Jack swore to himself he would do all he can to keep the darkness away.

The day progresses, and Jack is not willing to leave his box today. He does not feel like doing much. His mind is bored; his body is bored. Nothing really keeps him going today. Just another day on the streets.

Jack thinks about visiting the fox again just to get out of the streets, get some fresh air into his fur. Seeing the fox was like seeing an old friend.

The last visit, however, was disturbing as the fox keeps himself more and more isolated from the world. The fox talks now only to himself and ignores what is going on outside of his den. Worries brings Jack back again and again to make sure he is okay. Both have created a weird relationship considering that both tried to kill each other. One closer to it than the other. The fox tried to kill Jack physically, and Jack killed the fox mentally.

Though they are friends now, Jack is still using the fox to get closer to what really happened back then. He wants to connect the last view dots between the fox, Thumbs, and The Grey. Jack is sure this is not over. It was only the start of something bigger. But what? Jack thinks about the whole scenario over and over. He tries to find new hints by revisiting his memories of the escalation with fox and Thumbs.

Jack replays the conversations he had on that day and later with the fox on its own. Nothing new appears, but Jack is sure they can find answers deep inside the fox's head. All he needs is one clue to get to the next step to find the Grey.

Chapter II

A voice breaks Jack's concentration. "Jack, are you awake?" Azrael sits outside of Jack's box. "I need to talk to you! It is important! Something happened and we need your help!"

"Come on in, Azrael! I am up and was just wondering what to do with myself on this beautiful, hot summer day. Come in and bring me some news, old lad. I had a feeling today would be different somehow, but did not expect a stranger like you calling. Come in and tell me what is going on!" Jack says.

Azrael pushes the small fabric flap aside and jumps into Jack's little box. The space inside feels crowded with the two cats, but Jack did not feel like getting out just yet. Azrael looks disturbed. His eyes are wide, and his breath goes fast. Jack observes the Master of Spies closer. Emotions crossing Azrael's face are unusual as the Master of Spies is—well, any Master of Spies — always reserved and collected, hiding his emotions and intentions. A master of control. Right now, he looks like a mess to Jack. Whatever happened, it has shaken the world of Azrael to its core. The Master of Spies looks scared!

"What happen to you? You look like you faced the black cat and barely made it out alive." Jack is curious.

This day has shaped into a very interesting one. Jack cannot wait to hear the news Azrael has for him.

"A murder, Jack! We have a murder on the streets. The body was just found, and word is spreading at light speed. One of my spies was murdered in the middle of the night and they placed his body right in the middle of the car park. Jack, we need your help!"

"A murder, how interesting. This is definitely something new! How exciting! Tell me all you know, Azrael. Every little detail! Tell me!"

"Jack, do you hear me? We had a murder right here in our own streets. I think it is better for you to see the scene rather than me to tell you what I saw. Come on, let's go. I know you want to see the place. Let us not waste time." Azrael is already on the way out before he finishes his sentence.

Jack follows Azrael into the bright sunlight. A murder in the streets. Jack could not be more excited and worried at the same time. "I wonder how a place with a murder feels like. So exciting, it is indeed a splendid day," Jack thinks.

Azrael moves fast from 1st street to the car park in 2nd street. For Jack, it seems like a like déjà vu. The same place his first big case, his first mystery, ever started. It seems to start again with an event in or around 2nd street. It must annoy Gina to have another disturbance starting right at her doorstep. They turn the last corner together and stand in front of a large crowd of cats. The word must have spread like wildfire. Jack can even spot a few rats from the sewers trying to get a look at the dead body.

"Word really spread fast about this one. What have we done to contain the situation, Azrael? Why is everyone already here and knew about the murder before we knew?" Jack asks.

"A kitten found the body not more than an hour ago. I checked with the early morning shift at the food distribution, and no one saw the body. Somehow, the murder must have happened between the early morning food distribution shift change."

Azrael gives a brief report about the actions they took after they found the body. The kitten was a clever one and ran straight up to Azrael as soon as it spotted the body and the guards involved Churchill. Azrael came as quick as he could, but by then others had seen the body. It was too late to stop the news. Azrael identified the body as one of his spies and left the scene immediately to get Jack.

"It was the only thing I could think of. No one would be better than you."

Jack passes by a struggling Azrael. He walks straight into the crowd. They part in front of him, all the cats making space for Jack. He walks right through them. He can hear the whispers of his name, calling him Bright Eyes, a new nickname they invented for him. The cats move back into the shadows and watch Jack. Jack is yet again going to solve a mystery in The Five Streets.

Jack walks with his head high, showing himself to the masses. He knows it is important to show confidence. He is Jack the mystery solver, but he is also Jack the leader of 1st street. Again, both of his worlds are colliding, and Jack wishes he could just be one of the two. Jack knows which role he prefers, but giving up on being a leader is not an option right now. Again, he needs to merge both of his responsibilities into one. The safety of the streets is a priority, and if it takes Jack being the leader and the investigator, so be it. One day, he will leave the team of leaders and follow his true calling, but for now, he must be both.

Jack walks to the body on the ground with slow steps. He absorbs everything around him at that moment. His mind captures every cat or other animal around him: the sounds, smells, and even the colours. His mind creates a file in his head, something Jack can draw on immediately when needed.

Jack will revisit this moment in his mind and instantly feel as if he is there right now. Jack does not even think about this process anymore. It is automatic for him now; it all became more and more normal after each case he investigated in the last months. Now it is second nature to him. As soon as he enters the scene of the potential crime or mystery, his mind creates a special file. This file is then put into an extensive archive in his mind. They are all there, all the missing children, husbands or wives that ran away, stolen properties, victims, and culprits. All cases solved and archived like a good librarian for later reference if needed. The mind of a master detective. All thanks to Thumbs and the fox. And of course, The Grey, who or whatever he is.

Jack is deep in thought and pauses. He has reached the dead body of a cat. It is not the first time Jack has seen a dead cat, but it is still something different. Last time Jack saw someone dead, not by natural causes, was when the rabid dog caused havoc in the streets. He killed a few cats and hurt even more. It took a little army to take him down. Jack was young back then and did not see things the same way as now. Jack now and Jack back then are like different cats in the same fur.

Jack leans close to the dead cat. He inhales the smell. It smells sweet, not rotten yet. Death has not been here for a long time. The smell tells Jack the death must have occurred in the last few hours of the night, maybe very early morning. Jack leans closer to see the wounds that have killed the cat. Three deep slashes cross the midsection of the cat. The wounds are not bleeding anymore and the blood under the body is not enough. For Jack, it is imminently clear they did not kill the cat here. It was dropped here on purpose, but not killed here.

The slashes are big, too big for another cat claw. The rest of the body is intact, no signs of a fight.

Jack's first idea was an out-of-control cat fight, maybe rivals fighting for a female. Now Jack is not so sure anymore. The wounds are too precise and must have happened fast. The cat died suddenly and caught by surprise. It was a murder, not an accident. Jack walks around the body, trying to find some trace of how the body got here. The grounds are all concrete, nothing that would keep an imprint of any sort of paw. He looks up and around. The body got placed here with the guarantee to be found. Whoever did this wanted the dead body to be found. It was not a sloppy attempt to hide it.

"Azrael, come here, please. I need your help to move the body," Jack says.

Azrael looks at Jack as if Jack asked him to catch hot coals out of the fires of hell with his own paws. "No Jack, don't do that!" Azrael replies.

"Azrael, come here right now and help me move the body to the other side. I need to see what is underneath. I cannot move it by myself without touching it too much. Help me, please!"

Azrael looks at Jack with wide, crazy eyes. He moves closer to Jack. The cats around them whisper excitedly.

"Take the front and I take the back. We will roll him over on three, okay?" Jack instructs.

Azrael nods and takes a position at the head of the body. "1,2... 3" Jack counts out. Both turn the body, trying not to change his position too much. The body feels heavy, much heavier than expected, and it takes both cats' strength to turn it onto the other side. The body lays now on the open wounds and blood collects under the body.

Azrael inhales sharply. His eyes are wider now and he shakes visibly.

"Jack, I know this cat very well. It is one of my spies! It is Max! I talked to him just hours ago before he went into the Sewers for his shift." Azrael sits down, panting and sweating. He is in deep shock after he found out the identity of the dead cat in front of him.

"Out of the way! Everyone moves back and let us through! Seriously, what kind of clowder is this? Do you have nothing better to do? Show some respect and let us through! Her Ladyship needs to see the situation herself. Make space!" Churchill shouts, all over the place.

Churchill and Gina have arrived at the scene. Churchill wastes no time and takes control of the cats around. He tells them to go back to their homes, stay inside and let the leaders deal with the mess. Gina saunters through the masses gracefully, but her face tells a different story.

"Jack, Azrael, good morning to you both! Well, looks like it is rather not a good one at all. What do we have here, Jack? This is not your usual missing cat scenario. I could have guessed you were on the case already," Gina talks casually to him. Jack knows it's all show for the others. It is a big deal for all of them, but right now, the leaders must be in control. It gives everyone the feeling of safety.

"Gina, good morning to you too! It looks like an ordinary accident to me. Two cats fought, potentially over a female, and it got out of control. A shame, but nothing we need to worry about," Jack speaks loud and clear. He wants everyone to hear what has happened. A lie, but one that needs to be told to keep the calm in the streets. Azrael just sits on his hind legs staring, not saying anything.

"Glad you could confirm this so quick, Jack. Good to know nothing more sinister is behind this poor cat's death. Everyone please steps away, let us pay the last respect to one of us. This is not a show. One of us has perished before his time. We will take him and prepare him for the passing. The black cat will take him on her path now."

Gina pretends well. The cats disperse. Churchill moves closer to the three. They meet around the dead body, a close circle of cats looking at one dead cat. Jack moves his paw and shows the others what he had been covering. A written number in blood underneath the dead cat's body. A simple number one in blood. An indicator that the murder was not the key aspect. This is a sign, or better, a warning! They gave strike one to the streets. But for what and from whom? It excites Jack, the prospect of a new mystery case. His only worry is that more bodies will drop this time. This cat is not the last one to pay the price for living on The Five Streets.

Jack looks around the body and takes in every little detail. He will need the details for a later examination with a calmer mind. The other three cats stand around and wait for Jack. Gina, Churchill, and Azrael will have to wait for an explanation or assumption from Jack. For now, it is all about absorbing the environment. Jack puts his head low to the ground. He looks for traces of how the body got here. Someone must have dragged the poor dead cat's body here. They put a lot of effort into creating this scene, like the scene Thumbs and the fox created back then with the food in the bins. Their only purpose was to create fear, but now this one has a personal warning.

"One! What does it mean? Why now?" Jack thinks hard in his little head. But all he has is multiple questions with a few answers.

"Listen, all!" Jack speaks quietly to the three cats around him. "This is bad. I don't need to tell you this, but the cat in front of us got killed. What makes it so much worse is that they did not kill the cat here. They placed the body here as a message for us. Look at the symbolic 1 written on the pavement underneath the dead body. This is a set-up and a warning to us all. I am not sure yet why the warning, but I am sure Azrael can bring some light into this. Am I right, Azrael? This is one of your spies, correct?"

Azrael flinches as Jack mentions his name. "You are right, Jack. This is one of mine. Max was working on the sewer project. He went down there to check the many tunnels. We are still trying to map the complete system we found underneath the streets. It is massive. The rats living in the sewers are friendly, but cautious. They are shy, and we hardly ever see them. We depend on our own investigation and mapping of the tunnels. It is a whole new world on its own down there and I am afraid to say it also has a lot of new dangers for our streets up here," Azrael sights.

"Interesting, very interesting indeed!" Jack's mind races, digesting the news of the dead spy. "This makes more sense now. Someone wants us to stay away from the sewers. This is our first warning to stay away or worse, what will happen if we don't. Obviously, we cannot give in to this warning. Let me tell you, I will investigate the sewers now myself. Get everyone out there, Azrael. No need to put more lives at risk. I have the feeling this is more personal and directed at me. Shame, but this murder is creating the opposite result from what the person's intention might have been. Now I am curious and will be obliged to find out what is going on down in the sewers."

"Jack, are you sure you need to do this? I mean, remember the last time you got sucked into this kind of trouble? You got hurt, nearly killed. This time, it will not be a fox roaming the streets. This time, you will be alone in the dark down there. We cannot follow you down into the sewers. It is too dangerous. Jacky, are you sure this is what you need to do?" Gina says.

Jack is sure about this. He knows it is up to him. The sewers and what or whoever hides in there are calling for him alone. Jack must find the one responsible for this murder.

It is the only way to avoid further deaths. Like last time, he has no option. To protect the streets means to give his best. Jack needs to investigate this mystery. Like last time, he knows it deep in his little cat bones. But like last time, he has a strong team helping him in the background. Gina, Churchill, and even Azrael are part of his team again. Time to ask his last team member to join. Jack needs to see MooMoo, his most trusted assistant in solving mysteries.

"Listen, Gina, I am not alone. I have all of you. I know the places I must go to are only for me to go to, but I am not alone. All of you are up here. You are helping me. I cannot avoid the danger, to be honest I do not want to avoid it. It makes me feel alive. All these boring cases over the last few months, missing children, missing wives, and husbands. Stolen stuff. All this bores me to death. My mind yearns for a challenge. I dare say, this murder is the best that could happen to me. Oh, do not look at me like that, all of you! The attack Thumbs planned on our streets woke me up, and it is impossible for me to go back to sleep. I need this! Sorry, I know it is harsh, but our first case together never really got solved. The Grey is still out there, and he plans, and he schemes. I was expecting him to make his next move. I was waiting for it! This is it! I am sure he made his move, and he wants his revenge now. The Grey never stopped with us. And we, I am afraid to say it, are not finished with him either."

Jack points to the number on the floor. "Look at it, all of you! This is his sign, his warning. He wants us out of the sewers, out of the streets. We are the last that stand between him and his master plan. If we turn a blind eye now, we lose it all. Believe me! I know I am right. I can see it clearly in front of me. Stay with me as you did before. We can solve this, and we can protect the streets. We must stop him!"

Gina nods in agreement. Azrael, still shocked, looks at Jack with a blank expression. Azrael needs longer to digest the whole situation. He just lost one of his own spies, a cat that was under his direct responsibility.

Jack needs more time with Azrael to understand what the cat was doing in the sewers. They need to know about the last reports. Anything and everything can help to narrow down the search for the next clue. But for now, Jack will leave the three to themselves. He wants to see MooMoo.

"I will meet you all later. We have lots to discuss. Wait for me in Gina's place. Cheer up, everyone, this is not the end of it yet!" Jack turns around and runs away from the scene, leaving Churchill in charge of cleaning up now.

Chapter III

Jack runs all the way back to his box. From there, it is only a short stroll over to the garden, the place he can meet MooMoo. They like to talk and over the last few months, the bond between the two of them has grown. MooMoo has a lot of knowledge Jack still lacks, partially because of MooMoo's interest in human TV shows. She binges all the series about master detectives since she figured out that Jack is a much better sleuth than he is a leader of the streets.

Her strange behaviour was a torment, as MooMoo likes to call them, to her servants not owners. Whenever the humans skipped through the TV channels and MooMoo saw something that she might learn from and teach Jack, MooMoo would meow and throw a tantrum until the human would change to the right channel. It took her weeks to train her servants to do that trick. MooMoo took mental notes of everything she saw. Later, she would tell Jack about the techniques she saw. For him, it was a lot of nonsense to be honest, but it made MooMoo feel so proud that he listened with interest. A lot was totally impractical for their world. It might work in the human world with all the gadgets and rules, but here on the streets and for cats, things were too different. It helped Jack to understand more about himself and talking about it to MooMoo made many troubles sound less ill.

Jack loves talking to MooMoo. She always makes him feel normal. Not like the other street cats, always looking at him with admiration or fear. He differed from all the other cats around. Jack was involved in weird stuff, stuff a perfectly normal cat would not care about or understand. Often, he feels like an outsider in the streets.

A feeling new to him, it breaks his heart to see the place he calls home become more and more distant. Dark clouds are in Jack's head; he knows the future holds strange plans for him. He is still deep in his own thoughts when he pays MooMoo a visit. Jack shakes his dark thoughts off and looks around. Again, surprised that he entered the garden on autopilot.

Jack jumps onto the garden table and meows, calling for MooMoo. His left eye catches the fully loaded food plate on the ground. The Gracious Lady has not stopped feeding Jack. The garden is and always will be his favourite place. Jack knows he is in love with this place, and not only this place. But some things can never be. MooMoo is an indoor cat and Jack belongs to the streets. What both have together is special, both enjoying it but yearning for more, knowing it never can be.

"Hello, Jack. Thought I could hear your whining meowing from out there." MooMoo sits on the windowsill inside the house, looking at Jack with her big yellow eyes.

"MooMoo, good to see you! How have you been?" Jack plays casually, licking his paw while talking to her.

"Same old, same old, Jack. Not much changes in this house. Tell me, what is going on? I saw and heard a lot of noise. Something happened in the car park. Is everything okay?"

Jack is still amazed how often MooMoo knows that something is going on in the streets. Jack knows she has her own sources, not only him, but it still makes him struggle to understand how quickly certain news travel to her.

"A murder! Can you imagine that MooMoo? A murder here in our streets! One of Azrael's spies got killed and dropped off in the car park. How exciting, well how horrible, but I am so excited! Finally, a case worth the effort! I am so tired of looking for lost children or things. This is it, MooMoo! We have been waiting for this!"

"Jack, hold on. What are you saying? A murder? How sad! Tell me what happened. Tell me all, Jack!" MooMoo walks back and forth on the windowsill. Jack caught her by surprise on this one. News had not reached her yet about a murder. Not good, her network is normally top-notch.

"The spies Azrael sent into the sewers to mark and map the territory for us. One of them got murdered last night. Azrael wanted to be sure we have everything down in the sewers accounted for. His paranoia demanded that we have the sewers marked as our territory. But now this cat got killed. They placed him, yes, I say placed, in the car park for everyone to see. The cat got killed with three quick slashes, like a giant paw cut his side open. But no blood on the tarmac where we found him. Hence me saying he was placed in the car park. This cat is a sign. Did I tell you they painted the number one with his own blood underneath his body? We moved the body to the side and there it was, staring right into our faces, a big red one. I am sure it means this is only the first warning. A warning for what, I do not know. I will find it out, MooMoo!" Jack talks faster and faster. His mind is in overdrive.

He talks to MooMoo, but he revisits the crime scene, starts working on assumptions and possibilities. That is why he likes to talk to MooMoo, it helps him think. Being here now is what he needs to get his next steps in order.

"Okay, Jack. That is big! Wow, I just had my fur combed, but I can feel all the work was for nothing. Look at me, all my fur is fuzzing up! Jack, what do you mean it is a warning? Why? I remember some show where this happened as well. It was one of those old ones and the guy was warning this funny head with floppy ears on the side. I think his name was Sherlock or something like it. He was good, very good! You should watch him, Jack; he can teach you lots!"

Again, MooMoo references for Jack to watch something as if he could or even would make the time for it. Life is happening right here. He does not need to waste time staring at a screen through the window to show him a fantasy world. It is way more exciting out here, especially right now. No screen in the world can replace the feelings Jack has right now. The real world makes Jack excited.

Right now, he is on the brink of discovering a whole new world underneath his paws. The sewers! Jack cannot wait to get down there and discover what it is all about and why someone is trying to keep them out of it. MooMoo will not understand these things. The window between them right now is their biggest barrier and shows them both that they indeed live in different worlds. MooMoo lives in a world confined by walls and rooms. Jack lives in a world open and endless. No way they will ever get to live together as one. For now, it is good enough for Jack, and it seems good for MooMoo. Jack sits on the garden table and looks around him. The smells, the fresh summer air, and the sun warms his fur. His paws feel the wood. It is all real, this is true and exists.

"What is going on in your mind, little Jack? You have this look in your eyes. You are here, but far away. Care to share?" MooMoo asks.

"Nothing, my little princess. Just the usual troubles of the world on the shoulders of a cat!" Jack replies.

Jack does not want to talk about his feelings. He tells MooMoo everything about his morning and the ideas he has about why the cat got killed. MooMoo agrees with his theory of the cat's death being a warning to the streets. The number one makes it clear this is not just an accident. Jack continues to lie out his plan to visit the sewers himself, his eyes blitzing with curiosity. MooMoo is not as enthusiastic as Jack about the sewers, but she understands it is vital for the investigation. The thought of walking down there in the dark and the thought of the awful smells drives her nuts. She cannot even imagine what it would do to her fur being in that environment.

"You will be careful, Jack! Promise me you will be careful!"

"I will," Jack says. "I know it is a dangerous place to be. I cannot wait to get there!"

Jack says goodbye to MooMoo. He needs to get back to Gina and the others. Jack does not want to let them wait long. Jack jumps off the table and makes his way out of the garden. He feels MooMoo's eyes on him until he slips out of the garden through the small hole in the fence. He is back on the streets and his attitude changes as soon as his paws touch the hot tarmac.

The sun is now high up and heats the world. It will be a hot summer's day. Jack loves the long days of summer, keeping the shadows away longer. He struggles with the shadows and the things that can hide inside them since the attack of the fox. The pain he inflicted on Jack's body healed, but the damage it left to his mind is always present.

He walks around the corner and is on 4th street territory now. Following the 4th streets will allow him to get straight to Gina's home. He passes by the allotments that Cecile rules now.

A new leader with new ideas. Cecile tries to revive the allotments, but without the humans using them, it is a hard job as animals do not garden. But she tries, bless her. Her other ambition to educate more healers for the streets is doing well. Students have called plenty, and Cecile had to stop the rush, as it looked like every young cat suddenly wished to become her student. Having more healers took a lot of pressure off Gina. A welcome change for her and Churchill. Both could focus on other things, like each other. A long overdue event for the two. Jack still smiles when he thinks about Gina and Churchill. A knight and his queen. Finally, they got what they craved for so long.

Thumbs tried so hard to drive a wedge between all the leaders of The Five Streets. She would be well annoyed if she knew her actions resulted in the opposite. New leaders for 4th and 5th street, 3rd street destroyed. The bond is stronger than ever. The new leaders brought a different dynamic to the streets. A long-needed change to adapt to the way of living now since the city grew. The 5 streets are close to being absorbed into the busy city, no longer a slow paced, quiet outskirt of the town.

Jack thinks on this, wandering alone while his paws carry him to Gina's house. He needs the time to think, to sort through his mind and find the way into this new mystery. Right now, he still has more talking to do. He needs to talk to Azrael to get a better picture of the spy and his unplanned death. Just a few more steps and he is at the entrance of the tunnel that connects to Gina's home. As usual, Churchill sits in front of the tunnel, watching the day go on.

He still makes sure his Ladyship is safe, despite both having the same status now. Old habits never die. Jack can understand this more than anyone else.

"Jack, come on in. Gina and Azrael are waiting inside. Everyone is eager to talk to you about the murder. Any ideas yet? Care to share?" Churchill says.

"Not yet, Churchill. Let's go inside. The fewer ears around us, the better," Jack replies and walks into the tunnel.

The tunnel is still the place where the darkness swallows you after you entered a few steps. It puzzles Jack how a place can be that completely dark but lead to a nice place like Gina's home. The darkness and the tunnel are the perfect protection for Gina. Plus, Churchill is at the entrance, and no one can enter without notice. Now both walk across the tunnel, following the sound of each other's paw steps. It is only a couple of minutes in the darkness, but it blends out the rest of the world, a silent place, full of your own thoughts and sounds. Jack hurries to get into the bright lights of Gina's place. He is not in the mood for dwelling in the dark, not with the thoughts he was working with now. The light at the end of the tunnel is now visible and guides Jack. His steps quicken, and he rushes into the light.

Gina is laying in her favorite place, all stretched out. She looks up as soon as Jack steps into her home. Churchill follows a few seconds after. He always likes to stay behind in the dark, waiting and listening to the sounds. He wants to make sure no one follows uninvited.

"Jacky, my dear! What a morning! How strange to find this body in the car park. Would you have imagined something like that ever happening to us here? We are not in the city with all their crimes and violence. Come, sit down. I need you to take this case, but you know that already, don't you? I can see the excitement in your eyes.

You haven't been awake like this for a while. All these boring cases before must have numbed your mind."

Her words flooding out of her mouth like this shows how worried she is. Jack moves over to one cushion that fill the entire room and sits down. He tries to calm himself down. Jack needs to be in his respective mind now, listening and absorbing every spoken word. Filing it into his mind library for later, to be dissected and examined word by word.

"Gina, Azrael! Thank you for waiting here for me! I am sorry that I had to leave you all so suddenly, but I had to talk to MooMoo first before I talk to you all. As you know, this is a dangerous situation we have on the streets. This is not just a murder. You all know it. But let me not get ahead of it all. Azrael, please be so kind and tell me more about your spy. Why was he down in the sewers alone? Didn't we agree to work in teams down there?"

Azrael still looks shaken and uncomfortable. No wonder as he has just lost one of his trusted cats. He stares at Jack, shakes his head, and clears his throat. "I can't believe this just happened! Max murdered right here in our streets. He was under our protection, my protection! How could that happen? Jack, why us again? We had it all under control since Thumbs left."

"Get yourself together, mate!" Churchill says.

"Okay, okay, you are right, Churchill... Max was working on marking the sewers for us. He worked hard to have the 5 Streets mapped down there. He was passionate about this job from the beginning. The moment we mentioned it, he volunteered. Max had the idea to mark the sewers in the same way we marked our streets. Expanding our territory underground. He was obsessed with keeping strangers out of the streets," says Azrael.

Azrael continues to give a full report on Max's actions. "All he wanted was to make sure we are safe here. He was worried sick when he found out that we have a whole new world right under our paws and no one controlling it. I told him many times to stay within the vicinity of the 5 streets, not to venture out any further. Not for now. First, we must make sure we know what and who is living down there."

"When was the last time you saw him, Azrael?" Jack asks.

"The last time was not more than a day ago. He came up, all excited, as he found a new tunnel system. Max thought this tunnel would lead to the much bigger sewer system of the entire city. He called it our gateway into the city. All Max wanted was to find us a new way to enter the city without being seen. He is a spy, after all. Well, he was. The idea of moving inside the city and around it without being seen by one of the other gangs was all-consuming. I am afraid he ignored the warnings I gave him on multiple occasions and followed this idea. He must have walked too far off from our sentries. Wherever he went, all he found was his own death. Who would to this, Jack? None of the other gangs have ever been more violent than necessary. We got beat up or chased away if we entered their territory at the wrong time of the day, but they would never kill. This is wrong, Jack!"

Jack listens to all Azrael can tell him about Max and his duty in the sewers. The more Jack hears, the more excitement builds up inside him. The sewers hold a new mystery. He needs to get down there himself. Without a doubt, this is the next step for Jack. Going down there and seeing for himself. Azrael should have done this a long time ago, anyway. He was too busy with all the boring cases he had to solve to keep his mind at least sparsely busy. Now, Jack has a case on his paws that takes his full attention. Finally!

Azrael finishes his report and Jack has noted all the important little details for later. For now, he has enough to start his investigation. "I will have to go down there myself. Azrael, can you make sure the entry point will be open this afternoon? One of your spies needs to let me in. I need to see this place for myself. Someone wants us out of the sewer system. The quicker I can be down there, the better."

Azrael looks at Jack with big, shocked eyes. He thought his day could not get any worse. But now Jack wants to go down into the sewers, ignoring the warning they just received. "I hope you know what you are doing, Jack! I don't like the idea of my cats being down in the sewers. We must call them all back and I'll seal the entrance myself. The rats can fight for themselves. They have been down there for ages, anyway. Whoever is down there wants us to stay out of it! How can we ignore the dead body and message we just received? Max was one of us!" Azrael says.

"I know how this must look to you, but believe me, we need to get down there right now. Something is brewing in the sewers, and it will not stay down there. It will spill out into the streets quick enough. If I am right, we are under threat by none other than The Grey himself. This is Thumbs' last warning, the one we all ignored, come true. We need to find out what is going on or we will all be dead soon," Jack tries to explain. His thoughts are already steps ahead and it is difficult for him to stop and tell the others what he already can see.

Gina stares at both Jack and Azrael. She can feel the tension between them. It is time someone steps in and puts some sense to it. "Gents, please be kind. We all are in shock. This is not the moment to forget who we are. Be some lovelies and behave. Do not forget your manners. I will not tolerate shouting in my home! Both of you are right, by the way! We cannot ignore what happened, and we can leave no one in the sewers. Both is a danger on its own. Azrael, I agree with you, pull all your resources out of the sewers. Use the rats if you must, but no cat will stay down there any longer. And for you, Jack! I know you are on fire and eager to throw yourself into this exciting new mystery. Oh, don't look at me like that. I know how bored you were over the last few months. All this dull chasing after lost ones when all you wanted was the next big mystery, preferably with lots of danger. It does not matter to you right now who is suffering or has already suffered. You want this case? You have it! It is all yours! Keep us out of it. Report to me if you must, but I will not put any other lives at risk. This is yours, all of it!"

Jack is okay with that. All he wants is a case that finally challenges his intellect. Nothing mundane or boring, something with a thrill. Now this case is shaping up into something beyond his expectations. He nods at Gina to show her he agrees with her. This is all his and he will solve it.

"Very well, everyone. Enough of the talking. Azrael, if you would be so nice and have someone at the sewer entrance by tomorrow morning to let me in, I would very much appreciate it. For now, I will leave you all to your tasks. I, myself have some thinking to do. How exciting!"

Jack said his goodbyes to everyone and leaves Gina's place. The talk with Azrael was refreshing. It opened a whole new world to Jack. One he knew was there, but he never thought it would call for him to be discovered. A murder in their own streets. What bad times have come down on them all lately? He is sure The Grey is behind this. The murder is a warning to keep them out of the sewers. But why? This is the mystery Jack needs to solve. And he will!

Chapter IV

The next morning, Jack wakes up fresh and full of energy. No nightmares last night! His mind was too busy replaying the events of yesterday. The murder, the talk with Azrael, the discovery of the sewers and even the possibility of finally meeting The Grey. All was possible today!

Jack woke up exceptionally early today. He wants to see MooMoo before he spends the day hunting for clues in the sewers. MooMoo will be all excited, like him. She likes a good mystery. It keeps her entertained during her long day in the house. Sometimes Jack wishes she would just leave the house and run the streets with him. But this is his secret. He would never admit it in front of her or anyone. How would that look like? A cat from the streets and the queen? Jack knows a wonderful dream when he sees one; he likes to dream a bit sometimes. His dreams differ from his calculative mind. Here he can just enjoy a scenery without worrying about consequences and like in any dream he cannot influence the outcome. The element of the unpredictable is intriguing to him. Whereas the real world is all too predictable, too controllable for him. He knows already this new mystery is just the way of life to introduce change to their lives, the ineffable occurrence of change.

Jack's eyes are closed, and he purrs with satisfaction, savouring the last seconds of memory of his favourite dream.

He pulls himself back to reality. The temptation of escape is pulling hard on him. To escape in the world of dreams, leaving the real world behind. But no, Jack feels responsible for this world. It is his world. The streets need him. Later, he can escape and maybe a dream can come true. An experiment he will take on.

Jack stretches in his little box, turns around, and leaves through the small flap. He switches back into the real world the moment his paws hit the pavement of the streets. No time for dreams out here! Time to see MooMoo and check on reality. A murder needs solving. How exciting!

Jack inhales the fresh air around him. The morning is already warm, and the air promises another hot summer day. A nice hot summer after a long and cold winter. Jack enjoys the unfamiliar smells around him. Everything smells better with a bit of sun in the air. Jack prefers the summer over the winter, although a long dark winter night is not to disregard if you must hunt criminals. It adds to the mood.

Jack walks up the little path that leads from his box to the main street. From here, it is only a small stroll to his favourite garden. Nothing has changed here. The Gracious Lady and her husband still look after the garden and the house. Food is still available for Jack in the garden, and he is still a regular guest, if not the only guest. So far, he has not had to share his food with anyone else, not after the fox.

Jack slips through the small hole in the back of the garden and his body soon relaxes. It is a place of peace for him. Here and his box are the only two places where Jack can be Jack. No one bothers him here or in his box. These are the places he comes to think, to calm and fully open his mind.

Well, the gardens are not as quiet as his box. MooMoo is still present, but that is why Jack comes here, for the food and MooMoo. A feeling of safety and calm are welcome side effects.

The garden is in full bloom now. It is summer, but the lady takes good care of the garden. Fresh plants are growing; they spread out flowers of all colours in pots around the place. The grass is turning brown, not a surprise after the heat. But it is a well-maintained little garden. There is an outside sitting area right next to the house, well situated as the house provides some shade in the hot noon hours. The big table in front of the house is also Jack's food place. They place food under the table for him to keep it safe from the sun or rain. He also likes to sit on top of the table to talk to MooMoo. It brings them to the same eye level. This is where Jack sits right now. The sun on his back warms him, and he meows to get MooMoo's' attention.

"MooMoo? Are you up?" Jack meows.

Jack sits on the table and waits for MooMoo to respond. He knows she is not a morning cat. Jack is always up with the first light of the day. He knows, as the leader of the 1st street a day, has never had enough hours. In Jack's case, it is even worse, as he needs extra hours for his investigations. It seems everyone has decided it is his duty as a leader to offer his newly gained talents on top of his leader responsibilities. Jack tried to argue with the other leaders, but they would have none of it. Him leaving the circle of leaders is not an option. The streets need the famous Jack now more than ever. To protect and to lead 1st street. But for Jack, he wants to follow his new passion. His mind is starving for it. Every time he discovers a fresh case, no matter how small it is, it collides with his duties as a leader. He would love to be the mystery solver of the streets and nothing more. Jack would give up all his benefits and prestige as a leader. But it is not for him to decide. Not yet.

"Jack, what brings you here? It is not even daylight yet!" MooMoo yawns from upstairs.

She was still asleep in the bedroom when she heard Jack calling her name. Asleep or not, she will always hear Jack calling for her. But why did it always have to be in the early morning hours? The rest of her day will be a mess now. Woken up too early means a longer nap after breakfast, hence the brushing of her fur needed to be pushed back. And so on and on. Not the way MooMoo preferred her day to start.

"Good morning, my Queen! How was your night?" Jack replies.

"Don't you try to sweet talk me, Jack! You know it is too early for this. What is going?" MooMoo says.

Jack looks up at MooMoo, trying to see her cute little face. He loves seeing her just after waking up. Her face is her true face, no facade in these early hours.

"We have a new mystery to solve. I am sure you heard about it already. They found a cat murdered right in our streets. I mean, that is exciting enough to make me jump up and down with excitement. But this is not all. The body was a message from someone to leave the sewers alone. MooMoo, I think The Grey is finally taking the field. This is our chance to meet him."

Jack talks and talks. He gets so excited; he does not realise how much and how fast he talks. It is like all his thoughts are blurring out of him as soon as he speaks to MooMoo. He always stops at the right point, just before he would admit his dream to her. It is so easy for him to get carried away by just talking to MooMoo.

For now, he tells MooMoo all about the murder, the sign left and that Jack thinks this is a warning to not explore the sewers further.

"The cat that got murdered was one of Azrael's spies. The one he sent down into the sewers to map and mark the area right under our streets. We need to know how far these sewers go and how they may connect to other parts of the city. Someone does not want us to sniff around down there. I must find out why. MooMoo, I am sure it is The Grey. He is back after his trouble with the fox. My gut tells me it is him warning us to stay out of the sewers. And if it is him, for us to stay out would be the worst to do right now. I must go down there myself and see, feel. This is the big one we were waiting for all these months. What do you think?"

"Hold your paws for a moment, Jack! You sound way too excited about the murder. Don't forget, this poor cat was one of us. You guys sent him down there. The leaders wanted to check the sewers out. You should feel a bit more guilty about this death, don't you think?" MooMoo says.

That is what she always does to him. MooMoo is always good at pulling him back to reality. Of course, she is right. Jack knows that and cannot deny it.

"I know, MooMoo, I know. Sad thing, he had to lose his life. But can you not see it? It was The Grey's mistake to send us the warning. To murder one of us to keep us away. Or does he know I will come looking for him? Oh, MooMoo, the game is totally afoot now! He is challenging me! He is playing mind games with us. See how I already started doubting myself? Just by what he did?"

"Jack! Come back to me! Listen to what I just said! One of us died! No matter what the purpose might be, one of us got killed in cold blood. They will scare every cat in The Five Streets to death. The leaders need to step up and stop the fear from spreading. Don't you see? Fear is what The Grey wants, what he needs. Don't let him lure you in by thinking this is a personal challenge, his vendetta! This is so much bigger, Jack!"

Jack looks at MooMoo. How did she get this? He knows she is amazing, but today she is even more amazing, closer to being a mastermind like him. Jack feels happy he came to speak to MooMoo. Both of their minds together can solve everything. Not that Jack would admit it openly to her, but he always feels amazed by MooMoo's impact on him! Her words make sense, of course they do. This is a game well played on many stages. Jack is playing on one stage and MooMoo can see the other one. And The Grey seems to be the director of the whole play. He writes the scripts, and they all are only actors in his masterpiece.

"How do we get ahead of his mind games?" Jack asks.

"I agree with your theory, Jack. The sewers must be the place to investigate. One other aspect you need to be clear of is that the murdered cat was a warning. A sign to tell everyone to stay out of the sewers. You are ignoring the warning. Are you ready for the consequences?" MooMoo asks.

Of course, Jack was expecting this. MooMoo and Gina are on the same wavelength here. Both know that Jack's obsession with The Grey and this new mystery will put all the other cats living in The Five Streets and maybe beyond in danger. Jack knows this; he will do all he can to protect his street, all the streets. That is why he must go into the sewers. He knows to ignore what is happening below their streets will cause far worse. If The Grey is involved or not, is second to know. What is going on down in the underground is the priority.

"You know, you and Gina could be siblings. Both of you put the needs of all of us in front of your own. You would make an outstanding leader yourself. How would you feel about taking care of 1st street for me?" Jack is not joking when he offers his leader position to MooMoo.

He had been thinking about this for a while now. MooMoo would be perfect if she would leave the comfort of the house. Jack knew her answer before she replied to his offer.

"Lovely idea, wouldn't it be, Jack? Me in charge of all your shores and you are off and free to follow every mystery that runs past your little whiskers. No, for me, life on the streets is over. I am happy here. I like the idea of sturdy walls and warm heating. No one will get me onto the streets anymore. Not even you! Let's get back to the actual problem here. What is your plan with the sewers?"

"I have Azrael opening the sewers for me this morning. One of his spies will let me in. I recommended Azrael pulls out all his spies from down there, just in case. We do not want another incident. I am sure he put some sort of guard up at the entrance. Azrael is worried about the possibility of another clan using the sewer network to spy on us. You know how obsessed he is with conspiracies. Finding the sewers confirms one of his worst nightmares. Someone can move in and out of the streets without being spotted by his sentries. I am not sure if this is the case. The rats have few dealings with other cats. They still treat us with suspicion. The rats have this idea that we use them as an alternative food source. As if we have no dignity and eat rats!"

"The plan is for us to go right now. I just wanted to see you and talk things through. You are always good at spotting the unusual, and I feel we are missing something. I had the same feeling when we fought the fox. This is bigger, I know it."

MooMoo looks at Jack. How much he has changed since the fox attacked him. Now he is all about solving crimes. To keep his mind busy is more important than the streets. He lost his drive to be a good leader, replaced by hunting for the next unsolvable mystery. MooMoo worries about him. Jack is not a cute, small street cat anymore. He has grown into someone different.

His energy has changed and so has his appearance. He looks taller; his posture is stronger. Jack is more a leader when he solves crimes, much more than when he is back in his role as the leader of 1st street. MooMoo understands how much pressure it puts on Jack to be a leader of the streets. How much it puts him down, rather than builds him up. Now he is in his element, a crime that is so big, so new, that it requires his full attention and cunning. He is more himself than ever. Not pressured or pushed into a role by commitment and promises. That is what Gina struggles with. Jack is not leader material; she knows it, but she does not want to lose Jack as a leader. The structure in the streets is fragile. Leaders have changed already, and another change would rip the community further apart. MooMoo would not swap her place with Jack for anything in the world. His inner conflicts hurt her by only thinking or imagine them. Her heart reaches out to him, and she hopes it will help him find his way. MooMoo looks at Jack with all her thoughts swirling around in her head.

Her yellow eyes are full of affection. "Go, Jack! Solve this murder. Find out who is behind this and bring them down for good. Have a look into the sewers but be carefully. It is a dark place to be," MooMoo says.

Chapter V

A grey and black Siamese cat sits near the entrance to the sewers. His blue eyes stare at Jack with a crazy intensity. "Ah... Bonjour, Monsieur Jack! Azrael asked me to meet you here. It seems you require access to the sewers?"

"Hello, Lupine! Nice to see you! Indeed, the sewers it is for me! Kind of you to stay and watch in this uncertain time!" Jack replies.

Jack always liked Lupine. One crazy cat. He always pretends to be this strange character he adapted since he saw some sort of program on the human screens. A peculiar habit that intrigues Jack is the funny accent he puts on. He will inspect that habit another time. But it fits the crazy-looking cat. For now, Lupine is the gatekeeper to this new underworld of The Five Streets.

Lupine waves Jack to come closer. Jack sits next to Lupine, right at the edge of the street, and looks towards the entrance to the sewers. The gate had broken long ago; it looks like an entrance to a dark, unwelcoming place. No one ever noticed it before or paid any attention to it. It looked like a hole between the street and the pavement, nothing special. Now it is clear this is the entrance to a whole new world, and it stirred the curiosity of a lot of cats.

They had to put someone in charge of the sewer entrance to avoid cats getting lost or worse, other things coming out of the sewers.

Jack is not sure how they got past Lupine to place the body in the car park. Jack keeps a mental note to ask Lupine about that later.

"Look closer, Monsieur. This is the gate to hell. No living cat wants to be down there. It is dark, wet, and smells. A horrible smell. Allons-y, Jack, no time to waste. You want to be out of the sewers before dark. Believe me, you do not want to be down there when all the rats are up and hunting. Little they might seem, but do not underestimate them. They come in great numbers. Dangerous they are!" Lupine explains.

Jack looks troubled at Lupine. He is not sure if this is really a good idea anymore. Back at the dead body, it filled Jack with excitement to go down the sewers and investigate further, but now, seeing the black hole leading into the unknown is not very appealing. Something is down there, hiding and does not want Jack to come down looking for it. Jack takes a deep breath, calms his mind, and lowers one paw into the darkness. It feels cold, much colder than up here, and he only dipped his front paw into the darkness. Jack shudders.

"Lupine, how is it down there? Can we see? This darkness feels wrong!" Jack says.

"No worries, mon ami, our eyes will catch up in a few seconds. You will see as long as we have daylight up here. There are cracks and other outlets along the tunnels that let enough light in. Down there will be like night-time out here. Quick, mon ami, you do not want to waste the daylight. I will wait here for you to return. Not much more I can do, no?" Lupine says.

Jack smiles. The way Lupine speaks is just too funny, but it makes Jack feel better. He climbs down the hole in the street. Step by step, the dark swallows his body and Jack disappears into the underworld.

It is dark and smells unfamiliar. Jack's eyes are still adjusting to the fading light as he reaches the end of the climb. The bit of light shimmering that shines in from the opening in the street is enough for him to see. The hole is now merely a crack behind Jack.

Down here, it looks a bit like the streets, much older and humid, but at least something familiar. Jack follows the tunnel until his paws step onto a paved path. A trickle of smelly water flushes down in the middle of the path. A steady little stream of smell. Jack's whiskers twitch, and his nose wrinkles as he takes in the unfamiliar smells. Not a pleasant one, but it needs to be achieved and categorised for later.

Jack follows the path. There seems to be nothing else to see, only the water and the occasional crack in the ceiling to let some light in. Still enough for Jack to see, exactly as Lupine described. The path takes to a crossroads. He can turn left into the next path after a few more steps. Jack slows down and listens to any sounds. He hears the water dripping and flowing. Somewhere ahead the water is turning into a bigger stream, noisier than the small trickle Jack followed so far. The rushing water covers up all other sounds. Jack sneaks closer to the corner of the path. This is all very tense and exciting for the little cat. All his senses are on alert now. Jack nearly expects someone to wait for him and attack from behind the bend. The fur on his back is standing up, and his skin prickles. Jack knows that feeling too well. He is being watched. Jack jumps around the corner, a smooth movement, intending to catch the other one by surprise. Jack lands on his four paws, head low, and hisses. He is ready for an attack, but all that hits him is a lot of darkness. A lot of the same darkness. No one is waiting behind the bend for him.

Jack stands in the path, right on the corner that leads to another similar path. Water is flushing down much fast from his left side and combines with the trickle from behind him. The water smells awful.

Jack can see things floating in it. No pleasant things. Jack ducks as something bigger swims towards him. He lowers his head and hisses again at the unknown object in the water.

A black shape swims purposely towards the edge of the path where Jack stands. It bangs against the stone and bounces off the edge. Jack relaxes. It is only an old shoe floating along the smelly river. A sign of civilization in the dark, tinge catacombs.

Jack assumes the water must come from the human houses. It is full of human waste. That is the unfamiliar, yet familiar smell Jack could catch. Jack looks around. He stands at the crossroad of four similar paths joining. Three are full of water that runs down into the middle of the crossroad and down into an artificial funnel, created to collect the water and guide it deeper into the sewers. The path to this right looks dry, with no water flowing out from it.

"This will be my best chance, I guess," Jack thinks. But he is not sure how to cross from his point over to the other path. There is no visible bridge, and Jack dreads stepping into the water. Even though it is only a trickle a few steps back into the path behind him, no matter where the water is touching his fur, it will take a lot of work afterwards to get rid of the smell. The feeling of being watched is overwhelming now.

Jack looks around but no matter how hard he tries to find another way, the only way is to walk back the path he came until he finds a spot where the water is as low as possible. He turns and walks slowly back, keeping a close eye on the middle section of the path and the water levels. Jack is eager to cross and check out the only dry path of the sewers, but he is not ready to soil himself with the stench of human waste. He just got his fur clean after his last chase of the dragon. His food addiction got worst over the last few weeks and his body is a mess already after all the excessive food he ate. His mind goes back to the night before. Jack curses himself.

He forgot to make himself familiar with the layout of the sewers. He could have used Azrael and Lupine to describe the tunnels for him.

It would have helped him a lot down here now. He also forgot to ask for the marking system Max used. Jack realises how much the last trip down his food addiction costs his mind. He is still foggy and has not fully recovered. It gets more dangerous every time he gives in. Jack needs to be careful, and he needs to find a better way to keep his mind occupied.

He barely made it back to his box after his mind destroying food chase. How embarrassing it was at the beginning, but how quickly he lost consciousness and just let himself be carried away. This addiction will be his death in the end. For now, the case will keep Jack busy and his mind entertained, but Jack dreads the moment he solves this mystery and his mind chases for more food of its own. Jack walks the small path back to where he started. The dark of the sewers gets lighter the closer Jack gets to the opening. Just as he passes by the opening, a voice calls him from out of the sunshine.

"Jack? Monsieur Jack? Pardon me, mon ami, I could hear you strolling towards me, and must I say, how glad I am as it saves me from getting in there to look for you. Please, Monsieur, can you come out of the sewers most quickly and meet the Madam Gina? It is of utmost urgency, as her messenger just conveyed to me."

Jack investigates the bright sunlight. What a delightful sight it is after the darkness in the sewers. Lupine's shadow outlines in the sun. Jack smiles at Lupine's way of speaking. It always gets him.

"Hey, Lupine! Of course, why don't you come down here and help me up?" Jack teases Lupine.

"No, no, Monsieur. I will stay where I am for now. It is not good for my fur to get down there now. It would ruin all the work just done to my fur. Best for you to come up quick, mon ami!"

"All good, Lupine, just kidding. Make some space. I am coming up," Jack says.

Out of the dark and into the sunlight, Jack bends his hind legs and jumps up. Jack shakes his fur and stretches his neck. Just a few minutes down there felt like an eternity. Jack shudders. What a place, and he only saw the entrance and took a few steps in that all-consuming darkness.

"See you later, Lupine! I will be back as soon as I can. Lots more to see down there, but better not to let her Ladyship wait!" Jack nods to Lupine and runs off to see Gina.

Chapter VI

Jack runs up the street, no time to waste. He runs past empty streets, no cats or humans to see. Jack looks left and right, but he is all alone on the streets. Jack's fur goes up and stays up in many places. His senses are all on alert as he picks up a strange atmosphere. This is not a normal day. He sees hardly anyone until he reaches Gina's home. There are cats sitting in front of Gina's home, waiting for some sort of news. The cats are all nervous, moving around, hissing at each other. Hushed voices travel over the place.

"It only kills the humans, apparently. We have nothing to worry about!"

"Gina and the rest will know what to do."

"The humans deserve it!"

Jack wonders what is going on. He had left The Five Streets just for a few minutes to inspect the sewers, and now it feels and looks like the world has changed somehow. All the cats are here, anxious and many of them terrified. Jack makes his way through the cats.

"Looks, it is Jack! He will know!" one cats says and point in Jack's direction.

Jack looks at the cat and raises his eyebrow. "Excuse me, let me pass, please. I need to see Gina," Jack shouts.

Finally, Jack makes it past the many cats in front of Gina's home. He spots a familiar face at the entrance of the tunnel that connects Gina's house with the street.

Churchill stands guard and gestures to Jack to move into the tunnel.

"What is going on, Churchill?" Jack asks.

"Better to go right in, Jack. Better to go right in and listen to the news. Tell you, this is something never been. Better go in and see or hear for yourself," Churchill whispers, with a look on his face that worries Jack even more.

Jack jumps right into the tunnel. Darkness engulfs him instantly. A different darkness, not like what he experienced in the sewers. It is as if the darkness has many faces, depending on who sits on the other end of the darkness or in the darkness. Jack shudders again. This is getting stranger and weirder by the minute. He runs through the short tunnel and enters Gina's home; a feeling of dread and urgency pushes him through the dark tunnel.

The moment Jack leaves the darkness of the tunnel and he enters Gina's home, a wave of calmness floats over him. It still amazes Jack how this place makes him always feel like coming home. Gina's place is full of a welcoming, calm energy. The layout of the collapsed old shed amplifies the energy. The place has absorbed Gina's calm attitude. She decorated the whole place with a collection of colourful rugs and pillows, all spread out over the floor. Every time Jack arrives here, his mind calms a little and enjoys the silence. Not for long, but a little. The only disturbance of the calmness today is that all the leaders are in the same room.

They all are here: Cecile, Azrael, and Gina. The only one missing is Churchill, but he will not leave his post at the entrance of the tunnel. Not with that many cats in front of his Ladyship's place. He will watch and guard.

Jack is now sure something big has happened, and it has nothing to do with the murder they discovered earlier. Azrael is pacing nervously up and down, only stopping to wipe his head with a paw as to chase away bad thoughts, a nervous tick Jack discovered about Azrael whenever he feels under pressure. Cecile lays next to Gina; she is so like Gina. Younger still, but with the same calm attitude, the perfect student of Gina in all ways. Healing, leadership, and calmness. Jack is happy that Cecile joined them to lead the streets. The four of them, well, five if you count Churchill into the mix, rarely argue or debate. The atmosphere of the whole leadership council has changed to the better with the departure of Thumbs. Nina and Old Boy would be proud of them if they could see how the leadership is running the streets now. A harmony and logical approach are now guiding The Five Streets.

"Jacky! Darling! There you are!" Gina greets him.

"Gina!" Jack replies short of breath and walks over to Gina to rub his head against hers. A sign of deep respect and affection. Gina returns the head rub with a smile.

Jack looks around and greets the other two with a kind nod. Jack is curious about what is going on. His mind needs to know. This must be big!

"What is the matter, Gina? Lupine told me you want to see me, and I came as quick as I could. Azrael, Cecile, good to see you two! How are things?" Jack says.

"Azrael, be a sweetheart. Tell Jack what just came through the news, please. It might be good for all of us to hear it again. It all sounds rather disturbing and unreal," Gina says.

Jack looks at Azrael with wide eyes. "What is going on?"

Azrael stops pacing around. He sits still for a second, collecting his thoughts. "Jack, this is something. You would not believe it.

My spies were on duty as usual. Our media team was scanning the windows to catch the latest news on the human screens. We try to keep on top of the human news as well. I am not sure if you noticed, but a lot of what they do affects our life as well. I know they are humans, but they also decide about these streets, this city. Remember how we found out what will happen to 3rd Street? This one is way bigger! Funny, the one who got us the news first was Tabs. You remember him? Chubby, ginger fellow? Came to us at the same time Thumbs left. He is an excellent spy. Lots of experience from The Big City," Azrael chats on.

"Azrael, sweetie, please, you are getting a bit too chatty. Please keep it short. We have lots to discuss and time is not on our site," Gina pulls Azrael back.

"Yes, well, sorry Gina. This is so exciting, not so devastating. Never seen before in my life. Biggest news ever that travelled through the windows of the human world. Okay, okay. Here it comes, Jack. The humans have encountered a deadly virus. The entire city is in a sort of lockdown. No one can leave the house. Can you imagine, Jack? No humans on the streets, in the parks, in the shops. Nowhere! They are all confined to their homes. And the best of it, the virus is only affecting humans. No reports show it attacks animals. This is it, Jack; we are now ruling The Five Streets. It is all ours! How exciting is this? I know bad, terrible for the humans. But think about the opportunity for us!" Azrael stops to catch his breath. Jack has not seen him that excited ever.

"What Azrael says is right, Jack." Cecile chimes in.

"The humans are implementing the lockdown process as we speak. Azrael sent out some spies to check the area and shops are closed and people are rushing home. This is an unpredictable time and a very hard time for any healer in the city, no matter if human or animal. I cannot imagine the situation if the virus would attack us instead of the humans. We need to be on guard and prepared for the worst."

"Azrael, thank you for sharing the news with me. Cecile, I understand your concerns, but we also must deal with a murderer in our midst. We cannot forget the dead cat from this morning. The murder on its own is a bad thing; we cannot ignore it. I understand the circumstances have changed and we need to protect The Five Streets from the virus, but we also need to make sure the murderer is not getting away," Jack says.

Gina has been silent the whole time. Now all three of them look at her. Gina always knows more than the rest of them. It is as if Gina has a connection to a different source sometimes. Nothing physical, more spiritual. Maybe due to all the healing she has done with using the old way of healing has opened something else inside her. Now they need her view of the situation and guidance.

"You all are right. Sadly, this is beyond anything we know. A murder in our own streets is bad enough, but a pandemic outbreak at the same time is not what we need right now. Many will try to take the chance to do something stupid. I think the first thing we need to do is tell everyone what is going on. I mean both the murder and the virus. Let's get all the cats in The Five Streets behind us. We need to make clear this is not a time for riots or violence. Second, we need to secure our food supplies. With the humans being confined to their houses, food will become a problem. Lots of other things will not happen for maybe a long time. We need to be prepared and ready. Nothing worries the cats in The Five Streets more than food or the potential absence of food. We need to show control and calmness, or we will loss both. If we lose the streets, we will lose it all."

Gina looks at Jack, and Jack understands the message Gina gives without words. Jack needs to step up again to be a leader, the front of all of them. He is the famous one and the cats will listen to his words. Jack does not like it. He hates public engagements. He'd rather would crawl back into that sewer and finish his investigation. But again, being a leader collides with his favourite newly discovered talent for solving mysteries. But having the humans off the streets is indeed a danger that cannot be ignored.

"Okay, let's decide. How do we want to play this? As Gina said, we need to be quick in addressing this virus malarkey to the all the cats. How shall we handle this? Any ideas?" Jack says.

"Don't mind me," a voice says from the tunnel entrance as Churchill walks in. "Just letting you all know we have a sizeable crowd out there. All waiting to hear what is going on. Many cats and other small vermin too. Looks like this brings everyone together. My Lady, shall I disperse them? Sending them home? It makes me itchy having them so close to our home." Churchill sits at the entrance of the tunnel, his tail wagging around, showing his discomfort at interrupting the others.

"Thank you, Churchill! No need to apologise. Be so kind and let everyone stay where they are. We will speak to them all in a minute. Let's make use of the crowd to spread the word. Jack, you know it will be you this time telling them all what is going on. They all know you. You are the fox catcher. You helped many of them already by finding their lost ones or lost stuff. I know you dislike the jobs they gave you. For you, they are annoying little time wasters, but for them you are a remarkable cat. Do not forget, they are still your responsibility. Chasing your dream will have to wait. For now, we all need to step up and be the leaders The Five Streets are asking for," Gina says aloud what Jack would only dare to think. "Let's put our heads together for a few minutes and create a gracious speech for our famous cat here," Gina says, and winks at Jack.

Jack looks at Gina in surprise. He lays down and puts his paws under his body. He does not like it but must do it. Jack's head slumps down on his chest and he listens to the others drafting his speech, dreading every minute. Public speaking is his least favourite responsibility as a leader of the streets. Funny enough, it does not bother him giving his deductions and conclusions in front of everyone when solving a mystery. Jack the leader and Jack the mystery solver is like two different cats. Jack has the strong feeling that he needs to decide which cat he wants to be soon.

Gina, Azrael, and Cecile sit closely together, discussing the details of the speech. They want to make sure the speech is motivating but also a warning. It is crucial that the message delivers both.

A panic needs to be avoided at all costs, but it also needs to be clear that this is a strange and unpredictable time for everyone in The Five Streets.

"Jacky, darling, come over here. Stop sulking in the corner. We know you don't like it, but we need you right now. You need to be the leader of 1st Street. After that, you can go back and investigate this ghastly murder. I know that is what you want, but not everyone always gets what they want. Be a good boy now and come here. We have a nice little speech for you. Nothing too complicated. Let's prep you so you can deliver!" Gina says.

Azrael nods his agreement, but his eyes tell Jack he totally understands Jack's resistance. "Jack, come on. Let's get this done with. The crowd is waiting outside," Azrael says.

"Thank you for pointing out the crowd, Azrael!" Jack replies.

Gina smiles at Jack, trying to give him some comfort for his next task. Jack will address the crowd of cats outside and will give them the feeling that all is okay and under control. "Let's go all! Time to deliver the show to the masses!"

Azrael, Gina, and Cecile get up as one, and they make their way towards the tunnel. The darkness swallows them fast. Jack watches them leave. He is not ready yet. He needs a few more minutes to collect himself. Jack plays the staged message in his head over and over. He tries to expect the reactions of the crowd in advance. He creates a full detailed rundown of the expected show in his mind, dissecting the possible different scenarios, preparing replies and reassurances for the potential challenges he will receive during his speech. He knows there will be some cats who will try to challenge the plan the leaders will propose about how to handle the human virus situation. He imagines the responses in his head; he knows them already.

His mind is racing, indulging in the challenge ahead. At least one part of him seems to enjoy the challenge. A bigger part of his mind is still dreading the public display.

The only way for him to handle this is to see it as a matter of solving a mystery or a crime. Putting himself in the right mood, forgetting about being a leader and using the new him in this situation. Being a leader is fine, but he does not feel like one anymore. His subconscious mind is already a step ahead, the rest of him just needs to catch up. Jack gets up, stretches his hind legs first, bends his back, and stretches his front legs.

"Better to get on with it!" he mutters to himself.

"Jacky, darling? Don't let us wait here in the dark. Come on!" Gina calls out of the dark to him.

Jack drops his head and a deep sigh escapes him. He looks up quick; he hopes no one heard it. "Out of my way!" he shouts into the dark and follows the other leaders in the tunnel's darkness, Churchill's eyes following them.

Churchill sat still in the dark corner since he arrived and told the others about the crowd and the change in mood outside. But after that, he felt like Gina and the rest totally forgot about him.

They only focused on the speech they had to deliver and how to calm the cats of The Five Streets. Churchill saw the inner battle on Jack's face when Jack thought he was all alone.

Churchill kind of understands the conflict Jack goes through. Dropped on the streets with nothing else on him, only his own fur. Jack being picked up and raised by Old Boy, too soon left alone again, and put into the situation of accepting the leadership of 1st Street. And now, Jack has discovered his true calling. The true calling that collides so much with his responsibilities as leader.

A sad step of fate for Jack. Jack needs to find the courage to make a final decision soon. Churchill knows what he would choose, but he is not as lucky or cursed as Jack. Churchill never had the luxury of making a choice. He became Gina's number two, second in command, the day he laid on her. No questions about that and no regrets ever.

Churchill leaves the shadow and follows Jack on silent paws. He does not want Jack to know that he saw him a minute ago. This was a moment Jack needed for himself alone.

Jack enters the darkness; he can feel the others in front of him. His eyes adjust slowly to the dark. His other senses do not need to adapt. He knows they are waiting for him. Now it is all about showing a united front. Jack sees the picture clearly in his head. All the cats outside waiting, eager for the leader to appear. All eyes were at the end of the tunnel, staring and waiting.

Then, as if out of nowhere, the four leaders of The Five Streets emerge out of the dark. Gina, Azrael, Cecile, and Jack walk in unison into the light. Four cats, each different in structure and colour. Four cats respected and feared in all streets.

These four cats are the fate of The Five Streets. All yellow and green eyes waiting for them to be seen. Fluffy ears prick up, waiting to hear what the plan is. Jack feels dizzy. His imagination carries him away. He shakes his head, clearing his mind from the vision he just had. Now is not the time for his imagination to run wild. Focus is what he needs to show strength and assurance. All four of them. Jack stops for a bit, collecting his thoughts, and draws in a deep breath.

Suddenly, a voice behind him says, "I know, Jack! I know how you feel! Stay calm now. Remember the day we caught the fox and exposed Thumbs? This is a similar situation. It all depends on how we react now and how we present ourselves." Churchill walks very close to Jack. His voice was only a whisper now. Only Jack can hear him. "Be strong, Jack. We chose you for this moment. You caught the fox, you exposed Thumbs. You can manage this. I count on you!" Churchill passes by Jack and takes his place next to Gina. Now the five are ready to appear as one.

Jack squints his eyes as hard as he can. A bright light flashes in his mind. This is it. He is in the zone now. Ready or not, this needs to happen now. His mind focuses on the task ahead and zooms in on what needs doing. Jack is ready to face the cats waiting for him and the other leaders to make an announcement. He lifts his head, tail straight into the air and walks proudly behind Gina and Churchill into the daylight. The crowd's noise stops the moment Gina walks out of the tunnel. All that remains is an exciting, hushed whisper from the many cats.

Gina and Churchill are the first ones to see the cats in front of her house. The big parking lot is full of cats of all sorts. All streets have gathered here to hear the news. Gina and Churchill walk proudly on until they reach the end of the tunnel. Both sit down on their hind paws and puff up their chests, heads high, eyes firm. Next are Azrael and Cecile. Both follow the same attitude. Azrael positions himself next to Gina and Cecile, next to Churchill.

Four of the leaders are now visible to everyone, sitting and waiting for Jack. Jack steps out of the tunnel, his head held high, his tail straight in the air. His fur shines in the sun and his green eyes sparkle.

He stays right in the middle of the assembled leaders, Gina and Azrael to his left, Churchill and Cecile to his right. The cats in front of them get more and more excited. It has been a long time since they saw all the leaders together like this. No doubt something big is going to happen. Excited whispers reach Jack's ears.

"It is him, Jack!"

"Did you just see what I saw? It is all of them!"

"What's going on Daddy?"

There were many whispers, but all with the same sort of question, "What is going on?"

Jack looks around. He catches the many eyes staring towards him. It is a sea of blues, greens, and yellows. All cat eyes are on him now. His vision is clear and right, his ears are sharp, and he hears even the smallest of voices in the crowd. Jack feels the worries and excitement of all the cats in the carpark. It is overwhelming, but fascinating. His mind is screaming in happiness. It enjoys the multitude of other minds, all the thoughts that swish through his mind and the connection it can build by touching the others.

A picture takes form in his mind. The parking lot is full of cats, each detail captured. The different fur colours, body shapes, eyes, and voices. His mind captures it all. Cataloguing each cat in his view, filing them into categories and characters. Jack's eyes hurt; he feels like he has stared for hours at all of them. Breathing in deep, he closes his eyes and calms his mind. There is a second of complete stillness. Just Jack and his mind in unison. Jack opens his eyes again and tilts his head to the side. Jack is ready.

He knows the speech; he knows the mood, and he can deal with it all. His mind, again, takes charge when Jack feels the most helpless. He needs to trust himself more. The small kitten is long gone. He is Jack, and he solves mysteries for living. His mind is going to pull him down into hell if he doesn't have mysteries to solve.

Today is the first time that he realises that a mystery is not always a mystery connected to a case that needs solving. There are many more mysteries around him, every day, every night. He does not need other cats to ask for his help to find the mysteries he is looking for. The mysteries are always here, right in front of him. All he must do is decide what mystery to study first. The mystery of life on it owns. The mystery of the multitude of cats he is seeing right now. Even nature on its own is a mystery worth discovering. The sky, the rain, the wind, they all hold a mystery for Jack. His mind rejoices in this unexpected discovery. All it took was a deadly human virus and the pressure of public speaking to kick open another door in his mind. Jack is no longer the kitten he once was, he is no longer the cat he once was. Jack is now different. Beyond being a cat following its instincts of survival, Jack is now ready to solve the mysteries all around him. No matter if good or bad. For now, the speech he will give in a few seconds is another mysterious thing. His words have the power to influence the many. Just the words spoken by him will determine how the cats hear the speech and whether they go home assured of their safety.

Just words, his words, will create a feeling of peace and calm. The power of words is something Jack wants to study further. It is such a powerful instrument.

"But for now, on with my speech!" Jack thinks.

Jack takes another good look over all the cats in front of him, absorbing every moment in slow motion, filing details that might be useful later. When finished, he lifts his head and starts his speech, his green eyes reflecting the last of the sun, making them glow. He looks like a true leader.

"Hello cats from The Five Streets! Thank you all for gathering around. We know the news about the humans and the virus is more than frightening. It makes us proud to see you all so organised and calm. This is the way The Five Streets are. In times like this, times of danger, fear, or diversity, we come together. We solve whatever life throws at our streets together. We know the news about the virus is very scary. On the plus side, it seems only to attack the humans. I will not say we are safe. We should keep watch and be very careful about what we do over the next few weeks. Make sure you stay in The Five Streets. Stay with your families. Do not wander around. Let's make sure we keep each other safe. We—Gina, Churchill, Azrael, Cecile, and I—will keep you safe. All we ask from you is to be smart. Keep away from the humans. Avoid contact with them. I know we all love the affection the humans give us now and then, but keep in mind this one touch could be the one that puts your family, your friends, the whole Five Streets in danger. We do not know enough to say it is safe to carry on with our normal routine."

"Azrael and his team have their fluffy ears and busy paws on the ground, gathering all the information they can from the human screen devises and from the city. Let me tell you, cats of The Five Streets, this is a time of big change. We have the chance to make sure we are coming out on top of the change."

Jack takes a break, a well calculated one, to give everyone time to digest what they heard. They knew it, but they had to hear it from him. The moment Jack stops his speech, he realises something he had not thought of before. Misty MooMoo! How can he continue to visit her and avoid The Gracious Lady? For now, he must add the problem to his long list of problems to be solved. His speech needs to continue. He cannot lose the momentum.

"Listen to me, all of you! We are safe. We have enough food to cover for weeks without starving. Everyone has a place to stay, and we have each other. Cecile and her team are ready to deal with any discomfort or fear. If you feel overwhelmed, see either Cecile or one of her healers. We are here for you. You might feel these restrictions are too much, but we decided in the best interested of the streets to better be careful rather than regretful. We do not know how the next few days will be. Expect the worst from the humans. We know they tend to choose and show the worst behaviour. Stay away from humans, stay home, protect The Five Streets! Now go home, spread the word, make sure everyone knows what we expect from each one of us over the next few days. We will call again for a gathering as soon as we have more information." Jack finishes his speech with what he hopes is an encouraging smile.

Gina gives her nod of approval. He did well. The crowd disperses immediately after Jack tells them to go home. A good sign! No one challenged the imposed restrictions. No one panicked or got angry. In the end, all the leaders asked for was to stay home, stay in the streets. Few cats would leave anyway. The young ones would venture out into the city now and then, but The Five Streets has few young ones left lately. Another problem in the making, perhaps.

For now, it looks like the message has reached the cats and they accepted it. It needs to be seen what the next few days will bring.

All they must worry about now is what the humans are doing and how it will affect life on the streets.

All the leaders wait outside of Gina's home until the last cat has left the car park. They sit and watch, showing confidence and control until the end. Gina moves back into the tunnel as soon as the last cat turns around the corner and out of sight. For Gina, staying out in the open for that long is pure agony. Her fear of the open sky drives her insane, but she is mentally strong enough to fight the fear for the sake of The Five Streets. Another little mystery Jack has on his list. One day, he will ask Gina about that fear and the story that comes with it. The others follow Gina inside. They need to discuss the next steps. For Jack, it only matters that they find a murderer, but now it looks like they need to focus on solving two mysteries. How peculiar the day has become.

While Gina, Azrael, and Cecile debate the next steps regarding the new virus, Churchill keeps himself back in the tunnel. He wants to make sure no cat tries something funny out of panic. Churchill has seen it all in his lifetime and always expects the worst. And to be honest, he knows the others will be fine without his input. He is not a full leader of the streets, just a consort and protector of one of them. His one and only love, Gina. He lays down and enjoys the darkness that covers him, his one eye sparkling softly in the dark while he admires Gina from afar.

Jack is only half listening to the discussion Gina and Azrael are having. His mind is already back to the murder case. Having the streets deserted is perfect for his investigation. No one will disturb him or destroy vital tracks. All he wants is to get back into that sewer, to look for more traces or evidence. Someone down there must know something about the murder.

"Say. Azrael, what do we know about the animals living down there in the sewers?" Jack asks.

Azrael and Gina stop in their discussion and look at Jack. They both look confused about his question. "Sorry, Jack, what does that have to do with the virus?" Azrael asks back.

"Nothing, my old friend. Let me remind you, there is still a murderer out there. We cannot do anything against the virus, but we can do something about the murderer, like catch him, for example. Never mind the danger of the virus, we will have to deal with it if it becomes a real danger for us cats. For now, it is a problem the humans must get on with. Our problem is the dead cat, killed in our streets, by someone unknown. Can you imagine a murderer in our streets, running loose? Fear and panic are already on a new high. For the moment, the news of the virus distracts the cats out there, but they soon will remember the murder as well. What do we do then? Just think about how the cats will feel, isolated in their hiding spaces, scared about the virus, and to make it worst, suspicious about any cat close to them possibly being a murderer.

"I agree, getting the cats off the streets is a good move for now, but in the long run it will cause as more trouble. We cannot tell a cat to stay put and not roam around the streets. We need to find the murderer before it's too late."

Jack looks at them all with an intense stare. He cannot believe none of them made the connection already. Sometimes it is annoying how slow the rest of the leaders can be. For him, one goes along with the other in this case. The virus is only a distraction. They need to deal with it eventually, but not right now.

The cats of The Five Streets know what to do, how to protect the streets from the virus, but are they ready to face the fact that a murderer walks on the same streets as their families and friends? Jack's priority is right. Now he needs to make sure the rest of the leaders agree with his approach, or he must solve the mystery alone. Jack will find the murderer.

"Jacky, why Jacky, why?" Gina says. "I understand the danger of the murder and the effect it will have or has had on the cats outside. But the virus, Jack, the virus is a unique thing. For now, it's only hurting the humans, but for how long? What will happen if the humans transfer it to the animals? Our streets are in danger twofold, the murderer and the virus. The virus is what we need to focus on. If we make everyone stay home or close by, no one else can get hurt by the murderer. Nothing can happen if we all stay together, safe and warm in our homes."

Jack is not sure he heard right. Gina is all about staying home and being inside. It is her favourite thing to do. The virus gives her the perfect excuse to continue her isolated life. Jack is not sure, not entirely, but it looks and feels as if Gina is trying to use the virus to her own advantage. To keep everyone close by but also far away from her and her home. "This is going in the wrong direction!" Jack thinks.

"I know, Gina! The virus is dangerous, potentially dangerous for us. But a killer in our streets is not only a potential danger, it is a genuine threat. What will we do if we discover another cat killed off? What will we tell the families staying home, thinking we protect them? The killer is still here. He killed the cat and left him in the middle of the street for everyone to see. The killer wanted everyone to know about the murder. Don't you see? Even the traces left to lead into the sewers are a calculated risk. "

"He or she wants us to know that the sewers are off limits. What is the reason? Why the sewers? Why now? Gina, remember they marked the body with the number one! Does this mean it is the first murder of many? Is it the first warning?"

Jack's head spins with all the questions. He has so many unanswered questions about this murder and no one else seems to make the connections.

"The cat killed was the spy we sent down to map the sewers, to find out what is down there. What did he find? I tell you Gina, all these questions lead to a much bigger one? What if The Grey is coming back? He lost Thumbs, then lost the fox. But are we sure he left? We never explored what The Grey's true agenda was. Listen to me, all of you, what if this is just the begin of another sick play of the Grey?"

"Calm down, Jacky! We cannot assume everyone and everything connects to The Grey. I know it is still bothering not to have caught him back then. But to be honest, this are The Five Streets. Five little streets on the outskirts of The Big City. What in cat heaven's name would someone want from us and the streets? I am sure the murder is bad, a terrible thing and the timing could not have been worse, merely a coincidence, I am sure, as no one could predict the virus. Jacky, the cats we are looking after, are in danger. For me, the virus is way more threatening than the theory of a serial killer running around in our streets. I am sure there is a perfectly fine explanation for the dead cat. I am sure it was just one of those internal gang fights or territorial shuffles that went wrong," Gina says.

"My Ladyship, sorry to contradict your theories, but I am inclined to agree with Jack here," Azrael finally speaks up. "The murder was not a coincidence or a botched fight between two cats. One of my spies died, got killed in the line of duty. He got killed in the sewers and, as Jack pointed out, brought up to the streets and dropped as a warning. I am sure of it. No gang or territorial fights would have happened in the sewers. No other cats than mine have entrance to the sewers. Besides, all the other cats stay rather far away from the dark place down there. This cat got killed for what he found down in the sewers. He lost his life, and it is our duty to find out why. I agree as well with your point on the virus. It is potentially a danger for us here, but for now, it is no real danger."

"It attacks the humans, and the humans are told by law to stay off the streets. Obviously, this might develop into a different threat for all of us, for example, on the food supply, but for now, these are only theories. The murder and how and where it happened is a much bigger concern and we all should take it most seriously!"

Jack is glad to see at least Azrael is on his side. Everyone is looking at Cecile now, the last leader to make a vote for what the group should focus on. The virus or the murder. It is up to Cecile to tilt the scale and either support Jack's endeavour to solve the murder supported by the leaders, or if the leaders will focus their energy and time on the virus situation. Jack is worried. Cecile is well known for her compassion and healing. She is all about the health of the cats in the streets. Gina and Nina had an enormous influence on her development and training. Jack is not sure how she might vote.

"Gentleman and Gina, I am not sure how we came up to this so quick. I was not aware that a vote was necessary to decide for the peace and health of The Five Streets, but it seems we are well into it already. I understand both theories and must say it saddens me to see that we have different opinions about where our focus should be. Either way, I agree or disagree with either Gina or Jack. Both are moral theories, and both are an equal threat in my eyes. You all know, for me and my team, the primary concern is the health of all cats. Not only the physical health but also the mental health. The virus will have its toll on the humans, without a question, but it will also impact the mental health of the cats. My aim will be to make sure the cats in The Five Streets are safe and well. Healthy and with as few worries as possible."

"My team already has a lot to do with the usual day-to-day health issues. How the virus will impact us is questionable. How the murder will impact us is now. The murder has happened, and the cats know about it. Jack is right. How they placed the dead body has an undeniable purpose. The body was used to be seen by as many cats as possible. To send a message, to create fear. The virus, however, is right now, only a fictitious fact, nothing the cats out there can see or smell. The fear is on the humans, not on the cats. Not yet, at least. We need to find the killer before the news about the murder becomes a widespread fear. That should be our priority and is my humble opinion.

"I am sorry, Gina! I understand your points too well, but I need to decide what is best for my team and the cats in the streets. Having a killer in the streets, or just the story of a killer making the rounds, will create a bigger fear now. I can only go by the facts and the murder has happened; many cats saw the body. Stories will already make the rounds; fear will build up and suspicion will grow," Cecile says.

That was it, the deciding final vote from Cecile concludes the official voting. All leaders are present and have given their voice. Three to one in favour of the murder investigation to continue with the full support of the leaders. The Five Streets are still one leader, short; they are an entire street short until they reopened 3rd Street. But for now, this is the way, and they agreed that investigations of the murder have priority over the virus. Jack feels satisfied that Azrael and Cecile supported his point. It will make the search for the murderer much easier, especially having Azrael on his side. Jack only hopes this virus keeps out of the streets and is not hurting any cats. He knows he is up against an imaginary clock to solve this murder.

"But we need to make sure we protected every cat from the virus," Gina starts again, trying to get her point further across to the others.

"Gina, we know what needs doing. For now, let us focus on the murder, let us solve this problem, and then take care of the next. The virus is here, but for the moment, we are all safe. We do not know how it will be in a week, a month, or a year. We know the murderer is here. That is for sure. We can only make sure the killer is not hurting anyone else. The only way to do this is to stop him or her. Believe me, the virus creeps me out as well, but having a potential killer right here in our midst freaks me out more!" Azrael explains again to Gina.

Jack is only half listening. His head is already working on his next steps. Catching the murderer!

"I'll let you all to it! Discuss further as much as you all want. I for now have a mystery to solve! I will let you know when I need help and will report about my findings. Expect me back by tomorrow at the same time with some results," Jack says and as soon as he finished his sentence, he runs out of the home into the tunnel, past Churchill, and into the daylight.

Jack continues to sprint down 4th Street until he reaches the corner of 4th Street and 1st Street. He is not on the way home. He swooshes around the corner into 1st Street, his home street, and stops at the house at the corner. He slows down to a normal pace and looks for the hole in the garden fence to get into Misty MooMoo's garden. Jack thought about MooMoo the moment they mentioned the virus. Luckily for her, not much will change, but her servants will have to stay home now all the time. Jack wonders how MooMoo will get on with this recent development in her princess-like life. Jack is sure she will not be happy about this virus and the restrictions imposed on the humans.

Jack slips through the hole into the garden. His whiskers twitch with excitement about seeing MooMoo, but even more so as his nose just picks up the smell of fresh cats' food!

The Gracious Lady had served Jack's lunch. Jack forgot about food in all this excitement around the murder and the virus that attacks the humans. Now, Jack smells the food, and he wants the food. But only a little, not too much to make him sleepy. He cannot afford to knock himself out. Too much to do, too much to explore and discover. Jack takes a careful look around the garden. He still enters the garden with a strange feeling in his gut since the fox attacked him here. It is still his sanctuary, but the fox took a little of the calm and safe feeling away from Jack.

Jack still likes it here and he will never stop going to the garden to see The Gracious Lady or MooMoo and, for all that is worth, he will eat the food if it keeps coming.

That might change soon if the virus is as dangerous as they portray in the news, or as bad as Azrael and his cats say. In the end, the streets rely on the communication from the spies, telling what they hear and see in the human houses and The Big City. Jack is sure, no matter what, The Gracious Lady and her family will suffer from the virus. Jack is just not sure if it will be good getting too close to humans for the next few days. But he wants to see MooMoo now.

He finishes his routine of checking the garden from the entrance. He is sure no one lurks in the shadows for him. No strange smells, no paw prints on the grass and no weird markings of another cat. This is still his territory, his number one food spot. Jack walks on silent paws towards the wooden garden table in front of the living room window. His paws gliding over the wet grass, his nose fills up with the smell of the garden and the food. He jumps up onto the table and pricks his ears up, listening for noises from inside the house. Nothing all quiet for now. He peeks through the window and sees the big picture screen on the wall is showing humans running around, pushing, and yelling at each other. This must be the news Azrael and his spies talked about.

The humans going ballistic on the streets because of the virus and the restrictions. For Jack, it already looks bad with all this yelling and rushing people. The humans on the screen look angry rather than scared. Not a good sign at a time like this.

"MooMoo? Are you there?" Jack meows as quietly as he can. He knows the servants must be close by, watching the pictures on the screen. It still makes Jack feel dizzy if he watches the screen for too long. He tries not to, but something is captivating about this human technology. Jack sits back on his hind legs and waits for MooMoo.

"Jack! I was wondering where you were!" MooMoo replies, but not from the living room. MooMoo sits on the windowsill in the upper bedroom, her favourite place in the house.

"Sorry, MooMoo! Couldn't make it any earlier. Lots has happened in the last few hours. You obviously know about the murder and the virus. But we had to have a council meeting to decide how to proceed with The Five Streets. It is difficult having both happening at the same time. Gina was stubborn with her opinion that the virus is more dangerous than the murder. In fact, I am sure Cecile, Azrael, and Gina are still discussing this in her home. Long story short, we got the vote in favour of focusing on the murder investigation. Cecile and Azrael think it is the best to catch the murder."

MooMoo listens to the update from Jack about what happened in the last few hours. She knows about the murder, not much detail about it, but how much more do you need to be concerned? It is a murder in the streets, not an accident. The virus, of course, she knows about that. Her servants did not talk about anything else the whole day. For the humans, this virus is bad, terrible. She heard that some humans have already died from it. Expectations are that the virus will spread like a wildfire in the dry savanna in the next 48 hours.

Her servants are anxious, and this makes MooMoo even more worried. The energy levels in the house are all tainted with fear and anger. It takes every little trick of MooMoo's' craft to clean these energies.

Now, MooMoo is more a servant to the humans. She takes care of all the humans in the house, trying to take anxiety, fear, and anger away from them and convert the destructive energy into something better. Not an effortless task with bad news constantly coming out of the TV. The situation is grave, way worse than Jack can understand. Luckily, no one mentioned that the virus is dangerous for animals. Not yet, at least.

MooMoo pays close attention to anything the news shows her. She needs to know. Her servants were preparing to stay in the house for a long time. They went out to gather as much food and essentials as they could. They started the moment the first news trickled through. The constant in and out in the morning of her servants annoyed MooMoo at first, but now she is glad her servants reacted so fast. Going out now to gather food is like walking into a war zone. The pictures show many crazy humans fighting for the few leftovers in the stores. "It is terrible!" she thinks to herself.

"Interesting, Jack! I was not aware that the virus was already known by the cats out there. It is only dangerous for humans now. I am sure you are right, and the murder is a more pressing issue. Did you follow the traces into the sewers?"

"Indeed! I was down there myself! It is a weird place. Dark and wet. And it smells of human waste. Not a nice place to be. I am not sure why someone would attempt to keep us out of there. If not for the murder, I would never have set a paw in that place. Only Azrael is interested in this place, but more about the connection it might give with other streets and the potential threat it might pose to our streets. I get we must check it out, but we should just guard the entrance and make sure no one uninvited comes out of the sewers."

"Different story now with the murder. It makes me excited to go down again and discover more. I saw something that I think are blood marks on one wall. I had to walk all the way back, as the marks were on the opposite side of the path. The water was too deep and smelly to cross, and I was called to the council before I could figure out how to get across. Now I want to see the blood marks for myself.

Confirm that they are blood and hopefully they lead closer to the place the actual murder happened. Anyway, that's not why I am here. How are you? How is the situation in the house?" Jack asks.

MooMoo considers her answer for a second, but then she tells Jack how she really feels about this virus. "It is bad, Jack. The humans are going insane about the virus. My humans tried all day to get some food into the house and other stuff, but the shops are all either already empty and closed or full of fighting people. The Gracious Lady, as you call her, is terrified. She talks a lot to her husband about the virus and the TV is running all day showing pictures of the world out there. It gets worse by the hour. We all are staying in, no matter what. It will be difficult for me, as I like my alone time in the house, but I think under these circumstances I could make an exception. The humans are not well."

Jack thought as much, but it is good to hear how the situation is from someone inside. MooMoo lives with humans all the time, and she understands them better than Jack. Azrael's reports are all fine, but they are based on what the cats are seeing and their assumptions. MooMoo is someone who understands. Jack wishes he could take her to the council to share her point of view on some topics they discuss. In this case, it is good MooMoo cannot speak to like Gina; MooMoo's view of the virus would frighten Gina even more and back her up in her theory that the virus is dangerous to all the cats. Maybe it is, but Jack must focus on one thing at a time. The murder counts for now. Humans are in danger, yes, but he believes the cats are going to be fine and have nothing to fear from the virus. Jack knows that, and he hopes he can explain his thoughts to Gina better the next time they meet.

"What do you think will happen to the humans, Moo?" Jack asks.

"I think the humans will be fine, Jack. It will take some time for them to adapt, but if they are good at something, it is adapting. It will be hard and dangerous for them. A lot of things will change. The news is trying to prepare the humans for the worst. Scientist are working already on a cure, but it is unlikely to be a quick win. It will take months, maybe years, for the humans to recover from this. I do not know if you know, but this virus kills the humans quick and very painful. They call it a pandemic. And Jack? It is not only here but also everywhere in the world!" Gina says. "It moves quick, and no one is sure where it comes from. It is one of those things where humans say nature is fighting back and that scares a lot of humans, as it is a situation totally out of their control. No matter who you are, you cannot run from it."

Jack's green eyes light up at the potential of a global mystery. Is this something he could solve? Gina is right, this is bigger than the murder. This can be a total game changer for all the cats in the world. It means freedom for all animals in the world if the virus confines the humans to their homes forever. It would change a lot. Jack cannot comprehend the magnitude of what is going on right now. It is beyond his knowledge of the world, but he understands this is massive. MooMoo is worried, he can tell that. MooMoo being worried is what worries Jack. More than ever, Jack wishes he could reach out and rub his head against hers to give her some comfort. He snarls at the glass between them, tries to make it go away. MooMoo laughs from up in the bedroom window.

"What are you doing, Jack? Trying to tear the house down to get inside? Why is that? What do you want?" MooMoo asks.

Jack sits down again and looks up at MooMoo. He closes his eyes and takes a deep breath in. This is harder than he thought. He really, really likes MooMoo and seeing her in distress hurts him. All he can do is talk to her.

"I don't know. Lost it for a second there. Thought it would be good to give you a hug and cheer you up," Jack confesses.

MooMoo smiles at him and says, "I know, Jack. Believe me, I know. Sometimes I wish I could just leave the house and run with you. Discover the world with you on my side, solving mysteries, crimes, and looking for the lost cats. It would be wonderful, but I am a princess living in the bricks my humans built for me. I am here and you are out there. I am not ready to leave, Jack. Not yet, maybe never. Time will tell. For now, my humans need me more than I need them. It is time for me to do my job. And let's face it, your fur brushing skills are horrible! Look at your fur, all muddled up again and brushed against the trim line. You are such a street urchin, Jack!"

Jack laughs out loud. MooMoo did what MooMoo does best, made him feeling better about everything. Remarkable. How does she do this? MooMoo has a gift for caring and taking away all negative thoughts from the ones that are close to her. Jack feels blessed to be part of her inner circle of trust.

"Thank you, my little, spoiled princess! I will come and check on you as often as I can. I am here with you! My paws are yours!" Jack says.

"Go now, Jack. Find this murderer and be careful, please! We all need you, now more than ever! The murderer is out there, hopefully hiding and ashamed of what he or she did or planning the next one. We don't know, but we have you, the famous Jack, to find out and protect us from whatever comes next. I will be here waiting for you!" MooMoo winks and sends him off.

Jack winks back and turns around. He jumps down from the table and stops quickly underneath to get a bite of the food. It would be a shame to let it go off.

"JACK!" MooMoo shouts from above the window.

Jack pokes his head out from under the table and meows back. "No worries, MooMoo, just a little snack, and I am on my way. I promise nothing more!"

With that, he takes another quick two bites of the food. He pushes himself away from the food before his addiction kicks in and runs over the grass. He looks back one more time before he jumps through the hole in the fence onto the street. Moo was sitting on the windowsill as he left the garden. How much he wishes she could join him out here. How nice it would be if the two of them could run down the streets, chasing each other, discussing the cases he has and hunting the killer together. Jack wouldn't mind that at all.

Chapter VII

Jack is eager to get back into the sewers, but the day is ending, and he is not sure if it would be a good idea to climb down there in the dark. The sewers are a dark and weird place at daytime. In the night it must be a dangerous and wild place. Jack can see himself being hunted by shadows in the dark, shadows even darker than the night. "Better wait till the morning," he thinks and walks back to his box to have a wash and a rest.

Jack arrives in his little box and stretches all his legs. It feels good to be back. Here, at least he can sort his thoughts through without being interrupted. All his best thinking happens in this little box and at night. Many cases he had in the past required little thinking, that what made his mind restless. Lots of the cats who asked for his help had the answer for him already in the story they had to tell. Simple things. That's why he ended up chasing his food demon, trying to shut his mind up, asking for more and more mysteries to be solved.

Well, now his mind got what it asked for. Sometimes Jack worries that his mind fabricates all this trouble around The Five Streets, just to keep him entertained. Would that make him one of the bad guys? Certainly not, as he solves the troubles of ordinary cats. But now, a murder and the virus? That seems an awful lot to be solved.

The virus is not for Jack to solve anyway, but his mind still plays with the idea of investigating it closer. Jack knows that goes too far. It would involve a lot of interaction with the human world and that would be the biggest mystery ever. Cats and humans, how different their lives are.

Jack lets his mind wander. He learned he works best if he does not focus too much on the one thing he wants to deal with. Letting his mind wander around, he goes back to the original thought and over to other occurring thoughts, connecting what he needs and filing other thoughts for later. The murder was clearly a warning. Jack is sure about that. The number one written under the body was more than enough to make that certain. Whoever dropped the body on the streets tried to hide the marks of dragging the body from the sewer onto the street. They did poorly on the job, but was it intentional?

Another major detail was the missing blood from the cat. Why hiding the traces from where the body came from but not see to the detail of the missing blood? The murder looks like a nasty accident that someone tried to hide. Only the written number one under the body gives away that there is more than meets the eye. What is in the sewers? Does someone want Jack to go in or stay out? That is the big question for the day.

Jack needs to go back into the sewers to find more answers, more food for his brain. His thoughts move to the scene of the murder. He checks for more clues. He has a look at the cats present at the time Jack arrived. Is one of them the murderer? All the cats Jack had in his vision show different emotions. It shocked many; Jack can see it clearly in their green, yellow, and blue eyes. Only a few showing mild concern or even disinterest. These are the faces Jack marks for further investigation.

But not one face show anything that would tell Jack they are part of the murder. But some are worth looking into closer.

Next, Jack checks on Gina, Churchill, and Azrael. They are still on his list of suspects. He will never forget the betrayal of Thumbs. But here it is the same; all three are looking grim, trying to hide their emotions for the sake of the streets. But the eyes tell a different story. Jack sees the fear in all of them. Fear and the panic of the moment. No one shows signs of mischief or murder. For now, Jack lets them off the hook, but not totally. So far, nothing new, nothing that could help. It is too early to make good assumptions. The sewer exploration needs to continue tomorrow morning. Jack is confident more clues are down there. He only needs to find them.

Jack decides it is time for some fur care and a bit of sleep. For now, he cannot do more. Tomorrow will be another day, and tomorrow will bring him a step closer to exposing the murderer.

Azrael, Gina, and Cecile are still debating the risk of the virus. But all three get to no conclusion about what to do next. None of them have any experience with an event like this. Cecile will make sure her team of healers is on standby. She will make all aware of the murder and the virus and the potential impact both might have on the rest of the cats in the streets. Cecile has some excellent healers on her team that are focused on the mind rather than the body. They will need the healers over the next few days.

Azrael will put more spies in The Five Streets to make sure they are aware of any mood swings or conspiracies against the leaders. Churchill will be on guard all day and night. He already got Buddy to help. Both look ready for all potential troubles that might come their way. The Streets are ready for whatever may come in the next few days.

The sun is just about to rise when Jack opens his eyes. His green eyes look blurry into the new day. It is cold this morning, but Jack is still willing to go out and into the sewers as early as possible. Jack wants to use most of the daylight while he is down there. Not that it might help, but the feeling of being underground during the daytime is more appealing to him. It gives him the chance to return from the dark into the daylight. It will be a long day. Jack stretches and licks his fur. He starts with his usual ritual of cleaning, stretching, and yawning. His body complains at first but warms up quick. Jack stands up, stretches his back into an enormous arc and bends all the way down with his head held high. The big finale of his morning stretches. His claws scratch over the floor and he finishes the stretch with a big shake of his fur. He is ready now to face the world.

Today will be a good day. Jack feels it in his bones. He will find out about the blood spots on the other side of the sewer path, and he will find his next clue to solve the murder. Jack gets up and pushes the cloth cat flap to the side with his head. The chilly morning air makes him shiver. He jumps out of his box, back into reality, ready for the day. His paws touch the cold pavement of the streets, and Jack takes the chance for another round of stretches in the fresh morning air. Jack walks slowly through the morning. The streets are empty. Jack is not sure if it is just because of the early chilly morning or the new restrictions for the humans, but the whole place feels like a ghost town. It baffles Jack to have this virus show up out of nowhere. He will not admit it openly, but he is indeed worried about the virus in the streets. He is not only worried for the cats, but he also worries about the humans.

Gina and Cecile are right, of course. This will impact the streets. Jack is not stupid; he only likes to priorities his work to focus on one thing. This does not mean he doesn't work on other problems in parallel in the back of his head. He just does not like to muddle them all up into one big problem and get stuck.

The key to his work is to focus on the facts one at a time. Same with the problems. One at a time. No need to run around headless and make matters worse.

Jack blames emotions for this kind of behaviour. He knows he is not a master of his own emotions, but he knows how much of a distraction emotion can be. Often, they turn up at the worst time and in the wrong place to make problems bigger and you lose your well-established baseline. The best example was yesterday, with all the leaders arguing and wasting time and energy about what to do. It was clear to Jack as he kept his emotions in check. It did he is less worried about the human virus thing, but he kept his mind locked and focused on the murder case. One problem at a time! He knows he must apologise to Gina for his rudeness yesterday. It was not the nicest way of dealing with Gina's worries, but time is of the essence. Traces and clues might already be vanishing. Wasting hours debating about the virus made the matters in the murder case worse.

In the end, someone might still be around here that did the murder. Jack does not want anyone to forget that aspect. The virus is here and does to the human whatever it does, but a potential murder is right here in The Five Streets, and it might even be a cat. The scratch marks looked familiar, either a cat or a fox. Jack has not ruled out that an old enemy might have returned. Maybe the fox had a dreadful night and relapsed into old habits. You never know. Jack will have to visit the fox after the sewers. Just in case, to narrow the options down.

The claw marks look very familiar to Jack, and they worry him the most. The way they inflicted them shows Jack that the killed cat was not aware of being in danger, meaning it must have been an animal that the cat knew, maybe trusted, or a very good, planned ambush.

For Jack, it must be another cat or the fox. Any other animal would not have gotten so close to the spy without a proper fight. But the body has no signs of a fight, hence Jack does not agree with the theory of all this being just an accident. This was a calculate kill and a message.

Jack looks up. Time to make a move. His mind took over, and he stood frozen on the spot, analysing more thoughts and facts. He tried last night, but sleep took him before he could get his mind into the facts. Now, with the fresh air and a good night's sleep, his mind is racing. Jack pushes his thoughts to the site. Now it is time to focus on the investigation, collecting more facts and clues. The sewers first and, maybe later, a visit to the fox in the woods. Jack walks down the short stretch from his box to 1st street, his back warming up in the sunrise. It will be a good day to find a murderer.

Jack can sense the other cat way before they talk to Jack out of the shadows. "Jack, I thought I might catch you here first thing in the morning!" the voice in the shadow says.

"Azrael, I thought I'd meet you here at this time of the day. Care to join me in the sewers? Don't act surprised. I am as good at deducting as you are a spy," Jack replies.

Azrael moves out of the shadow, his black and white fur licked clean and laying slick on his skinny body. He is not the most pleasant appearance, but Azrael makes up for it with his character if you get to know him better. Jack thinks highly of Azrael and his network of spies. They are vital for his two jobs, as a leader and as the mystery solver in the streets.

Jack concluded last night that it would only be logical for Azrael to join him on his second trip down to the sewers.

In the end, it was one of his spies who got killed.

At first it shocked Azrael, and he did not want to go down there for the first time, but by now, his curiosity and duty demanded it. He knows he needs to keep his personal feelings and emotions out of this.

"Agreed, Jack. I know I cannot play the game with you, so better I am cutting right to the chase. I will go with you. Make sure not all you see makes it back up to be shared with everyone. Some things down there need to stay down there for the better of up here. You will see," Azrael says.

Now it is Jack's turn to be curious. What else is down there that Azrael is not saying? In a time like this, that sounds highly suspicious to Jack, and he keeps a mental note to look closer into Azrael's activities, just in case. For now, Jack will play along and take the advantage of having a guide for the sewers. Someone who will be down there in the dark with him. Someone with a bit more knowledge about the place. The day turns out to get better and better. "Let's go, Azrael!"

Jack and Azrael walk side by side down the street. Both are silent and busy with their own thoughts. The rest of the street cats have not woken up yet. It is this time Jack prefers the most. The silence and freshness of a new dawn. It is the perfect time to find the ones that do not want to be seen. Sneaking husbands trying to get home before the wife wakes up. Thieves were on their way back to the lair to hide the fruits of a night's work. Jack saw it all, knows it all. Many got exposed, but some got away, so they thought. Jack knows them and he will tell when the time is right. Calling in favours for silence. This is how it works on the streets.

Jack glances at Azrael. "This one has even more secrets than all of us together," Jack thinks. "Azrael must know a lot about the darker side of the streets and the city. I wonder if I could gain more of his trust and make better use of his network. There must be something I can help him with, something I can use for a favour later when it becomes handy." For now, Jack is content with Azrael's help, but he knows it is not a selfish act, either.

A short walk later, both cats arrive at the sewer entrance. Lupine is already waiting for them. He looks tired and his eyes are spinning with confusion as soon as he spots Jack and Azrael walking towards him.

"Bonjour, mon Amis! Early start for you both. What brings you to the gate of hell at this ungodly hour?" Lupine shouts.

"Good morning, Lupine! How was the night?" Azrael asks.

"A silent night, mon capitaine. Nothing to report. Did not see a paw or claw entering or leaving the sewers," Lupine reports back.

"Very good! Let us hope it stays this way. Go now and have some rest. We will be down there for a while. No one will leave their homes today. The leaders made sure they confined all cats for the moment. Few will dare to move around today. Get some rest."

"Merci beaucoup! Alonsi, the quicker you both are down there, the faster I get some sleep. No worries, I will sleep right here. It is my favourite place in the universe!"

"Thank you very much, Lupine. We all feel better knowing you are watching this space. Speak to you later!" Jack says and slips into the darkness of the sewers.

Azrael follows Jack into the dark. The place still makes him sick. The smell is horrible, the humidity disgusting. Azrael cannot imagine anyone living down here. This place signifies all that is wrong in the entire city for him. It is a dark, dangerous place, full of shadows and unknown passages. His spies are still trying to map the whole place. So far, they have discovered one direct tunnel leading all the way into The Big City.

The exit is right in the middle of an old junk yard. Luckily for the spies, the yard has been long closed and gave Azrael the chance to build a base camp for these spies right in the middle of The Big City. So far, that was the only good that came out of the sewers. He and his spies found a hidden way in and out of the city.

But how many other tunnels are there and who else knows about them and uses them? The security risk is immense, and it causes Azrael many sleepless nights. At least Lupine stays on his watch and makes sure no one leaves the sewers undetected. Not at this exit. But this is the only one the cats here in The Five Streets know about. There is still so much more to explore. That's why Azrael joined Jack on his trip today. He wants to see the sewers for himself again. Maybe helping in finding out who did the murder will hopefully prove it was nothing that lives in the sewers trying to protect its territory. The Five Streets have enough to do alone with the cats from The Big City. The last thing they need is another player in the territorial cat wars fought in the background.

Sometimes Azrael wishes he could tell everyone what is really going on in the streets and the world of the cats. It would surprise them all how often his spies avoided an enemy takeover at the last minute. The big bosses from The Big City are always keen on absorbing the outskirts into their own territory.

For now, The Five Streets have been safe, but the sewers might change the plan. Azrael needs to see for himself at this point what is going on down there and on the other side of the tunnels.

"Jack, hold on for a second, please. When you are down, wait for me. I need to talk to you before we dive deeper into this sewer network. It is important you understand what is at stake."

"Okay, Azrael! It is your tour anyway. You are my guide. I am only here for the murder, but I am sure you are already on your own agenda!" Jack replies.

"If you only knew, Jack! If you only knew!" Azrael thinks to himself. But he will try to show Jack as much of the truth of what is going on as he can. Jack needs to know, or he might make wrong turns later and that will put everyone in danger.

Jack arrives at the bottom of the sewers after a quick climb down the hole in the street. He can hear Azrael right behind him, climbing on silent paws. They both are careful and move slow. The last they want is to scare anyone off by making noise and announcing their approach. Jack is back for a second time and is curious about what he will find in the sewers with Azrael as a guide. It will be much easier to cover some ground down here with Azrael helping. Jack is sure Azrael knows the tunnels like the back of his paws.

"Jack, wait a bit for now. Let me tell you something no one knows yet. You need to know. I trust you, but I am not sure if anyone else will understand the situation we are in here."

Jack turns to Azrael; his eyes are still adapting to the change in natural light, but he can see Azrael like a shadow against the opening. "What's the matter?" Jack asks.

"I am not holding you up for long. You know we found these tunnels and we are trying to map them all. Checking where the tunnels lead to, who lives down here? What kind of animal they are? Many things. It is a whole new world for us to discover. One tunnel we found is leading directly into The Big City. I know, I should have told the leaders by now, but it is such an enormous opportunity for my team to establish a direct link with the city and the spy network over there. I could not bear it to be shut down, as some of us will find it too dangerous."

"Don't get mad at me. We have been setting up in an empty building on an abandoned yard. No one knows we are there. We have established no contacts in the city yet. But we can move back and forth without being seen. This is our advantage. I had to use it before I tell the other leaders about this new way. Listen, Jack, this is part of my job, keeping secrets. This new base camp helped to map the other tunnels, as we did not have to turn back every night. I have a more than capable team at the other site. They observe everything and prepare to blend in. City life is so different from our way of living."

Azrael talks and talks. He does not want to stop out of fear Jack will interrupt. "We learned so much more about the structure and how the other cats live. I have a full report and will share it with Gina and Churchill later. For now, I want you to know that we found more evidence about The Grey. Jack the Grey was one of the big leaders in The Big City. Was meaning until he disappeared one afternoon. Listen, Jack, The Grey was there, and he is more than real! No one knows what happened to him, but considering Thumbs and how she talked about him, we can assume he is somewhere here in The Five Streets. Hiding or planning whatever he wants to do next. He left the city."

"Why? We are still working on the why's and how's, but it is for sure he was a big one. He was the leader of many districts, and he had his ways of making cats and other animals do his bidding. Someone told us, him vanishing was the best that could have happened in the city. Jack, we need to be careful here. We are not one hundred percent sure The Grey that disappeared from the city is the same that might hunt us, but it is a possibility, and we need to consider we are up against one of the best the criminal world had!"

Jack listens and absorbs the information just shared with him. Azrael has just verified what Jack suspected for many weeks. The Grey is real and a threat to all of them. Jack knows Azrael discovered more about The Grey in The Big City. It fits his theory about The Grey. It would have been impossible for a cat from The Five Streets to be the mastermind behind Thumb's actions.

It had to be someone from outside and with more skill. Jack's curiosity has been sparked to a new high, but he needs to speak about the problem that Azrael kept secrets like this. He was told to share everything he discovered about the sewers. The leaders can only function and protect The Five Streets if they all work together. Trust is the key to all the decisions they make. Azrael has just put this trust in grave danger. Maybe more than he realises. His actions didn't come from bad intentions, Jack can believe that, but he damaged the fragile trust. Thumbs was the first and all the other leaders fear who will be the next to break the leadership's trust. Not good, but for now, the danger is still content. Jack needs to think about how both he and Azrael can spin this problem around and make it seem an advantage.

"I get it, Azrael. No worries, I understand your motives. It is important to know The Grey's story even more. The tunnels and the one in the city are a great discovery. Keeping it from all of us is a big problem that can turn into an even bigger disaster. Have you told anybody about this before? Who knows about this? We need to contain the information and any leaks. Gina will break if she hears about this from anyone other than you or me. She will lose the little trust that she has left in us. We need to protect the little we have. Thumbs made it clear to everyone how important trust is and how quickly it can turn against us leaders."

Jack can feel how Azrael relaxes. His shadow-like silhouette loosens its tense position, and he gets up on his four legs to continue the path down into the sewers. "Okay, Jack, for now, let's focus on this investigation of yours. Follow me into the darkness, my friend. Let's see what we can find out here and maybe I can show you one or two secrets we found down here. More secrets, Jack, but not as hidden as the one I just told you about."

Jack follows Azrael deeper into the tunnel. It is the second time Jack enters the sewers from this point, and his perception has not changed. He does not like this place. Too dark, too wet, and all smells covered by the horrible stink of the human waste that flows down here in the middle of the path. It is hard for Jack to imagine someone choosing to live here.

Both walk up to the crossroad, but this time Azrael takes the right turn so they can walk over to the blood spot Jack saw on his first visit. Jack lowers his head to sniff the blood. It has the same smell as the dead cat they found. The cat had been here, but it is still not the place the cat died.

Jack looks around and, based on the position of the blood, he can see that the body must have scratched the wall while someone transported it towards the sewer exit. Jack checks the ground; he sees drag marks on the wet floor. Very faint traces, but still visible to him.

"Look, Azrael, they dragged the cat this way. The traces are still there. We can follow them. Do you know where this tunnel leads to?"

"This is the tunnel that leads to The Big City, Jack. Looks like they killed our spy as he was on his way to the city!"

Jack is getting excited again. A new clue and a clear one. Jack keeps his head low, following the marks on the path. Azrael walks behind him, checking for potential other traces and danger. Azrael is concerned that the cat got killed down here. He knows the animals who live down here. They are small and shy. None of them could have killed a cat like that.

"Be careful, Jack. Whoever killed the cat might still be down here. Let me tell you, the animals who live down here wouldn't be capable of killing the cat with the injuries it had. The ones who live down here are small animals and are always frightened.

The mice we know in the streets are a different race. They lived all their lives down here, trying to keep away from the daylight most of the time. They are small and not strong enough to kill anything bigger than an ant."

Jack considers the advice Azrael gave him, but he needs to continue the investigation. "Interesting fact, Azrael. So, you met some of these rats down here? Where do they live? Where are they now?"

"They are watching us, Jack. Can't you feel their presence? The overwhelming feeling of being watched the moment we entered the sewers?"

Azrael is right, of course. Jack felt the same way the first time he came down here. He put the feeling away because he thought it was only the strange environment that made him jumpy. But now, as Azrael mentioned it, the feeling is back and stronger than before. Maybe superimposed by Azrael's revelation, but it is there now. Jack imagines little eyes watching him from the darkness. Curious little black eyes. Just the thought creeps him out. That's why he pushed it aside for the first time. Jack shakes his head and fur; he tries to shake the feeling off. It is a distraction, and there is nothing he can do about for now. He closes his eyes and clears his mind. "Focus on the trace in front of me. Ignore the eyes in the darkness," he whispers to himself.

"What's that, Jack?" Azrael asks.

"Nothing, just talking to myself. Let's carry on. I have the feeling we are close to the next clue."

Azrael takes the lead again, and Jack follows him deeper into the sewers. The light is now nearly gone, only present through a few cracks in the ceiling. Jack wonders what part of the streets is on top of him now.

The path they walk on is narrow and Jack needs to pay attention otherwise he will step into the brown, smelling water running in the middle of the path. The smell is overwhelming now, and Jack sees more and more pipes spilling water from the walls into the middle, combining small spills into a flowing river.

Azrael walks in front of Jack and neither the absence of the light nor the smells seem to bother him, confirming Jack's suspicion that Azrael has spent a good deal of time down in the sewers already. The Master of Spies keeps all his cards close to his chest. Jack will remember that from now on.

They walk on for a while; the light diminishing with every step, the smell increasing with every breath.

Azrael stops again as two paths cross, each leading in another direction. He looks up, left and right.

"Hmm... I do not remember this part well. Give me a second, Jack."

Jack takes the time to inspect the path. The tracks of the body have stopped for a while now, but they followed the only possible way they could have dragged the body. Until now, at least. The crossing has two options: a turn to the left and a small bridge crossing over the water. Crossing the bridge would mean they continue to follow the straight path; turning left will lead them away from the path. Jack tries to find any marks on the path to tell them the direction. Jack lowers his head as much as he dares, his whiskers touching the cold stone. His green eyes scanning the floor, he moves his head to the left and right, checking every inch in front of him. His little nose twitches as he absorbs the new smells of the sewers. He tries to filter the smells; he hopes he can catch some unusual smell. Maybe a cat, maybe the smell of blood.

He crouches low on the floor now, his belly on the cold and he moves little by little. His eyes focused, his whiskers straight, and his nose twitching. Suddenly he stops. "What is this?" Jack leans closer, his eyes drawn to a spot in front of him. His instincts tell him to stop and to look closer. A bit of black fur sticks on a stone. Not a lot and hard to see.

Jack sneaks closer, careful not to touch the fur. He smells it and his mind tells him it is the same fur as the dead cat. Jack looks up. The fur is right on the edge of the bridge. They must have dragged body over the bridge and the fur got stuck in the gap where the bridge joins the path. A lucky event.

"Look, Azrael, some fur right here. I think we need to cross and carry on."

Azrael comes over to Jack and leans low to have a look at the fur. "Well spotted, Jack!"

"Where is this bridge leading to?" Jack asks.

"It will bring us deeper into the sewers. Turning left here would bring us to the exit to The Big City and the new base camp my spies are using. It would have surprised me if the trace leads us there, but you never know. Everything is possible down here. We will enter unfamiliar territory if we carry on over the bridge. I have never been there; my spies have not checked this area either."

"The trace is clear; we need to follow it. Let's go!" Jack says.

Jack and Azrael cross the small stone bridge. They walk slowly and listen to any noises that might tell them what lies ahead. The light is now gone, and both walk in the dark. The other side of the bridge smells less and the water in the middle of the path is all dry.

"Azrael? Say, do you know the purpose of those pipes coming out of the walls? The smell is awful. I wonder what they are doing?"

"You know, Jack, it took us a bit to figure it out ourselves. These pipes transport the dirty water out of the human houses. The water is full of waste and dirt. You can compare them with the rubbish containers outside. It is just another way for the humans to put their worst back into nature. The water they use is not good for anything after what they do to it, so they decide to bring it down here and give it back to the earth. I am sure these pipes are going deep down into the earth, and they collect the dirt water somewhere and then pushed it into the deep and smelling sea," Azrael explains.

Jack is not surprised by Azrael's theory. It makes sense if you know the humans. Wasteful with many things and less considerate of their impact on the surroundings and nature. Selfish creatures.

"Seems like the water dried out here. Look at the pipes. No water is running down in this section. Do you think we are heading out of the streets?"

"You might be right, Jack. Looks like this part of the system is not used very often. Maybe no houses are above us anymore. It is hard to guess in which part of the streets we are. It is easy to lose track down here."

They walk on for a while until they reached another crossing. Both Azrael and Jack try to find further tracks, but they discover nothing, not by smell or sight. They decide the best would be to walk on straight, not to take any turns to avoid getting lost. On they went for another few minutes until Jack sees a small light appear at the end of the tunnel.

"Look, there is light further down. Looks like another entrance or exit?"

"Interesting, Jack. Let's check this out!"

Both cats start running towards the light. Paws and claws scratch over the now dry path. Whiskers twitching with excitement and tails lashing left and right, both arrive out of breath at the source of the light. It is a gate and behind it is the outside world again.

The bars of the gate are wide enough, so they decide to slip through and see where they are in the normal world. To Jack's surprise, they are right at the edge of the fields, next to the woods. Jack looks disturbed, as this means one of his suspicions could be correct.

"Another entrance, Jack. This is not surprising, but unexpected. Reckon we need another guard at this end of the tunnel. Just in case. The big black cat knows who else could have come this way. Look at the woods over there, the farms on the other side. Many animals could sneak in here and make our life harder. We have been very lucky over the last years. This could have been a nightmare in the waiting for all of us!"

Jack agrees with Azrael. This is not the worst but also not the best situation.

"Could you imagine if Thumbs knew about these sewers? She would have had her entire operation down here, undermining us from right underneath our paws. Indeed, we have been very lucky! But I also think we have found our prime suspect for the murder. You know who lives right across these fields? I wonder if your spy followed this tunnel to investigate where it leads to, and he might have found someone unexpected on the other end. I do not want to conclude right now, but for the moment, it is a logical assumption that your spy might have caught our old friend with his terrible temper and things developed into something bad. Not sure how the number plays a part in this and why they would drop the body back in the square, but irrational minds do illogical things. Azrael, I think we need to pay him a visit. See what he has been up to? It has been a while, anyway. We owe it to check on him. Just for the sake of peace for the streets."

Azrael gets immediately who Jack is talking about. "I agree. The trace is too close to be ignored. It is a possibility. Not a welcome one, but never less one that is possible. I must confess, I pulled the resources back from observing him because of the sewers, but maybe it was too early to assume he would not trouble us anymore. All past reports showed he stays in the woods and lives the life of a loner, since Thumbs tricked him, and Gina absolved him from his crimes. Gina's gesture has broken him somehow. Sad enough, but better than having a bloodlust driven animal close by. But and let me be clear, maybe we have been under the wrong impression, and it was only a temporary stop. Let's go. We need to make the most of the remaining sunlight. Last thing I want is to meet him in the darkness in his woods. Just in case he has turned back to old habits."

Jack totally agrees with Azrael. Better get this visit done as quick as possible and with as much daylight as possible.

Chapter VIII

Jack looks over the field towards the woods. The woods seem dark and uninviting. Big fir trees stand guard at the edge of the field. It has been a while since Jack crossed this part and ventured into the woods. He looks up at the enormous trees, feels the cold earth under his paws. No, this is definitely not one of his favourite places in the city.

"Come on, Azrael. Let's get this done with. I haven't been here for a while, and I do not intend to stay for a long time here."

Jack crosses the field. Luckily, all the corn has been harvested, and the field is left to rest. It makes the crossing much easier, and they have a clear view. Both cats walk slowly, each one with their own version of dread in their minds. It feels as if the woods amplify the negative thoughts in their minds. For Jack, it makes sense as not one part of the field or the woods has splendid memories for him. He tried a few times to face this fear and pay a visit to his first real enemy. Seeing the fox after he got expelled out of The Five Streets was part of Jack's healing process. It was difficult the first time Jack came over.

Jack remembers it well; the moment they entered the woods, a voice called out for him out of the dark. The same voice still gets Jack every time he hears it. It is a voice that told him he would die back then is now calling his name as if they would be friends for a lifetime. The fox had refused to leave the woods.

He had rather stayed and contemplate his life. Jack thinks it was the fox's way of dealing with what he did to the cats on behalf of Thumbs. During one visit, the fox admitted he regrets his involvement with the cats and the streets. He said if he would have known about the cats without Thumbs leading him into the streets, he would have been sure the cats would have understood him and would have helped him to find back to his true self. In one way, they did, but at a much higher price. The fox is or was sure a cohabitation would have been possible between him and the cats, as all he would have asked for was just to belong to some sort of community. He would not have depended on the food from the streets. No food he had plenty. What drove him nuts was the loneliness and the constant influence of his bloodlust. No one was ever present to stop him or tell him he did wrong. His skulk rather left him alone when they found out his tendency to violence. The leader had to protect the rest of the group. They moved on and left him behind.

Not the best that could happen to a young fox alone in the woods full of smaller animals to hunt and kill. But now, the fox told Jack many times, his bloodlust has been gone, vanished the moment Gina touched his forehead with hers. Jack couldn't believe it, but he got healed from deadly wounds inflicted by the fox, from nothing more than a purring technique forgotten by many. For Jack, lots of things are now possible that had been beyond his imagination back then. Who would have thought Jack could do what he is doing now? Not even Jack knew.

Both cats take a brisk walk over the resting field. The cold earth sticks to their paws. Azrael looks tense. Jack is still deep in his own thoughts about his first visit to the woods many weeks ago to face the fox after the case got closed.

Jack remembers walking through the field of corn, a different Jack now, a different Jack then.

He arrived at the end of the field and had to sit down for a long moment. All he did was stare at the trees.

He sat there and stared. His little body was not willing to enter the dark woods, but his mind told him he had to. He had to face the fox, see for himself the evil that still haunted him at night. He finally got up and crossed the invisible line between the fields and woods. His paws crossed the border, and it felt like the woods swallowed him in full. The trees dimmed the sunlight. The only pleasant memory was the smell of the woods. Clean air, the total opposite from the daunting sight of the high trees.

Jack took a long breath of fresh, unpolluted air. He still remembers the smell of pinecones, fresh air, and the trees. It was an enjoyable experience for his nostrils. His mind conserved the smells brilliantly in his memory. He walked deeper into the woods, recalling the path from memory to the fox's den. It was not long before Jack heard the voice out of the dark. It spoke directly to him.

"Well, well, if this is not Jack, the famous cat. What brings the kitten into the dark woods? Haven't you heard? It is full of dangerous, wild animals out here!"

The voice startled Jack. He was not aware of the presence of someone else. But he would recognise this voice above all voices. The fox had again sneaked up on him. All of Jack's senses are over occupied by the unfamiliar smells and sights of the woods. Not a bad trick of the old, sly fox. He clearly knew how the woods affected outsiders; the same way Jack knew how The Five Streets would distract new arrivals.

Jack tries to hide a smile. Regardless of the dire situation, it is good to see the fox out and about.

"I am not sure if you should be here, Jack. Better keep going back to where you belong, little kitten," the fox says. "Just a friendly warning!"

Jack turned around, trying to spot the fox. The voice seemed to travel out of the shadows, bouncing off the trees. Jack had not expected this, and it made him feel nervous. Alone with the fox again, what was he thinking? He should have taken Buddy with him. Just in case. Too late now.

"Fox, come out and let me see you. Is this how you greet an old friend? Sneaking up on him and talking from the shadows? I am sure if you wanted to hurt me, you would have already done so," Jack replies.

Nothing moved in the shadows. Jack turned around and around. Suddenly, a shadow released itself from behind a tree. The fox stepped out and walked towards Jack. Jack was happy that his bluff paid off. He was not sure the fox did not want to hurt him. No one had seen the fox or heard anything since the last time he was in the streets. This had the potential to be wrong for Jack, but he had to try.

The fox stopped short in front of Jack. He sat down on his legs and stared at Jack. Jack checked the fox. He looked tired and thin. Not as threatening any more. He looked beaten. Jack was sure this fox is not a danger any longer. An act of kindness had broken this wild animal. What Nina did for the fox seemed like a generous gesture for everyone who witnessed it or heard afterwards about it. Nina understood the fox only did wrong because of his nature and not with true evil intentions. He was a victim himself rather than an instigator.

Nina got all this in a second and tried to rectify what the streets did wrong to him. She tried to make good of what Thumbs did badly to him.

It was The Five Streets' responsibility to help and not to judge. Nina understood this right then, but the other leaders struggled to see it this way. Even Nina.

"What are you doing here, Jack? Coming to see what I am up to?"

The fox sat in front of Jack and stared with dark, sad eyes. Jack saw the fox was not the same at all. The only thing that was left from the old viciousness was the voice the fox tried to use. Jack did not buy it. The fox looked awful.

"How are things? I know coming here does not seem right, but I had to meet you. Get things sorted in my head. You still spook me in the nights, and I want to get this out of me."

The fox tilted his head and looked at Jack with new curiosity. "Say, Jack, do I look like I want to have anything to do with you? Do I look like I could harm any of you anymore? Whatever this tiny, old cat did to me, I do not know, but I can tell you, she took it all from me. Only thing left is this old fox, feeling sorry for himself. All I do now is try to get on with the one I have become and the one I was. Do you know how it feels when the evil part of you has left but left all the memories with you, just to be sure you remember all you did? I can hear something laughing inside me.

Deep inside, someone has a pretty good joke about me. I am done, Jack. The bloodlust is gone. Nothing drives me mad for a kill or for blood anymore. All I want is to hide my sorry self and forget. But they do not let me. The memories do not let me forget."

Jack looked at the fox with surprise. He was not expecting that. Jack was hoping for a sort of different confrontation and not being accused. Jack wanted to accuse the fox of still being the evil one haunting him in his sleep. Jack wanted to tell him how he still flinches every time he passes by the dark corner on the street where he got beat up by the fox.

"How dare you make me feel bad about what happened to you!" Jack said.

"Do I, Jack? Why is that, I wonder? You and the other cats did this to me. Maybe not you personally, but you did. You should have killed me back in that park. I would have appreciated a quick kill rather the absolution from that granny cat!"

"Don't you dare talk bad about Nina! She saved your sorry ass, you fool!" Jack shouted back at the fox. He really got furious about this animal trying to blame him and the cats from The Five Streets for what happened to him. "All we did was get Thumbs out of the streets for good. She deserved it. What she did to you was not fair. I give you that, but it was your choice. Your greed led you to team up with her. It was your choice!"

Now the fox was losing it with Jack. He jumped up, paced around Jack like an angry dog. Tail up in the air, all fluffed up, he hissed at Jack, showing yellow pointy teeth. A weird howl slipped from his lips. Jack stared at the fox, amazed at the weird display. Jack wondered what animal the fox really is. All his behaviours mixed up. He howls like a dog but threatens like a cat. That is one weird animal. Jack was more and more concerned about the mental state of the fox. He does not act well.

"Shut up, you little kitten! A choice? How could I have had a choice in all this? Thumbs came to me, caught me, and threatened me. Can you believe that? She told me to join her and do as she said or I will be dead. Did you see the black cats she had? They beat me half dead. What about those cats, Jack? Did you bring them with you to finish the job? Not brave enough to do it yourself? I am ready. Take what you want from me, but be quick about it. I am done with all of you!"

Jack was astonished by the fierce response of the fox to his visit. All Jack wanted was to close the chapter on the two of them, but now the fox accused Jack of what happened to him, as if it was Jack's fault. All Jack did was to protect The Five Streets, nothing less and nothing more. How could he know they pushed the fox into working for Thumbs in the first place? No, Jack was not taking any of these accusations.

"Stop it right there, you sly fox. You did what you did. I am sure it took little encouragement to come to our streets and cause trouble. Thumbs used you fair enough, but you still attacked me, nearly killed me. I am not here to finish anything or anyone. I am only here to face my fear of you sneaking back and killing me in my sleep. I do not care about you. This is about my sanity, not yours. Complain somewhere else about your unfair life and choices. Talk to the trees or some of your cadavers after your hunt. I am sure the dead animals are perfect listeners," Jack spats back, annoyed with himself, letting emotions boil over, but he had enough. "You are a fox. I am a cat. We both could not be much more different from each other. Our worlds collided in the worst possible way. All I want is for this to be finished once and for all. It drives me crazy knowing you are here in the woods and planning something. Even if not, my head tells me you might. Once betrayed, the trust is gone. Simple!"

The fox stared at Jack. He looked like he was thinking about what Jack had just said. His face changed as the words sunk in. Jack saw the fox breaking down, showing his true self. The mask dropped rapidly. Jack saw the fox was no longer a bloodlust-driven animal. The fox lost it all. All that he had left was the guilt of what he did over the last years in his life. The killing, the cruelty of other animals. Now, with no protection through the bloodlust, the fox's mind was breaking. The fox tried to deal with the new consciousness that has developed in his mind after the bloodlust faded away, but it was too much to comprehend for him.

His mind broke the moment Gina let him go. Being alone in the woods was not the nicest thing that could have happened to the fox. Jack saw this clearly in the fox's eyes. The fox stared into Jack's eyes, a silent plead for help.

The fox let his head fall, his posture showing defeat. Jack still felt angry, but slowly the feeling of guilt was creeping into him. This is what they did to the fox. Once a viscous, dangerous animal has become a broken, lifeless shell of its former self.

"Look at me, Jack! Take a good look! This happens if one's passion is taken away from you. I can't sleep. Can't eat. No hunting, no drive to do anything. All I want is to silence the voices in my head. The voices shouting and accusing me of having taken lives. Enjoyed the killing and the hunt. Tell me, what is still left of me? Even the vermin in the woods mock me now. They would never dare to cross my path in the past. I beg you, Jack, finish what you and the others have started. I cannot go on like this for longer."

"Shut up, fox. I am not here to take any lives. I am here for my sake. You show me what I feared the most. You are the one I fear the most. Stop being so soft. Shout at me, attack me. Show me why I have feared you in my dreams."

"Don't call me a fox. I am no longer worth being called a fox. Call me Reynard. That is who I was back then and the one I am now. The fox is gone. I am only Reynard now."

Jack's face lost everything after that revelation from the fox, not from Reynard. The fox had a name. A name Jack will not forget. Reynard! His nightmare just became more real. Until now, the fox was just that, a fox, an animal. Everything changed after the fox shared his name with Jack. Now this bizarre meeting changed into a more personal affair. Jack was not sure how to handle this situation and thinking back now to that point, he is still not sure what had happened back then in the woods.

Jack had always dreaded the first time he would meet the fox. Jack avoided the woods out of fear. Now the fox seemed to be more afraid of Jack rather than the other way around. For Reynard, Jack embodied everything the fox has lost.

"Fox, listen to me. Please listen, Reynard. I came here to make sure you do not haunt me in my dreams anymore. I needed to see you and to see with my own eyes that you are still real and not just a fabrication of my mind. I was not expecting to see you like this, always thought you are still a danger to the streets. I am not sure what to think of you right now. You confuse me. This is not going the way I hoped for. Let me help you so you can help me get over the past. I will forgive you, but you will have to live with what you did and who you were. I cannot change this, but I can promise you, you will not be alone. The Five Streets are off limits for you, but that does not mean The Five Streets cannot take care of you," Jack talks while he thinks. "What we did to you is our responsibility. No matter how Thumbs got you into this. Thumbs was one of us. Her mistakes are ours to redeem. Do you agree to let us help you?"

Reynard sat down on his legs. His head is full of the voices, telling him to run, to hide. The loudest voices shouted at him not to listen to Jack. He needed to suffer for what he did. Jack offered help, but could he really help Reynard? Nothing is like it was and nothing is like it should be. A cat and a fox in the middle of the woods. Once enemies, now haunted by each other's existence.

"Only one way to find out, Jack. I am out of options and will claw at any straw. Help me and I will see if I can help you," Reynard said.

Jack still sorted through his mind. He tried to find a solution where both could win.

"Reynard, listen," Jack said. How weird it feels to call the fox by his name. "I came down here to see if my memory is playing tricks on me and if I can get you out of my mind for good. Like you, I spend many hours waking up in the middle of the night, haunted by my memories of you. You messed me up properly. The same way we messed you up at the end. Believe me, if I tell you, I am here to help you. I am not here to seek revenge or bath in your misery. I am sure I can get beyond my fear by helping you to get on with your life again. A different life as you know it, but that does not mean it is a bad living. Let me try to help you and in return you will help me clear my mind from the fear your former self-created in my mind."

Reynard was not sure if Jack really meant what he just offered, but he would claw for any straw right now. Reynard missed his old self, the hunting, the freedom. Now he felt trapped in the open woods. Trapped by his own mind and memories. Haunted by guilt. Guilt he never had to worry about before. It was as if Nina's gesture ripped through the walls. He'd built over the years apart with a single strike and now everything was flooding through this small cap. The small cap widened day by day from the sheer amount of guilt, and memories tried to flood through. Now the wall was gone. Only a small fraction remained, a memory itself. Nothing protected Reynard from seeing and experiencing what he did to all the other animals. Now it was he who was haunted. Haunted by the memories of each kill he made. His nights filled with eyes of the killed animals staring at him, judging him.

Voices shouting his name, cursing him. Words inflicting pain straight into his brain. The memories are a constant flow of pictures in his mind, bright highlights of all the dead animals he killed, like flashes in a thunderstorm.

Reynard dreaded the night-time; in his sleep, the pictures came to life and accused him of all he did. His dreams were never-ending nightmares. After days, the only way out he could find was to take his own life or to go insane. So far, he was not brave enough to take his life, so for now, he travelled the route to go insane.

For now, it was his preferred path, and he still had the hope that this path would lead him to silencing the voices at the end of his trip.

Jack remembers the first meeting with Reynard after he caught and exposed the Food Thief like it happened yesterday. Thinking back to the first day makes Jack realize how much impact his change had on many others. He enjoys solving crimes and mysteries, and he will continue to pursue his newfound passion, but it also made him aware of a different world. Before, he did not know how many bad things happen alone in The Five Streets daily. Lots of things happen without the leaders being aware. Now Jack knows, but only because of others involving him and his talents, not only for help but also trying to gain advantage of others.

Jack doesn't always take the case. It takes a careful approach of the case and the cat involved. Jack had to learn that there is evil in many facets out there. For now, Jack is sure of who he can help and who he needs to keep a close watch on. His new line of work gives him access to distinct characters in The Five Streets. The fox, Reynard, was one of many that took Jack's curiosity to a new level, at least for a while.

Jack went back many times to the woods and continued his conversations with Reynard. Jack learned more about Reynard's past and what drove him to become the deadly animal he was for many years. Jack tried to listen a lot, asking questions, and giving advice as much as he could. Reynard seemed grateful for the company and the chance to get some bits off his chest. Jack built a complete profile on Reynard based on stories he heard and the time they spend together.

Sadly, Jack figured out that as Reynard opened up more and more to Jack, he also isolated himself more and more from the rest of the world. At the beginning, Jack and Reynard would talk for hours, walk through the woods, and just talk.

That was in the beginning, where the talks had been light and refreshing. Both shared their vision of what had happened in The Five Streets and how it changed their lives. But later, as Reynard took a step further and told Jack about his past, the walks became shorter. Reynard tried to stay in the shadows most of the time. It felt like he was too embarrassed to talk about what he did and be seen doing so. It got worse the deeper they went into the details of his past. The last meeting had been at Reynard's den, Jack sitting outside listening to the voice coming from the dark inside the den.

Reynard seemed to get weaker each time they met, while Jack grew stronger. His fear about Reynard subsided slowly, and a desire took over to help this poor creature. The desire to help moved slow into the direction of analysing a strange mind. Soon Jack had decided and could see the outcome of Reynard clearly in front of him. Jack knew he could not help fixing the fox. Reynard the fox had given up on himself and was beyond helping.

It became apparent to Jack that all he could do was make sure Reynard had company as much as possible. That's when Jack involved Azrael and his team. They allocated cats to take turns sitting in front of the den and listening to Reynard. Jack heard no complaints from Reynard, and they kept going for many more weeks. It helped to make sure they looked after the fox and The Five Streets knew all about the fox and his whereabout. This continued to be the procedure for many weeks until Azrael had to pull off the cats to investigate the sewers. It was a hard decision, but keeping both tasks covered was impossible. The leaders used all available cats for the sewer investigation as they did not see the fox as a danger for The Five Streets anymore.

Now, Jack is not sure if the decision was a good one. What if Reynard has turned again and is back to his former evil self, now out for revenge? Jack had to see Reynard for himself.

All these thoughts and memories crossed Jack's minds as they walk off the field to the edge of the woods, his mind working already on the worst-case scenario.

"Azrael? We might need to be ready for the worst. We might be in trouble if Reynard is the killer. He might expect us, or worst he might have already laid his trap out and is waiting for us to step into it. Let us be as careful as possible."

"Right, Jack. Maybe it's best we split up, so at least one of us will surprise the fox if he is busy with the other. He would not catch both of us in one go," says Azrael.

"Right, you stay away, and I will sneak right up to Reynard's den. You stay hidden if you can. You will be a little surprise if things go wrong," Jack agrees.

Azrael jumps quickly to the left and runs a few meters away from Jack. Not far, Jack can still see Azrael through the trees. Both lower themselves low to the ground and sneak toward Reynard's den.

They move slow and careful, trying not to make too much noise. Walking on the leaves and sticks covering the floor of the woods is tricky for the street cats. Every step could be on a stick that will break with an ear deafening sound, announcing their arrival to Reynard.

Jack never thought it would be hard to sneak into the woods, but his senses are on high alert and every noise he makes amplifies by a multitude, and he feels like a thrashing giant. Jack looks to his left and tries to see Azrael, but there are too many trees now in between them.

Jack is sure Azrael is much better at sneaking up on Reynard. It is Azrael's job to move like a shadow through the world. Sneaking on the hard tarmac of a road is nothing compared to sneaking on the soft floor of the woods. True, the soft earth swallows every sound your paws make if you can find an uncovered spot of soil. The floor is full of small sticks that might break under your weight, leaves that move with a crinkly sound if stepped on. And stick covered by leaves are the worst of them all.

The floor in the woods is covered with thousands of natural noise-making traps. Jack tries to move as slowly as he can, avoiding all these traps. Jack stops. What was that?

A snapping sound flashes through the woods, followed by a muffled curse that makes Jack smile regardless of the situation he is in. Even Azrael struggles apparently to move like a shadow in the woods by the sound of it.

Jack continues to sneak towards the fox's den. He is not sure if the hiding is necessary but better be careful than regretful. His paws never leave the ground. Jack tries to push his paws quietly through the leaves and sticks, rather than lifting his paws up and crashing them down into the noisy ground. Now he can see the entrance of the den. So far, no sign of Reynard.

All is silent in the woods. The few animals remaining still stay away from the den. The memories of the evil fox still live on.

"Now I understand why Reynard struggles so much. Forgiveness is hard to find here in the wild. Different rules, different way," Jack thinks to himself.

Jack can now see the entrance of the fox den. Many times, he sat in front of the entrance and listened to the voice coming out of the dark. The last meeting with Reynard had been weird. Reynard was moving more and more to being as isolated as possible, only talking to Jack out of his den.

Jack tries to remember the last time he saw Reynard and not only listened to the voice. The last time Jack recalls seeing Reynard was way back. Reynard looked skinny and haunted. His eyes were dull; his iris had taken on a milky white. Jack assumed it had to do with Reynard staying below ground for too many hours. Jack asked Reynard about it and the fox said it was better for him. The voices were quiet in the darkness.

It worried Jack a lot back then, but he paid little attention to it. Maybe he should have interfered here already, but Jack was more concerned about his own observations rather than the health of Reynard. Now Jack is not sure if he has neglected the opportunity to help Reynard and fix him. He instead left this to the cats Azrael commanded to stay and watch at the den.

"Heavens knows what Reynard has been up to since we pulled the watch off."

Jack reaches the entrance of the den. He sits down and listens, trying to catch any sounds coming out of the den. His eyes try to pierce the darkness. No sound comes out of the hole in the ground. All Jack hears is the birds and the wind brushing through the trees. Jack closes his eyes; he tries to listen closer to the noises. Nothing. Reynard is not at home.

"Azrael? Think we are too late. Reynard is gone."

Azrael walks over from behind the tree he was hiding, startling Jack a bit as Jack thought Azrael behind a different tree. Somehow, Azrael moved without Jack noticing.

"Don't do that! Sneaking up on me like prey!"

"Sorry, Jack! Thought I might try the different underground to work on my sneaking. You know, kind of important as a spy," Azrael replies with a big smile on his face. "So, where is our prime suspect? Any ideas?"

"Honestly? I do not know. Maybe you can go in and check? I mean, as a Master of Spies, it would be good to check out the underground as well. In the end, it is all new for you," says Jack.

Azrael looks at Jack with his funny look. His head tilts to the side and his eyes look as if they are calculating if Jack means it or if it is a joke. Jack saw this a few times in Azrael.

Azrael's ears twitch and he jumps around, facing the source of noise he caught. "Someone is coming!"

Jack signals to Azrael to hide again, and he gets ready for the someone to arrive. Azrael sneaks back behind the tree, hidden and out of sight. Jack sits down again and tries to put on a calm posture. He sits and looks at the noise. He can now clearly hear something walking through the woods towards the den. Whoever it is, it does not move carefully or try to hide. Branches are snapping, leaves are rustling, and Jack can even hear faintly a voice talking to itself. This is no threat. Jack knows the voice. It is Reynard coming home.

"Hey! Reynard! What have you been up to?" Jack shouts through the woods, shouting to inform Azrael. Telling him to be ready for the fox.

"Hmm…? Is that you, Jack? What brings you into this part of the world? Checking if you will find me dead, finally?"

Jack waits for Reynard to arrive at the den. The fox is moving slowly, much slower than the last time Jack saw him. Reynard's fur is now a lot more grey than reddish. The fur is all over the place and Reynard walks like an old cat. His head moves from side to side and Jack can see him whispering to himself.

This fox is nuts. Jack shakes his head in pity. Jack knows it is due to what they all did to him. One way or another, it was the cats' doing.

Thumbs, Jack, Gina and all the others contributed to the fox getting a broken mind. Forgiveness did not work for Reynard the same way. Reynard needs to forgive himself. It did not matter if the others forgave him; it made everything worse for him.

"Just came around to see how you are doing, old friend. Haven't seen you for a while and thought it would be good to catch up. Sorry that I have not been around a lot lately, but you know, The Five Streets keep you busy sometimes."

"That is well and true, Jack. Any other creatures invaded your streets? Maybe someone you can send over here, and we can suffer together? I am sure you cats are good at forgiving the new dangerous animal too and it could come around and sit with me here. Waiting for the voices to drive you finally nut and into the endless dark. Tell me, Jack, does Nina still give out her absolutions so freely?"

"Reynard, you know Nina is no longer with us. She left The Five Streets ages ago. Her gift to you was her parting gift from all of us," Jack says.

"Very well, as you say. I am not always sure what is real and what is not. What brings you here, Jack? I have the feeling this is not a visit from an old friend. I haven't seen any of you in the last few weeks. Looks like you cats decide I am no longer a danger for you all. Very well, you might be right, you might be wrong. Who am I to tell?"

"Where have you been, Reynard?" Jack asks. "My, my, you never were one for a cheap chat. Straight to the case.

What happened? Is your food bowl empty again? And the first one to check on is old Reynard here? Jack, you should know better. Would I tell you if I did what you think I did? Come on, Jack, another hunt, just the two of us. For old times' sake."

Jack steps back and looks closer at Reynard. This is not the fox he left behind weeks ago. Reynard looks weak, but Jack feels the voice and mind of the fox got stronger. Reynard would not have challenged Jack in the past. He would talk and talk and talk if Jack would stay in front of his den. Now Reynard was not in his den. He was out in the woods, or even worse, out somewhere else. The fox might look weak, but Jack is no longer sure if this is the case or just a show. Is the old fox back? Playing his part in the game again?

"Reynard, tell me where have you been? I am sorry, but I need to know. No time for hurt feelings," Jack says.

"Calm down, Jack! I still must eat. We all do. I went deeper into the woods, looking for small vermin to still my hunger. Yes, vermin! That is all I can hunt nowadays. Eating them still makes me sick with guilt, but I must eat. There is no way around it. Believe me, I try to hunt as little as possible. It gets harder and harder. My body is suffering the same as my mind. I mean, look at me, Jack! Look properly! Do I look alright to you? My fur is getting grey, my teeth losing their sharpness. My eyes are not the same either. Do you think I could see you from over there? No way! Your smell gave you away. My nose works as it always has. A little blessing in disguise, as my nose also tells me I am not right by the way I smell myself. No secrets here. Look for your murderer somewhere else this time."

The outburst Reynard just delivered catches Jack by surprise. Jack was expecting some sort of argument or stupid comments, but Reynard giving him a full rundown of his situation. The little speech Jack just heard makes Jack realize how bad Reynard really is. All that Reynard mentioned is visible to Jack. The fur, the weird colour of Reynard's eyes, and the smell, too. But one thing makes Jack stop feeling sorry for Reynard and letting him go back into his den.

"Murderer? Reynard, I mentioned nothing about a murder. What makes you think I am looking for a murderer?"

Reynard jumps a few steps back and lowers his body as if to jump at Jack. A deep growl slips from his throat and he shows his rotten teeth. Jack does not lose any time and sprints behind the same tree Azrael is hiding. Azrael signals Jack to be quiet, not to give away Azrael's position. Jack runs out from behind the tree and back in front of the den. Reynard has not moved at all. He just stands there like he is frozen, growling and hissing.

"What is the matter with you, fox? Have you finally lost it all? Stop being stupid. You know we are beyond fighting each other. Even if you want to try, you know you will lose."

Reynard shows his yellow, stained sharp teeth. Saliva drops from his jaw. He lifts his head and tries to howl, but all that coming out of him is a tiny sound. The scene makes Jack sadder than anything. It shows how confused Reynard is, but Jack also has discovered something vital for the murder. Reynard knows something about it. And Jack needs to step carefully to get the information out of Reynard. He needs all his skills, even if it might take time to get Reynard to talk.

Reynard stops throwing his threats towards Jack immediately. Jack can see the fox's face change from wild to questioning as if he is just realizing what happened here. Reynard drops his body back into a sitting position, staring at Jack with lost, milky eyes. Jack does not like the look of it at all. Reynard is much worse than the last time Jack saw him. This whole guilt trip is taking its toll on the fox.

"Reynard, what do you know about the murder? Tell me what you know. It is important," Jack tries to reach the fox.

Reynard keeps staring at Jack. Just staring with those strange eyes. It makes Jack uncomfortable.

"What just happened? Jack, where was I? It felt like the old days. My mind went black for a bit, and I could feel being pushed aside. You triggered something in me I haven't felt for a long, long time. It was a few minutes without me feeling bad. It felt good, like being me again!"

"I am not sure, but I tell you I had the same feeling. You freaked me out there a few second ago. It felt like facing you again back in the dark street corner. What ever happened, I was sure you would attack me like in the old days. What is going on, Reynard? Where have you been just now and how do you know I am after a murderer? Be honest, Reynard."

"Believe me, Jack, it was not me who killed that cat. I know why you are here. I understand. It is the first logical choice to be here and check on me. But I can tell you, it was not me. Believe it or not, all I can tell you is that whatever killed the cat came out of the sewers. Don't look so surprised. I know about the sewers. There is an entrance over the fields. I used it myself twice. For nothing specific, just kept going back and sneaking underneath the streets. It has been a little like being back and on the hunt."

"The thrill of knowing no one could see me and being so close to you all up there. Don't get me wrong, I could have done it if I wanted. All these cats walking around in the sewers like they know where they are. Do you know how often they passed by me? They did not suspect a thing. The shadows are deep down there. A few times I was considering moving in there, just to have a new place with fewer memories. But it is too wet, and it smells weird. But it crossed my mind. That was before your cats discovered the entrance and started poking around."

Now Jack is even more surprised. He was not expecting this at all. Not any of it. This is going in a different direction. Reynard and the sewers sound for Jack like the perfect match.

If Reynard was still the old fox from back then, this would have been a recipe for disaster on a different scale. Jack hopes Azrael hears the whole conversation and takes mental notes. His spies had one of the most dangerous animals sitting in the shadows, watching them while they explored the sewers. If it would have been anyone else, the spying cats could have been in a lot of trouble. The whole Five Streets could be in a much worse scenario by now. Jack feels his mind side-tracking, losing focus on the one topic he came to discuss here with Reynard. Now his one question has brought up hundreds more.

Reynard stands up and walks towards Jack. He moves slowly with low, dropped shoulders. Nothing remains of the vicious fox seen a few minutes ago. They all are responsible for Reynard; they all helped to break Reynard; the same Reynard Jack left in the woods alone. Reynard looks at Jack with his sad, empty eyes as he walks past Jack.

"I am going home now, Jack. I am tired. Seeing you was nice, but I believe it is best if you stay away from me for a while. I am not sure what you did, but it is clear you did not bring out the best of me. As nice as it was to feel like me again, I know it is not what I should feel," Reynard continues to talk while he walks to his den. "I do not know what happened to that cat. All I can tell you is it was not me. Someone else did it and this someone is your problem, not mine. Leave me alone now. I am tired."

Reynard retreats into his den. Jack watches the fox being swallowed by the darkness of the den. Jack sits in front of the den and still thinks about the endless questions his meeting with Reynard has brought up. It was not what he hoped for at all, but he also got some interesting new leads to the murder. Reynard confirmed what Jack suspected; the cat died in the sewers.

Someone killed the cat to hide something from the sewers. It is not much, but it is a beginning.

"Goodbye, Reynard!" Jack says and turns around, away from the den and the fox.

Azrael was listening to the whole conversation between Jack and Reynard. His hiding spot was ideal to overhear every word. This was his world, hiding in the shadows, spying on others. This is what he does best. There was a moment of fear inside him when the fox turned against Jack. Azrael was sure this was going to end badly. He was not sure if Jack could handle the fox and pull him out of his sudden rage. But Jack did well. He jumped and ran at first, but then he thought better of it and stood up to the fox. It was a moment of weakness from Jack, based on the experience with Reynard. Jack was quick to remember and face his fear.

The information Reynard had was not much, but Azrael understood that the problem and the solution is in the sewers. It is all connected to the world underneath

The Five Streets. He needs to speak with Jack about the next steps. There is no way Azrael is letting Jack wander around alone in the sewers. He will go with Jack, no matter what. In the end, no one will stop him. It was one of his trusted spies that got killed because of the task Azrael gave to that poor cat. He had all the right to be part of the hunt for the killer. It was partly his fault that one cat from The Five Streets has died. What if he and his team of spies have missed something? Azrael knows he can't change the past, but he can make sure nothing further happens because of his decision to investigate the sewers.

Azrael follows Jack back to the field, keeping a distance between them. Better to keep the appearance until they are far enough away from the den. Just in case. Jack walks like nothing has happened.

Azrael sneaks from tree to tree, staying under cover wherever possible. He trains his sneaking skills in the unfamiliar surroundings, a welcome opportunity. Here in the woods, every step needs to be placed carefully. There are so many factors to be considered, from placing your paw down for one step to checking out the best possible cover at the same time. Azrael sneaks and tries to keep his prey in sight. He enjoys being out here in the woods. It is so different from the streets and the city. Azrael see Jack stop to scratch his ear, so he takes the chance to get ahead of Jack. He jumps out of his cover and runs silently past Jack, stopping behind a little bush just at the edge of the woods. Here he waits for Jack to catch up with him.

Jack knows Azrael is somewhere around him. He would not leave Jack alone, not after meeting the fox and seeing the reaction. Jack tries to listen for Azrael, but so far, the master spy is doing well in the woods. All Jack hears are the noises of the woods. Nothing suspicious reaches his ears.

"Well, let him have it," Jack thinks and moves on. He wants to get out of the woods. He has lots to think about. More questions than answers. Jack feels annoyed as the visit and talk with Reynard has not ended up as he hoped. All he knows is that the sewers are the main reason that the poor cat died. But why? What is down there that needs protection? Why killing a cat for it? And how could a fox hide down there with none of them knowing? Gina and Churchill will freak out when they hear about that. It will give the rest of the leaders a good chance to close the sewers for good. Maybe not a bad idea, especially with the virus around that kills the humans. But what if the sewers could be the only safe place for all the cats during this unpredicted time with the virus? Who knows how this will play out? Jack's mind is racing. It is refreshing after all the dull cases he solved in the last few weeks. This is a real challenge!

Jack stops to sort his mind. He scratches his ear and takes a deep breath. His stomach rumbles. It is time for some food. Food and a catch up with MooMoo would be a good thing right now. The sewers will get too dark soon, not the best place to be in the dark for hours. Whatever happened in there will still be there tomorrow. Jack's ears twitch. He hears someone moving fast behind a line of trees. Jack smiles. He just caught the master of the spies spying on him. The game is on!

Azrael waits until the last second and jumps out from behind the bush with a big grin on his face. "Got you!" Azrael shouts.

"Wow, really? I heard you already back there behind the trees, thrashing around like a mad dog. I think you need to stay in the woods longer and train your skill," Jack replies.

"You might be right, Jack. I can tell you looked way more scared when the fox had a good go at you. Maybe you should stay longer in the woods and work on your inner fears," Azrael counters.

Both look at each other, puzzled and a bit annoyed. Then suddenly both laugh out loud, and the tension of the woods evaporates.

"Definitely time to get out of here. Let's go back home. I am a hungry cat, and it's too late for another exploring round in the sewers. I think I will see MooMoo, check in on her and the humans. How about you go back and update Gina and Churchill? I will join a bit later. Need some food first."

"Sounds like a plan. Let's move. The quicker the woods are behind us, the better. We can cross the fields to get back to The Five Streets. Better air out here than down there, anyway."

Both cats turn their backs to the woods and walk towards the field, tails and heads held high as to show the woods who is boss here.

Jack and Azrael had a good day together and both know it will not be the last time. Jack has the feeling Azrael will not leave Jack alone on this murder hunt. It suits Jack well.

Reynard sits in the shadow of an enormous tree. He watches the two cats joking and finally leaving his woods. He nods to himself and turns around into the darkness.

Chapter IX

Azrael and Jack split up when they reach The Five Streets. Azrael will go straight to see Gina and Churchill, maybe even Celine, to give his update on the sewer trip, and Jack is sure he will tell them about Reynard and his behaviour.

Jack turns left and runs towards his beloved little garden. He hopes the owners had time to leave some food out for him. Jack knows these are unusual times, but often humans stick to their routines when other things are not as well. It helps them to feel in control. Jack notices how silent the streets are. No humans are to be seen. The streets are empty. The noise is different too. No cars, no kids playing around. It is silent. The streets feel like a thing of the past.

Sounds echo in Jack's head, projecting what he should hear, but whenever he stops to listen, nothing. He did not meet any other cats on his walk to the garden either. It is a weird atmosphere. Jack would have never thought that silence could feel so threatening and unwelcome. He continues his walk and thoughts until he reaches the hole in the fence. He slips through and is in the little garden of The Gracious Lady.

"Back home!" Jack thinks with a smile.

Jack stops in the middle of the garden. Something is missing. He looks around, his little ears up like radar antennas scanning the area. He sits still, only his ears moving around, catching noises and his whiskers twitching, feeling the atmosphere. His noise sucks in the air.

"No, something is definitively not right!" Jack talks to himself and still scans the garden.

But it is true, no smell of food in the entire garden. All he can smell is the stench of cleaning products spilled all over the garden. His nose is full of the smell of bleach. He stretches his neck to see the patio area. Someone has cleaned it all. No, not cleaned, disinfected it. And it is not summer!

"That is odd. What is going on? Where is my food?" Jack thinks and walks over to the patio. They even removed the table, his place to converse with MooMoo and the table that protected his food from the weather. This is indeed not good at all. Jack moves over to the window and jumps up onto the sill. He looks through the window and tries to spot someone inside the house. The TV is running, but the living room is empty. Jack can see the TV and the pictures it shows are not very good either. It shows people fighting in car parks, burning stores and lots of police and army moving in the streets. Jack understands that this is the outcome of the first day with the announcement of the virus. A typical overreaction of humanity, as he thinks.

"Where is MooMoo?" Jack tries to find her in the room, but he can't see far through the window. He misses the table already. It was much easier to sit on and shout for MooMoo. Jack jumps down from the window and looks over to the back door of the house. It is not closed as usual; it is open a bit, maybe enough for Jack to squeeze in and check it out.

He has never entered the house; it is not what he ever wanted to do, but it is different now. Something is going on here and he really wants some food. Jack is not in the mood to wait at the line for the food distribution. Not for what he calls leftovers, anyway.

It is not the same if you know you can get fresh food. No way he is giving this up now.

Jack sneaks to the door. Slow movements, bit by bit. His belly touches the ground as he tries to lie as low as he can. His ears are up, scanning again for noises. He will make a run for it if he hears any sort of movement behind that door.

"It could be a trap," Jack thinks to himself. He stops, listens, and carries on moving. The short distance takes him ages, but he finally arrives at the door. He turns his head and stretches to look inside through the small opening. His eyes widen in surprise. He sees mountains of food packs in the room. Not only human food but cat food as well! Tins of delicious wet food and cartons full of crunchy snacks. It is a paradise!

Jack feels drawn into the room. All the foods make him forget about the danger of entering the house. All this food is so close to him. And all for him. His paws carry him closer to the entrance. He lifts his paw and tries to open the door more. The door swings open easily and suddenly Jack stands in the room. He sits down and let his eyes wander over the packs of food. His mind is full of all the flavours he can see.

This was clearly unexpected for Jack and is more food than he ever discovered in his life. He didn't even know that so much food could exist in one place. This is nothing compared to the bins that The Five Streets are so proud of. This is new food, fresh and untouched.

Shame they stored it inside a human's house. Jack would love to lead the other cats here so they all could have a big party. No one would worry about food for a long time.

Jack sits on his legs, and his head swivels back and forth. How to take the food? What to do? A noise makes him jump up; it come from the other side of the second door. The humans are back! As much as he likes The Gracious Lady, he has no intention of meeting her in this room. He turns and jumps out of the room like a flash.

Back in the garden, Jack sneaks back to the living room window. He still wants to check on MooMoo. Even more now, as he wants to ask her about all that food. But there was something else he wanted to talk to her about.

"What else was it? Right after the murder, Reynard, and the sewers. But all I want to know is if MooMoo is safe and well. The virus, of course. How could I forget?" Jack knew how. The food is all he can think of. It took over everything.

Jack sits on the big patio; he looks up to the window on the second level. No MooMoo in sight. "MooMoo!" Jack meows.

"MooMoo! Are you there?" Jack has no other way than to shout up and hope MooMoo can hear him. He knows his meowing might attract the humans, but he sees no other way to tell MooMoo that he is here in the garden. It was easier in the past as MooMoo often sits either on the window down here or up there. But not today.

"Where is she?" Jack wonders.

He walks along the patio, trying to get a better angle to see inside the room. He moves onto the grass and looks up, hoping to glimpse her upstairs. Just as Jack feels like giving up, a black shadow swooshes onto the upstairs window. A slim, tiny cat jump onto the windowsill and looks down at Jack. MooMoo has arrived.

Jack smiles up at her. It makes him happy to see MooMoo. Happier than he would admit to her. He sits back down on the patio and looks up.

"Hello, Moo! How are you? How are the humans?"

MooMoo looks at Jack. He finally came to see her. It felt like days since she last saw him. He looks well. MooMoo was worried sick knowing he was going down into the sewers. The sewer is a dangerous place on its own but in a time like this, with all the humans out there going crazy, the whole outside world is nuts. Jack does not know how much danger he and the others cats out there are in. But for now, she is just happy to see him. Not that she would tell him this, but she is. For now, MooMoo must tell Jack something way more pressing.

"Jack! Nice to see you, but you must leave! Leave the garden!" MooMoo shouts down from the bedroom window.

Jack is not sure if he heard right what MooMoo just said to him. "Me? Leave? Why should I do that? I am hungry! Where is my food?"

MooMoo looks down at him with a look that should burn Jack down to a rubble of cinder on the patio. "How can he be so thick?" MooMoo thinks and then she tells him exactly that.

"Jack, leave now. The humans are out of control. My servants don't want anything that comes from the outside near the house. They disinfect everything, even themselves, repeatedly. The house smells like a hospital. My nose burns from all the vapours in the air. They even bleached the patio! I am sure you have noticed that! I tell you, Jack, they do not want to see you right now in the garden. They will freak out and do whatever comes into their crazy minds. Leave now, please!"

Jack gets it. He saw the pictures on the TV in the living room. All these fighting and angry people in the streets everywhere. It must be scary for a lot of the humans. Jack cannot imagine how it feels to face such anger and violence. It must be a hundred times worse than facing a wild fox in the streets. In fact, it must be like facing a thousand wild foxes in the streets in the middle of the night. But he really wants some food.

"MooMoo, are you okay? I am not sure I understand what is going on in the human world right now, but I am worried about you. And my food. Oh, don't look at me like that! You know how important food for all of us is here in The Five Streets. If the humans go crazy like that, it will impact us out here in the streets. First the dead cat and now a food shortage. How can we control this stuff and keep everyone in The Five Streets safe? Crazy times are coming for us."

"I know, Jack. Believe me, I know what all this means to you cats out there. But for now, I need to take care of my servants. They are my family, too. Please leave now and do not come back until all this is over. I can't bear the idea of you getting in trouble with The Gracious Lady. Both of you will regret what might happen. Please, Jack, leave now. There is more to worry about than just food. You are right, times are going to be tough, and you still must catch a murderer. You can't control what's going on with the humans, but you can catch the one that killed one of you. Focus on the murderer, Jack. Make The Five Streets safe by finding the one who did that. Go, Jack, run!" MooMoo did not wait for his reply. She jumps down the windowsill and disappears out of Jack's vision.

Jack is alone, sitting on the cold, disinfected patio slab. He shakes his head, not sure if the fumes from the disinfecting chemicals made him experience what had just happened or not.

MooMoo just told him to leave the garden. Not to come back, not for food, not for her. That is ridiculous and cannot be true. Jack sits there and stares up to the window, hoping MooMoo jumps up on the windowsill again and tells him how funny his little face looks after she tricked him. A few minutes pass and nothing happens. Only Jack, sitting alone on the patio. Jack drops his head and strolls out of the garden. If MooMoo tells him so, it is better to do so. He knows better. Not listening to her will end up in an argument, or worse. In the end, he would not win. This is her territory. She makes the rules here.

Jack walks over the grass, his paws dragging, his head hanging low. He is not happy to follow MooMoo's pleading, but he will leave. He turns his head around, hoping for someone to call him back. All he sees is the big TV through the window, still showing pictures of people scared, angry, and sad. Jack sneaks out of the garden through the little hole in the fence and the last view of his beloved garden is full of angry people fighting and shouting.

"Maybe they do not deserve better," Jack thinks with a deep sadness inside himself.

His paws touch the pavement of his street. Here it is he who rules! 1st Street is his territory! He is back home and all he wants now is his little box in the corner. The last hours have been very eventful, and Jack has a lot to think about. The world he knows, they all know, is going to be very different tomorrow. It already started today.

Jack wonders what all the other cats and animals think about what is going on with the humans right now. For all he knows, he hopes all the animals in the world are safe for now.

Humans are in danger, but for how long have animals been in danger from the humans? Maybe it is time to turn the tides.

Jack decides that this is a problem for a later time. He must find a killer right here in the streets. That danger is way more present than any other in the world. Time to get himself together and report to the other leaders about the sewers and the fox. At least Jack is sure his first suspect is in the clear. The fox did not do it, not this time. Jack stands in front of his little box and all he wants is to go in, close his eyes and be by himself. His mind demands silence to think. It wants time with him to sort through all that he saw today. Laying out the next steps based on the facts. But Jack cannot give in right now. He has a duty as a leader and needs to speak to the other leaders first. His ongoing conflict between being a leader of the streets and a mystery solving cat comes up again.

"Of you go, Jack!" He sighs deeply and turns his back to the box, making his way to meet Gina, Churchill, Azrael, and Cecile. And Jack cannot wait to get an update about how the cats in The Five Streets are after the announcement of the virus. The little cat walks away from his home, his head hung low, his shoulders slumped. A tired and worried Jack walks the 1st Street. It feels like today has been one endlessly long walk.

The streets are still empty of human and cat. It is eerily quiet, as no cars are moving. No one is coming home from a day of work or driving out for dinner. Everyone stays home. Jack thinks The Five Streets are one of the safer places to be right now. They have no big shops people can come and steal from, like he has seen on the TV in MooMoo's house.

Jack cannot imagine how it might be for the animals living near those areas or right in it.

All the fighting, noise, and fear. It must be dreadful. But regardless of that feeling, it feels sort of safe; the change is visible.

Jack wanders the empty street, trying to sort his mind before he meets the other leaders. Somehow it is what a lot of the conspiracy cats from the former 3rd Street always told them. One day, the humans will go down and the cats will take over the streets. Who could have guessed they were so close to reality with their theories? He continues to walk away from 1st Street into 5th Street, avoiding the building site 3rd Street is now. It would be faster to cross through 3rd Street, but Jack did not feel like jumping and climbing over rubble and building site machines. Besides, he welcomes the longer walk. Even though he is tired, it gives him some time to sort himself out.

MooMoo hit him hard with chasing him away. He understands her a little; but it was not nice to do so. Jack just lost his most reliable food source and a place where he felt safe and at home, like his little box. The garden was the place it all started. That place changed his life more than once. First, he found The Gracious Lady and her food. Second, he met MooMoo. Last, it gave him the chance to catch a food thief and show him his true calling—chasing mysteries for the greater good, well, kind of greater good. Mostly for Jack and his ego, but also for his mind. Since then, his mind has been racing. He solved more cases in the streets than anyone before him. He helped many cats find their lost ones or uncovered plots and thefts before they could get out of hand. It was a good thing that he did. But now the garden changed his life again. It took itself away from him.

"Well, two out of four isn't that bad," Jack thinks and off he goes to meet with the others.

His walk takes him through 5th Street, but he knows Azrael won't be there, so no need to stop. He will see him in Gina's place. Jack is sure Azrael gave his full report already.

Jack is curious about what the spying cat thinks about the last few hours they spent together. For Jack, it was a real eye opener. He thinks Azrael is the perfect companion for his cases. They work well together and to combine their knowledge and skills makes them a perfect team to work on the murder case. Jack hopes Azrael thinks the same and will continue to work with Jack. "It would be good to have someone else out here with me. Having Azrael will open different doors and sources, that's for sure."

Jack walks in the middle of 5th Street and pauses. He wants to think the situation through before he arrives at Gina's. Would it be good to have someone tagging along with him all the time? So far, Jack was good on his own, with the occasional help from MooMoo. But MooMoo is different. She stays inside and gives advice where she can whenever Jack asks for it. But having someone beside him all the time may distract him from the primary task. Or not? Jack wonders if this can work, but he cannot see anything against it. He knows this can be a one-off teamwork, anyway. No one expects anything from him in that direction.

They both are leaders here in The Five Streets, busy enough with their own streets. Jack decides there, in the middle of 5th Street, that he will try it if Azrael is up for it. Jack can learn a lot from Azrael and not only about The Five Streets. It makes Jack smile to himself. He is looking forward to the time with Azrael in this case.

He jumps up and walks with a lighter step towards the end of the street and turns into 2nd Street, Gina's territory. The end of the day suddenly became a much better day. He lost MooMoo and the garden, but he seems to have gained an unexpected companion. Not that Jack feels the same about Azrael as he feels about MooMoo. This is his little secret he tries to hide.

MooMoo is his special little secret, one he needs to keep away from Azrael and the others as much as he can. For now, all the other leaders know about MooMoo is that she is one of Jack's sources of information.

He needs to tell the leaders about MooMoo's behaviour and warning. The humans are losing it with this virus, and Jack cannot blame them for doing so. To Jack, humans lost it a long time ago. There are few he knows, humans that is, but the few he's met have been strange. Only The Gracious Lady was different so far.

Jack rushes now along 2nd Street, passing by the car park and bin storages. A few cats are out here, waiting for the food distribution to start. But there are fewer cats than usual here at this time of the day. The impact of the virus has made it into the heads of the cats. Another big problem The Five Streets need to address soon.

Jack follows the street until he arrives at the small hedge that separates Gina's home from the street. He jumps on top of the hedge and looks around from up there. He can see the cats waiting for the food to be shared and the tunnel that leads into Gina's home. The tunnel looks uninviting and dark. Jack always feels weird entering the house that way. It is so not Gina. But Churchill loves the tunnel. It is his domain.

Jack can see one eye glowing back at him out of the tunnel. Churchill is on his watch. Jack takes a moment to look around the street. From up here he can see the spot they left the cat to be found by anyone. Jack can clearly connect the dots from up here. The entrance of the sewers, the dragging of the body, and the point where it got dropped. The question remains, why and how does the marking under the body play a part in it all? It is a message, but for what purpose? Jack wished he could meet the other leaders with more answers than questions for himself.

Not yet, but he will get behind this all. The trace is there. Whoever did this is not as clever as they think. The drag marks leading to the sewers. The blood drops in the sewers. It is all there; all Jack must do is put it together. He needs another trip into the sewers tomorrow, that is for sure. Answers laying below the streets this time.

He jumps down the hedge and as soon as his paws touch the ground on the other site, the glowing eye comes closer through the tunnel but never leaves it. A scruffy voice greets him out of the dark.

"You took your time. They are all waiting for you. Azrael already gave his full report. What took you so long?" asks Churchill.

"Back off, old cat," Jack replies with a smile. "I am not late. You all are impatient and worried sick. Don't you have to be somewhere else and watch other cats out there? Making sure they behave?"

Churchill chuckles at Jack's reply. He likes the little banter the two have. For now, it is good to see that Jack has not lost his humour, but Churchill can feel how tense Jack is. It will be worse in a few minutes when he must face the others.

Churchill has listened to Azrael's report, and it does not sound very good for any of them.

"Come on in, young one. Everyone is curious about what you will report and how you spent your day in the sewers. Azrael gave his take; you know how dramatic he is. Now we need you to cheer us up or pull us further down. I can't wait to hear what you think about this murder. Heard you met the fox again? How is the old bastard doing? Could have gone and visited him myself a few times to sort out what stands between us, but you know Gina and her view of such things. Would have broken her heart."

"We all must do what we must do. Let me go in and make my report. We are not at the end of his murder yet, Churchill. I am afraid we are only at the beginning and the next days will not be easy for any of us," says Jack as he walks past Churchill into the tunnel.

Jack continues his walk through the darkness of the tunnel. He dislikes everything this tunnel stands for. The darkness and feeling of being caught always gets him. As usual, Jack tries to cross as fast as he can and hopes Churchill will not stop him for a little talk in the middle of the tunnel before they step in front of Gina. Jack is not in the mood for it today. He spent too much time in dark places, or places he did not want to be. The only place he wants to be right now was taken away from him minutes ago by his most loved cat. No, Jack is not in the mood for little chitchat in the dark tunnel. Jack feels Churchill behind him, following him. Jack sighs with relief when they pass the middle of the tunnel with no stopping.

"I heard that!" is the only thing Churchill says.

Jack relaxes more and more the closer they get to the end of the tunnel. He can already see the cosy light of Gina's cave. The partly fallen apart sheet has created a nice little cave for Gina and Churchill to live in. Jack is still amazed how much time and effort Gina put in to making the cave feel and look comfortable.

Jack steps out of the tunnel and into the small cave. The floor has recently been updated with new colourful rugs and bits of carpet. A lot of colours are on the floor. The broken ceiling lets enough sunlight in but is covered enough by a tree to keep the rain and wind out. The whole cave greets everyone who steps into it with Gina's kindness. Everyone feels immediately welcome. That's why all the important discussions happen in Gina's cave. It helps to keep the temper down.

"Hello, Jacky! How nice of you to step by, darling! Come on in; have a seat. Look, Azrael is here too. He just told us about your short trip back to the woods. How is the nasty fox doing? Hope he still stays out of the streets as agreed?" Gina greets Jack as he steps into the light of her cave.

Jack walks into the cave and smiles at Gina. She never misses the chance for a grand entrance. Calling him out the moment he arrives and giving him the latest and greatest in a short version, so he knows where they are with the update. Jack walks over to a yellow piece of carpet and sits down. He looks around the cave and takes a moment before he replies to Gina. He needs to choose his next words wisely or it all will end up in an all-out discussion that could take the whole evening.

All Jack wants is to give his update and continue with the investigation of the murder, nothing more, nothing less.

Jack checks on Gina; she looks composed. A good sign after Azrael gave his report to them all. It looks nothing Azrael told was upsetting any of the cats in the room. Jack wished he had been here earlier so he could have listened to Azrael. Now he needs to assume Azrael's report was not holding anything back, but Jack has the feeling he gave them all a lighter version of the event from today. Jack follows Azrael's lead and keeps his report brief with fewer details. Better to keep some details for himself for the big reveal later when he has solved the murder. Why make everyone nervous right now with his assumption of what is really going on in the sewers and The Five Streets? "Stick to the facts and basics," he tells himself.

"What's that, Jack?" Cecile asks.

"Nothing really, Cecile. Just sorting myself out. Give me a second."

Jack takes his time; he knows the other cats are waiting for him. He wants to get this right and out of here as quick as he can. He wants to be back in his box now and go to bed. Finish the day and hope tomorrow will be a better one. He lets them wait a little longer, taking time to prepare his report. Jack gets up and paces along the carpets. He feels the other cats staring at him. Gina, Cecile, Azrael, and Churchill sit in the cave waiting for Jack to tell them what happened that day. After his report, they will decide on the next steps. But Jack does not need the other leaders to tell him what to do next. This is his murder case, and he will solve it. No matter what the council of the leaders decide.

"Very well. I can see you all are eager to hear about our little expedition. As you all know, Azrael and I went down into the sewers. Azrael was so kind and offered his help as a guide in the sewers. He was a great help indeed. You have not been down there, and I can tell you, try to stay out of the sewers. It is not a place a cat should stroll around. Azrael could guide me through the tunnels, but even he struggled to remember the right turns by the time we were down there in the darkness. We followed the marks the cat's body left as far as we could. We even found some blood spots guiding us further into the sewer system." Jack stops his report and lets everyone digest the news he just shared. Jack is sure the blood spots will help to get the leaders on his side again.

"We followed the trace as far as we could, but soon lost ourselves in the darkness. We got to a point where we either had to return and try to find the last traces of the blood on the floor or we press on and see where the tunnel leads to. Azrael and I carried on, and after a few more steps, we could see a light at the end of the tunnel. We had all the motivation we needed to carry on and find out where the light came from. I am sure Azrael told you about all this already. We ended up just below the field, near to the woods. My main suspicion was confirmed. The tunnel was leading us to our prime suspect. We all had it in our minds from the beginning, no need to deny it. We all thought about the fox when we saw the body. I cannot blame you for this quick conclusion, as I did the same. But let me tell you, we or better, I spoke to Reynard. Azrael hid and overheard the entire conversation and can confirm I am speaking the truth. Reynard is still weak and far from his former self. The only time he showed some sort of strength happened when I challenged him directly and accused him of the murder. "

"It was a short flashback, but it cost Reynard dearly. He has no will to be alive and continues only purely out of the stubbornness of his body to give up. Anyway, I do not want to regress. Reynard is another topic for another day. During our conversation it transpired that Reynard knows about the sewers, indeed he was even using them to travel under The Five Streets. Still too scared to come out and face anyone. But he knows them and has spent some time down there himself. He was watching our cats from his hiding place and none of our spies even knew about it. It shows us how much more dangerous the sewers are. Everyone and everything can hide there without us knowing." Jack catches his breath. He talked much more than he wanted to, but he wants them all to understand that this is the beginning and not the end of the murder investigation.

"I know what you all are thinking now. A murder happened. Someone used the sewers to kill a cat and tried to make it look like it happened on our streets. This act of crime has the same taste as events we had in the past, driven by individuals who are now banned from The Five Streets. But what if I tell you they killed this poor cat alone for telling us to stay out of the sewers? A warning from someone down there who does not want to be found? Imagine someone like this living right below our paws! Whoever sent the message is still hiding in the sewers. We do not know who it is and why that someone is down there."

"We need to continue to investigate the sewers, but I would recommend we pull all our cats out of the area. Make it look like we left the sewers alone. Only Azrael and I, if he wants to support me in this case, will venture further into the sewers to find the murderer. The true meaning of why one of our cats had to give his life for The Five Streets."

Another well-timed break in Jack's speech. Jack waits for the first protests or questions, but the leaders keep quiet, looking at him with worry in their eyes. Jack continues. He does not want to lose his momentum. "I am sure we can find the killer, but we need to proceed with utmost care. It is vital that nothing we say leaves this room. All I ask from you is to leave it to me to catch this killer and do not interfere. I need all of you to carry on taking care of the cats in our streets. Tough times are coming our way. I saw the human's storing food and locking themselves up. Soon we will be on our own to find something to eat. This virus will be our problem soon enough, and I need you all to work on this together. We have no time or energy to waste. The Five Streets are under threat again, multiple threats, and it is up to us to make sure everyone is safe. It is our responsibility!"

Jack stops talking and lets his eyes wander over the Gina, Churchill, Cecile, and Azrael. He checks each of them for their individual reaction. Gina is half asleep on her pillow. Her eyes are closed, and it looks like she was not listening at all. Churchill sits at the tunnel entrance and his one eye is sparkling with excitement. He is all up for the hunt. Jack sees that clearly. Cecile's face is a frown of worries, a garden of deep wrinkles while she thinks over the next steps and what it might mean for her healing corps.

Cecile worked hard with her cats to get the allotments up and running. A hard task for cats.

They cleaned up as much as they could, making it look more attractive for the humans to return and use the allotment like in the old days. Providing the cats with another source of food. The humans have been slow to realize what happened in the allotment, but some of the older ones had already started coming back and planting things on the earth. All that is now close to collapse again.

The virus will make the humans stay away.

Jack knows Cecile is all about caring for the streets and all living beings. She is not interested in catching a killer. All that counts for her are The Five Streets. That's fine for Jack. He needs someone back here in the streets to hold it all together when he and Azrael are out on the hunt for the killer. Azrael licks his paw and cleans his ears; he is eager like Jack to continue and leave everything else to Gina and Cecile. Jack sits back down and sighs. His job here is done. Now someone else needs to do the talking. All Jack wants is to get back onto the streets hunting for the murderer and this time with less distraction from his job as a leader. He wants the freedom, and he hopes the other leaders will grant it.

Gina was the first one to speak. Not asleep, as everyone thought. She listened to everything Jack said. She opens her eyes and stretches her long legs.

"Jacky, what a nice way to tell us all what to do without telling us what to do. I know what you want, and I will give it to you. But under one condition: can you make sure we will feel safe again in our own streets? I hear you and agree, the sewers should be off limits. But what if we ignore the warning and let you continue to go there? How can we know we are not making matters worse? We must think about all the cats we are looking after. The virus is bad enough, but having another threat looming out of the sewers? Wouldn't it be better to lay the murder to rest and focus your combined energy on the threat the virus poses? Tell me, Jack, how can we know for sure you will stop the killer before it gets worse? Can you promise? If you can, I will let you go, and we will deal with the issues up here." Gina stretches again and lays down, closing her eyes again. She looks tired already, and the trouble has not even started yet.

Cecile takes her turn before Gina even finishes. "I agree with Gina! The safety of our streets must be the major priority. We need to avoid anything that can cause more harm to us. There is enough for us to do with the humans and the virus. We already see the impact this virus is having. Humans go crazy about food and supplies.

It is just a matter of time until the paranoia kicks in on our streets. We cannot afford a panic like this. And dealing with a killer, or worse, stirring something up from down there that should have left asleep. I get where you are coming from, Jack, but it is a risk. We already have the rumours spreading about the fox being back in the streets and hunting us down for revenge. This must stop right now. We should declare the murder as an accident and let it be."

"I agree with Jack!" was all Churchill had to say.

All heads spin around and look at Churchill. No one was expecting him to take any side that early. Normally, Churchill followed Gina's lead, but not this time, it seems.

"What? Don't look at me like I am the fox! Believe me, I would happily forget about it all and keep my lady safe," Churchill tells them. "But we need to be true to the problem here. We have a murderer on our streets. Ignoring it does not make it go away. For me, the murderer is a threat to my lady's life, and I will do all I can to protect you, Gina. Even if it means getting behind Jack's plan to solve the murder. I know you will be upset, but this is not the time for it."

Gina gives Churchill a mean look and turns her head away, suddenly more into cleaning her fur.

She does not give him a reply, just plainly ignores him for what he just said. Jack's little heart is jumping up and down.

Getting Churchill on his side is a delightful bonus, unexpected but very welcome.

Now the situation is a draw. Two cats are for it and two are against it. The last one to give his vote is Azrael. Jack is sure what Azrael wants to do, even before he hears it. Jack knows the spy cat cannot let it finish like this. One of his own cats got killed for something Azrael asked. Letting it stop here would make no sense at all. Jack tries to catch Azrael's eyes, but the other cat is evasive, as usual. Not giving away any of his intentions, not yet. The air in the little cave is getting tighter second by second. They all know what will happen next. The cave is full of tension between the leaders' emotions. It feels like you cannot breathe in here at all anymore.

For Jack, the feeling is unbearable. This is one of his favourite places and right now it feels like the most uncomfortable place to be. The murder is already doing the worst for The Five Streets. It divides the leaders. A murder and the human virus, no one could have planned both happening at the same time better. That would be too much to ask for. But Jack knows someone is thrilled right now, and that someone is not here in Gina's home.

"Alright everyone, let's calm down. This is not the time for us to break apart and make matters worse. We need to stick together to save the streets. I know we have different perspectives on how this should be done. We can't always agree, but we still can work together to get the best for the streets. All the cats out there must be kept safe. Let us not loss ourselves and make matters worse." Jack says and tries to stay as calm as he can. He shows them he is in control of his emotions.

"All I want is what is best for our streets. We are here to protect and to guide. We are The Five Streets! No one can take this away from us, only us." Jack stops talking here. He hopes his words will help to make them all understand what is on the line. This is another moment where the leaders can fail and lose a lot if some of what they have said here today makes it out. Jack sits back down and tries to relax himself. He really hopes the others can see the danger as clearly as he can. If not, all will be lost, and hell will break loose soon. If the unity of the leaders breaks here today, the streets will fall and the lives of every cat in The Five Streets will be different. Anarchy will replace control. The right of the strongest suppresses the weak. Jack hopes this will not be the end, not after they survived the fox, Thumbs, and The Grey.

"Please let us not fail now!" Jack thinks to himself and lays his head to rest on his paws, waiting for Azrael's last words on the matter and the fate of The Five Streets.

Azrael stands up and paces around the cave. He looks around himself without looking at any of the other cats around him. The decision to continue with the murder investigation will be driven by his words. He wants it to continue, but at what price? Azrael wants to find it out!

"Well, here we are. All of us again. Feels familiar, doesn't it? Last time we were like this was after we found out about Thumbs and her plans to take over the streets. Now we have another threat looming on the horizon. Well, two. For me, the only concern is the murder. The virus is something we cannot control. We have no other option than to roll with what happens next. The murder well, this is something we have total control over. We can find the one who killed one of us. We can make sure this does not happen again. Can we live knowing that maybe someone we live with on these same streets is a cold-blooded murder? I cannot. I would really like to know why one of my spies had to die. What had he found? Who had he seen? Why did he have to die? This question weighs heavy on me. It was I who sent them down there to map the sewers, to find out more. It was a good idea back then and is still a good idea. We found the connection between our streets and The Big City. What possibilities do this gives us? We found a hidden passage between both worlds. Can you imagine if we never found out that everyone can come to our territory unseen?

"The tunnels under our streets are the biggest threat right now, as big as having a murderer in our midst. I agree with Jack. We need to find the murderer at all costs, and we need to continue to watch the sewers." Azrael finishes his little speech with an aura of confidence.

He hardly ever steps up for his own needs or tries to be heard. Talking now to all the other leaders shows how important this topic is to him. They all will listen to Azrael. He does not speak often, but when he does, it is important.

Gina is the first again to object. She still feels bad about the murder and the sewers, but for her, the virus is more threatening. An unseen danger that will cause the cats on the street to lose faith in the leaders. "Thank you, Azrael. Indeed, a very detailed and eye-opening viewpoint. I will agree partially on your view, but I feel we need to focus our strength right here, on our own streets. There is talk already, fear spreading. The cats know about the virus and what it does to the humans. They know we will run out of food soon if the humans stop supplying it. Why don't you leave the sewers to your shadow cats?

They are perfect for sneaking around in the dark. No one will enter our streets undetected. They can handle everything that might be down there."

"A good point," Jack thinks. He had not thought about the shadow cats. A little detail that slipped his mind, but they would be very helpful right now.

"My shadow cats are busy otherwise," was all Azrael had to say to Gina. That was not enough for any of them.

"Where are the shadow cats, Azrael?" Jack asks.

Cecile is not holding back either, "Right, tell us Azrael, what is so important that you have them not in the sewers? A second ago, you made us believe the sewers are the most dangerous and important place to watch. How come you did not have your best cats on this?"

Azrael takes a step back; he tries to hide in the few shadows of Gina's cave. His eyes glow yellow with mistrust, and he hisses back at all of them. "It is of none of your concerns where I sent my cats. I am the Master of Spies and I decide what tasks my spies need to attend to. I make sure The Five Streets are safe, safe from any outsider and from within. My shadow cats are where I need them the most right now. I do not need to tell you until I am very sure you need to know. For now, all you need to know is that they are out on a mission more important than the sewers or the murder itself. They are undercover in the city. That is all I can tell you right now!"

"Oy, calm down, mate! No need to talk to her ladyship like that!" Churchill steps closer to the middle of the room, positioning himself strategically between Azrael and Gina. Churchill does not like how Azrael is behaving. For whatever reason, the Master of Spies looks cornered and loses his usual calm.

Churchill is not sure what will happen next, but he will make sure he is in the way if things get nasty. "Azrael, relax. We are all friends here. No one will harm anyone," Churchill tries to play the outburst down, but he feels the tension in the air.

"Azrael, no one tries to threaten anyone here. Why are you acting like this? We understand your line of business, and we are the last ones who want to tell you what and how you should do your job. Remember, we are all on the same street at the end. Tell us, why have you sent the shadows away rather than using them to protect us? Why now?" Jack is asking all his questions as they come to his mind.

His mind works on the overreaction Azrael just showed. Unusual, these are the signs Jack looks for in his fellow leaders. Something is off with Azrael, and Jack does not like it. Until now, he thought he had a companion to join him in his investigation, a precious companion to help him solve the murder. Now Jack is not so sure anymore. Azrael pushes to find the murderer, but does he really want to find the killer or just want to make sure he is part of the team hunting for the killer to make sure nothing comes out that compromises the master of the spies? Another challenge for Jack has just come to light. A new suspect begins to form in his head, an unwelcoming one, but still a new lead to solve the murder. The case is moving forward by the hour and Jack is eager to find out more about Azrael and his motive to hide the whereabouts of his shadow cats.

"Tell us, Azrael. Please tell us why you kept it secret what the shadow cats are up to? Our whole leadership is based on trust. How can we continue to lead if we distrust each other? Please, darling, let us be part of whatever it is you are working on," Gina pleads to Azrael to play fair and share.

Churchill still doesn't move from his space between the two cats. His body is relaxing, but he stays on guard. He never trusted the spy. Azrael is always sneaking around in the shadows, trying to find out all the secrets everyone is involved it to use them to his advantage.

All apparently for the greater good of The Five Streets, but Churchill never believed that for one second.

The spy is too far out in the dark all the time. Maybe he finally got swallowed up by the darkness and is now following a new master? Whatever it is, Churchill is ready, watching the Master of Spies. Churchill has his own way of spying on the cats in the streets. Azrael is not the only one who can play that game.

Azrael keeps pacing around in his corner, his eyes small slits of yellow shining in the dark. How could it happen that they could corner him like this? He is not sure why his calm betrayed him just now. A terrible choice and an even worse timing. Now they all will have a reason to stop trusting him, more than before. He curses himself for being so impulsive; it always takes all his self-control to keep his temper in check. A Master of Spies needs to be calm and collected, calculative and controlled. Azrael does not need emotions in his line of business. He blames Jack and his sewer trip for his overreaction. It took a lot of his focus to keep Jack going in the direction Azrael wanted him to go to. Away from the part of the sewers that lead into The Big City. Last thing Azrael needs is Jack in The Big City. Or even close to it.

No way he would let Jack take away that mystery from him.

Azrael will be the only one to know what is going on in the city, and he will decide if the rest should know about it. What made him really lose his temper and jump on the others is the loss of communication with his shadow cats.

It has been days since he had an updated report of their doing. For days, it has been silent around the cats and the progress they made to infiltrate one clan in The Big City.

Unusual and a concerning, that much Azrael can agree on. But should he share this with the rest of the leaders? It will open him up to more and more questions. Questions Azrael does not want to answer or has no answers for yet. But he needs to give them all something right now, or they will not let him go. He needs to make sure Jack is still willing to take him with him to continue the murder investigation. It will make it much easier this way. Azrael has no resources to spare. To put one of his spy cats on Jack would be too tiresome right now. The best option is Azrael being with Jack wherever his investigation might lead him.

"You all are right. Please accept my apology! The last few days have not been easy for any of us. The pressure is growing by the day and keeping The Five Streets protected from the outsiders is getting harder. My spy cats are tired, and we fight in multiple areas at the same time to ensure no one slips into our streets without noticing. Our streets have not been the same since we had the fox to pay us a visit. I had to spread our resources very thin to keep up with all the potential dangers.

Around the clock surveillance of the fox in the woods, keeping the sewer entrance covered and having cats down there as well to make sure we know every single dark corner of the sewers and, as we like to forget, the ongoing search for the ominous Grey. Who and where he is? He remains one of the biggest threats to our streets.

"I know you all want to hear something good, something positive, but I can't really give you that. The Five Streets are in danger. We must be ready for the next attack from the outside," says Azrael.

"My spies have confirmed the worse, the next attack will come from The Big City itself. Don't get me wrong, this is not a war or something like it. The attack we expect is organized and kept in silence. Not an all-out invasion like in the old days. No one will fight other cats in the streets. No, this one will be another attempt to infiltrate us from within." Azrael takes a little break to give everyone time to catch up with his report.

"That's why I sent the shadow cats into The Big City. They are the only ones capable of dealing with the life in The Big City. We need intel and they can give it to us. They are our only hope at a time like this. And believe me, now with this virus, The Big City will be a powder keg waiting to explode. This is all I can tell you right now. I am waiting for a more detailed report and will update you all as soon as I can." Azrael takes a big breath and settles himself down again, his calm restored. "I am sorry for my outburst earlier and maybe I should have shared this earlier. The murder is just the cherry on the top for us on 5th Street. We are already under threat every day. Nothing physical but it takes its toll on my spies like every living being in The Five Streets."

Jack takes a step back in his mind. This new revelation from Azrael is worse than any of Jack's deeper fears. What does Azrael mean by The Five Streets are under attack from various threats? It intrigues Jack about what Azrael might know and, more importantly, what Azrael does not know and does not admit to knowing. Jack will make sure he keeps Azrael close for the next few days. Looks like working together on the murder case will have more benefits after all.

Churchill sits on his back legs now, his head spinning with what Azrael just said. A threat, many threats for The Five Streets? What is going on? Who is threatening his lady?

All Churchill can think of is Gina and that she might be in grave danger. And why hadn't Azrael told him about it? What is going on here? First a murder, then the virus, and now another anonymous threat? How should Churchill be ready for all this? His security team is already small, much smaller than it was. He really needs to get Jack out there as quick as possible and catch the loose killer. At least they can take care of one worry. For now, Churchill will keep his concerns quiet, but he will have a serious word with Azrael later.

Cecile and Gina stare at each other in silence. Gina nods to Cecile to continue and let them all know what they think.

"I, or better, we, agree that the murder investigation needs to continue. Jack and Azrael should find out who killed the poor cat. Azrael is right. We face many threats lately. We know some and some are unknown to us. For now, we should focus our energy and teams on the threats we know. The murder and the virus. For the rest, we will leave for Azrael and his judgment. We could argue all night long about the way you handle these threats and keeping your secrets, Azrael, but we think it would not help us at all in this situation. We must deal with this another day. For now, let us try to fix what we can and hopefully the streets will be safer by tomorrow. It will help everyone in The Five Streets to know that Jack is back, and he will find whoever did it. We all know what to do. Let us go home and rest. Tomorrow will be another long day for all of us."

All the others agreed, it was enough talk and revelation for tonight. They need a good night's rest to get everyone ready for the next few days. Jack cannot wait to get back to continuing his search in the sewers.

Jack is the first one to leave Gina's house. He wants to get some fresh air and think about the day. A lot had happened, and he needs to get his mind in order.

He walks through the dark tunnel to get out of the house and arrives outside to be greeted by a cool night. The stars are out, and the moon is starting his journey through the sky. The streets are still quiet, no humans out, no cats strolling in the moonlight. It is indeed a strange time.

Jack sneaks through the hedge that borders Gina's home and is on the street. He looks up and takes a deep breath. The air is fresh. Jack takes a stroll over to the car park in the section where they found the cat. He wants to cast his eyes over the scene again. What better way to animate his brain about the scene than by being at the same spot he wants to remember and analyse? It is only a short walk and Jack arrives at the scene of the murder. He notices a big change already. A lot more cars are now parked here, making the normally big open space rather crowded. Must be all the humans that have to stay home now.

Jack never saw that many cars around here before. Only a small square in the middle of the car park is empty. Strangely enough, it is exactly the space where the cat had died, or better, been placed to be found dead by someone. It is as if the energy of what happened there made the humans avoid it. Jack sits right in the centre of where they found the cat. He sits in the same spot the cat had laid earlier. His eyes are closed, and he recalls the scenes of the morning in his head. He sees it all as if they're there right now. His little head moves around as he tries to see different things in his head. He is at the murder scene and inspects the area. Not only at the scene immediately in front of him, no, he checks the scenes his mind captured that are further away. All the cats that had been around the setting of the car park.

He looks for something that is out of the norm. Something they might have missed the day.

Suddenly Jack jerks back, his eyes flash open wide. His mind turned against him, and he got attacked in his mind by the fox and the old, rabid dog. Here in the car park. That was not part of his achieved memory about the murder scene. It caught Jack by surprise and made him jump up and look for cover. The memory felt too real.

"What was that?" Jack says aloud to himself, his voice still shaky. He turns his head around, making sure no one saw his weird behaviour. He checks for any danger that might be around him. Maybe his mind picked something up and wanted to warn him while he was in his trance. But nothing to see, only cars, and a lot of cars. Everyone could hide behind or underneath them. Jack sniffs the air, still clean. No fox smell in the air or dog. "Why the old rabid dog? That is all very weird."

Jack settles down again and tries to be calm. It has to mean something. His mind would not do this for fun. Jack closes his eyes again and visualizes the murder scene once more. This time, he focuses on the nearby scene. The dead cat, its position, the marking on the floor, the wounds that killed the cat. There it is! The wounds. Jack inspects the wounds that killed the cat. They are long and have big clawed marks. Jack can see now that these marks are even too big for a fox claw. Or any cat that Jack knows of. It is now clear to him that the fox was never an actual suspect in this at all. Neither could it have been any normal cat. These marks are way too big. Thinking of it and seeing it in front of his inner eyes, they look just about big enough to fit a dog, an old, rabid dog. It would fit. Jack jumps up, all excited this time.

That is fresh evidence, and he cannot wait to share it with the one who would know best about the dog's claws.

"There are few dogs in The Five Streets. The ones I know are all kept inside, and the humans keep them on a short leash when they are outside. I wonder if it could be possible for one of them to sneak out and kill a cat?"

Jack continues to follow the new theory in his head. It is a possibility he must consider. Given the evidence of the claw marks, it is more likely to be a bigger animal. Cats are no longer a suspect here. Jack gets up and starts walking away from the murder scene. His steps are now swinging with excitement. Now he is ready to take a good rest and tomorrow will be a new day with new possibilities. He cannot wait to share his theory with Azrael. But before that, Jack thinks he should talk to someone who knows dog claws and injuries the best. Churchill will know more about these kinds of claw marks. Jack wonders if Churchill already knows, but decided not to say anything.

This case is becoming more and more entwined with individuals.

Jack walks down the road, deep in his own thoughts. He does not see the cat hiding in the shadows, watching him. Jack passes by the cat hidden in the shadows and the cat follows him hidden and on silent paws.

Azrael can see by the way Jack walks that Jack just had a break though on the murder case. Azrael needs to know what Jack just discovered. He followed Jack after he left Gina's place. Now he is glad he did so. Seeing Jack like this is raising his level of concerns. Jack is on track to discovering the murderer, and Azrael is dreading the moment Jack does, as it will change everything Azrael works on right now. He tried so hard to get into the Big City to investigate himself and find out more about what is going on there in the city and how it might impact The Five Streets.

If Jack finds out the murder is from the Big City, all of Azrael's work will be stopped by the other leaders.

Jack is on his way back to his box. The day is ending, and Jack feels exhausted from the events the day has brought up. He has lots to think about, but his body also needs rest for the days to come. Jack knows this is still only the beginning of the hunt for the murderer. He will need all his wits and energy to catch the killer. It will not be easy; the numbers of suspects are still large and the only clue he has might hide somewhere in that sewer. Jack needs to find the place the cat died, the place where it all started. That will be his task for tomorrow. For now, all Jack wants is a little of food and some good rest. He hopes his mind will let him rest. For the moment, his mind works at a high speed.

The discovery of a different animal as a suspect is challenging enough to keep his mind occupied for the night. Some food will clearly help to calm his mind, or to numb it a bit at least. But thinking about food makes Jack realize he has another problem to consider. His favourite food source is off limits. No more visits in the garden. He promised MooMoo, but can he keep his promise? Jack needs food, food to keep him going. Food makes sure he can function without being distracted by the need for it. Jack stops at the edge of the streets, where it narrows into the side street to his little box. The garden is right there, the entrance just around the corner.

"Did the lady leave me some food?" Jack wonders. Jack is not sure if the lady will still leave the food for him. All of this might have changed because of the outbreak of the virus. The humans have changed already because of it. Fear is in the air around the many houses.

"I am not sure what to do?"

Jack walks over to his box. He still hasn't decided about the garden and the food, but he does not want to be seen sitting in the middle of the streets. Better to go home and lay down for a bit. Thinking will start as soon as he lays down. He knows it and for now it is his best option. Jack needs answers. Some are better to get right now and others later. But he needs quiet time for some serious thinking.

He continues to walk down the road and takes the turn onto the little side path between the two big houses. There it stands, his little wooden box, the former home of Old Boy, Jack's mentor and teacher. What a good time the two had together back then. Now it is Jack's home, his place. And there is no better place like home for him.

He slips through the cloth that covers the entrance and he relaxes the moment his paws touch the soft carpet inside the box. All the tension leaves his body, and he just stretches out on the carpet. All covered, all protected. The box keeps the warmth of the sun and Jack stretches his front legs, clawing into the carpet with a satisfying purr. He drags his claws over the carpet repeatedly, as if digging for some hidden treasure. His purring gets louder and louder and he sinks his body down onto the carpet. His claws are still moving but his eyes are now closing, and the movement gets slower and slower until he lays still asleep in his little box. That went much faster than Jack hoped for.

Azrael sees Jack stop in the middle of the road. Something made him stop right there. Azrael moves deeper into the darkness, making sure Jack does not see him or smell his presence. The wind is low and blows into the wrong direction to be smelled, but you never know. Better be careful than regretful. Azrael is sure Jack will not take it nicely if he finds out that Azrael tails him.

It would raise many questions. Questions Azrael is not ready to give answers to. Not yet. First, he needs to know more about Jack.

Tonight, Azrael wants to see Jack as how he really is with no one around him. Not that Jack has anything to hide. Well, everyone has something to hide. That's what keeps Azrael in his job. Secrets are his calling and getting others to admit their secrets is what Azrael is good at. Not all secrets are useful, but it is always good to know. Knowing them can be handy at some point. You never know when, but they might. Right now, Azrael is wondering what secrets Jack is hiding. Maybe a murder or a bigger conspiracy? For Azrael, this is not out of the possible. He must do his job, even if it means to go against his own kind. His own partners.

They all have sworn to protect The Five Streets, no matter from what or whom. Insider or outsider. Azrael is just doing his job.

Tonight, it is Jack, tomorrow, maybe someone else, if the observation satisfies Azrael. If not, Azrael will stay around and investigate Jack out of the shadows longer. Shame he cannot use one of his shadow cats. Doing this job himself takes too much precious time, time he does not have. A virus threatening the humans and murder in their own streets, why both at the same time? What unfortunate timing!

"Or is it?" Azrael thinks aloud. He doesn't have to believe that this is just what it is, a coincidence. No one would have the power to pull this off. No animal in the world could do that.

Azrael looks up. Jack is on the move again. Jack disappears behind the corner of a house; he took the turn towards first street. No surprise for Azrael so far. All actions look like Jack is going home. Azrael relaxes a bit. He follows Jack. He wants to make sure he sees Jack enter his home before he makes any conclusions. Azrael peaks around the corner, his body pressed against the house wall, using all the shadows he can to avoid anyone seeing him.

His eyes follow Jack, taking another turn into a small side path, the path between the two big houses, right where his little box is. Azrael moves further on silent paws. He sneaks over to the corner and lowers himself low to peak again. He sees a tail slipping into the box. Jack is home now. All Azrael must do is wait here and see if Jack stays home. Azrael really hopes this is the case. He is not in the mood for a long night of stalking behind a murder suspect.

Azrael hides in a small bush next to the road. He lays down with his front paws crossed and his head resting on them. He is ready for a long night. It will be worth it, as he needs to know if he can trust Jack or not.

Jack is fast asleep, not knowing that Azrael has been watching every one of his moves since he left Gina's home. Jack's sleep is full of dreams about Old Boy, the rabid dog, and the dead cat in the car park. Somehow, his mind sees a connection and tries to tell Jack what to do next. Jack's little legs twitch in his sleep as the dreams intensify. His mind uses Jack's sleep to analyse the past happenings and builds a connection to the present murder.

The claw marks on the killed cats have triggered the memory of Old Boy and the rabid dog. His dream shows Jack the wounds the dog inflicted on Churchill and Old Boy. They are an obvious match, the same claws that killed the cat. There is no doubt. A dog is the killer. Jack needs to find a dog in the sewers. The sewers are a perfect hideout for an animal like this. It will cover all smells down there. No one could single out the smell of a dog in the sewers. But to what purpose is a dog hiding down in the sewers, and why did it have to kill the poor cat?

Jack stays in his unsettling dream. He knows it is just his mind trying to help him solve the case, but it feels all so real. The crazy dog is being fought by Old Boy and Churchill.

Jack the kitten joins the dream right now when the dog turns his heads and spots Jack, the little kitten. His head flies around and the eyes burning with hate stare at Jack. The dog takes a step towards Jack, his mouth dripping with blood from the other two cats. He barres his teeth, old, big yellow teeth, and growls at the kitten. He bounds towards Jack now, running to get the easy prey. Jack stands frozen on the spot; his legs won't move.

He curls up into a small fluffy ball and hopes for a quick ending.

Jack closes his eyes. His ears hear the dog running, hear his heavy breathing, his big paws flying over the tarmac. It took only seconds but for Jack, it all moved in slow motion. Jack hears the crunching sounds of another body colliding with the dog, a big crunch, and a yelp from the dog. Churchill took him by surprise. Both animals crash to the ground. The rabid dog rolls over Churchill and lashes out with his claws. Churchill tries to turn and bite back, but the weight of the dog pins him down.

Jack watches all this between his paws. His head covered by his legs, he peeks through and watches how the dog lifts his big paw and slashes over Churchill's face, ripping the cat's eye open and hitting him again and again until the cats lay unconscious on the ground. The dog stands over Churchill; the cats laying between his front legs. He opens his mouth to bite the cat's neck, finishing this cat for good. Old Boy jumps out and attacks the dog from behind, just in time to avoid the death of Churchill. The dog spins around, facing the other cat. Old Boy throws wild and fast attacks at the dog. His paws flash over and over to hit the dog. He drives the dog back bit by bit with his fast attacks. The dog is trying to block Old Boys attacks, but he fails often and the claws slash at his fur, making him bleed out of hundreds of tiny wounds. Churchill still lies on the ground, not moving. More and more cats are now joining the fight.

They heard the noise and decided it was time to take matters into their own hands. Churchill and Old Boy tried, but they could hear both needed help. Now the cats circle the dog; he has no way to escape. All the cats hiss and lash out at the dog.

Jack watches the scene with horror. He never saw violence like this in his whole little life. The dog begs them to stop. His eyes have turned from hate to fear. He tries to protect himself as much as he can, not fighting back at all anymore. It looks like they are going to kill the dog right there in front of Jack. It is the law of the streets. The Five Streets have agreed to take care of the dog and protect the streets. The cats get closer the smaller the dogs make himself. With one last outburst, the dog tries to free himself. He jumps up, throwing paws and teeth at everything that moves. He pushes two cats out of his way and runs. He runs for his life. The cats following quick on silent paws.

That was the last time Jack saw the dog for real, but it will take years for them to stop meeting in his dreams.

The dream makes Jack very agitated, and he thrashes around in his little box. Azrael can hear Jack moving, but he does not interfere. For Azrael, it is only important that Jack stays in the box. This is the only way for Azrael to judge if Jack is innocent and not involved in the murder. Jack relives the scene with the rabid dog over and over in his dream. But the details he sees change little by little.

The focus shifts away from the actual fighting and violence, closer to the details Jack needs. He sees the teeth of the dog, the claws, the wounds the claws inflicted on the cats.

That is the important part. Jack wants to see the wounds; he wants to see if they match the wounds of the dead cat, even remotely to the dog he knows. Jack's focus is all on the size and pattern of the wounds.

He can see clearly the bite marks the dog left behind and the scratches his claws make. It is obvious to Jack that the pattern and length of the claw marks match the dead cat ones.

Jack is sure a dog was involved in killing the cat in the sewers.

Jack leaves this horrible dream and drifts finally into a deep sleep. His body is relaxing and the trashing in the box stops. For now, Jack will rest a few hours. He does not need his bad dreams any longer. He found the proof he needs to continue his investigation.

The next morning is fresh, and Jack feels the chilly wind drifting into his box through the cloth cover. He tries to curl himself tighter, resisting the cold air and the early morning trying to wake him up. It was an intense night for Jack. Managing this kind of dream with all the details is challenging for him and his mind. He feels tired and exhausted. All he wants is to carry on sleeping. His body complains about the cold. His eyes will not open, but his mind stirs. He remembers the discovery from last night in his dream. The claw marks of a dog on the little dead cat in the car park. He has a new suspect for the case. No one physical yet, but better than nothing. A dog must hide in the sewers and Jack wants to find him or her. Jack decides that sleep will not come again and stretches his legs wide and long. He cleans himself with his tongue and paws, washing his ears and snout, clearing the nose of unwanted smells. Today he will go back into the sewers, and he will spend the whole day searching if he needs to. Azrael will be with him, an expert help and guide down there.

"Shall I tell Azrael about the dog?" Jack thinks it through, but decides for now to keep his discovery a secret. Better to leave everyone out of it until he has proof. Jack gets his cleaning done and leaves his box with a spring in his step. Today will be a good day to find a killer.

Chapter X

Azrael waits for Jack at the sewer's entrance.

"Hi, Jack! How was your night? Ready for another trip into the darkness?" Azrael greets Jack.

"All is well, Azrael, all is well! Slept like a kitten. Ready by all means! Let us find that murderer and close the case before this virus thing makes our life's way more complicate."

"Very well. I was thinking about today and how we should approach the search. I think I would like to introduce you to one of our contacts who lives down there. It would be good for you to meet Basil and his family. He knows more about the sewers than anyone else we have met. Basil was born down there and spent his whole life scavenging the sewers for food and other things," Azrael says.

"That sounds interesting. Lead the way, my friend," Jack replies, and his tail twitches with excitement.

Azrael doesn't want to waste any more time and slips through the hole in the pavement into the sewers. Jack looks around and it surprises him that there is not a guard at the sewer entrance today, not even the crazy French cat. He takes a mental note to ask Azrael about this later. They agreed they would watch this entrance all the time from up here. What has changed? Jack shakes his head and follows Azrael into the sewers. Sometimes Jack is not sure who he can trust anymore.

Things like the missing guard is only helping Jack's suspicions that every leader follows his own agenda, regardless of what the others think.

The darkness welcomes Jack and Azrael as soon as they slip through the hole. First it is just a small shade, engulfing the cats softly. With every step, the darkness becomes fuller and pulls them deeper into the sewers. The darkness fully embraces both cats as they arrive at the first crossroad. Azrael stops there and sits down, waiting for Jack to catch up. He wants to tell Jack a bit more about Basil to make sure Jack is ready for the meeting.

"Wait here a little, Jack. I need to talk to you before we meet Basil. There is a thing or two you need to know before we continue," Azrael says.

Jack sits next to Azrael, his head tilted slightly with curiosity. "Go on," Jack says.

"You will meet Basil soon. He lives down here with his family. He spent all his life down here. I know I mentioned this before, but listen, please. It is important that you know as much about Basil as possible before you meet him. Basil is a rat, not a cat. I am sure you guessed as much already."

Jack nods in agreement and signals Azrael to continue.

"His family goes back a while, and he knows parts of the sewers that are now closed off but still accessible by smaller creatures, like rats. Which means me and my spies have not seen these areas yet, and we do not know how to get into them," Azrael takes a breathing pause and continues, "But they pose another threat. Something you and I might need to work on, as the killer could hide in one of these places. Anyway, Basil was or is the only creature from down here that approached us and offered help. I must admit we have not had a lot of other contact from the animals that live here. He is our link between our world and theirs. It is important that we treat him with care. We cannot afford to lose his trust or help. You need to understand this, Jack; it is important that we have an insider down here to make this work."

"I get it. The network of tunnels is very important to you and the spies. I can't wait to meet this fellow. Never talked to a rat in my whole life. I know some of us hunt them and even eat them if they catch one. How come Basil is not afraid of us?"

"You will know when you see him. Basil could follow unnoticed for days down here. He could have been a danger to all of us if he wanted to. Not physically, maybe, but by spying on us for someone else while we try to figure out the tunnels. He watched us for days, only to decide if he should join us or hunt us out of the tunnels. His words, not mine. How he would do that, no idea, but if you hear him talking, you will believe he is capable of it. This is much bigger than we think, Jack. That's why I am so eager to continue checking these sewers out. It is a whole new world down here, right under our paws. The potential is limitless. We just need to connect with whoever is living here."

Azrael's words and openness intrigue Jack. It makes more sense now why he wanted to join Jack on the hunt of a killer. Especially if the killer comes from down here. It would put everything Azrael has tried to build up now in danger.

"Very well then. Let me see this rat. I am more than curious now. By the way, I think you really should share this all with the rest of the leaders. It will make it much easier for them to understand what you are trying to do."

"Gina will be more on your side if she knew about the animals living down here. She will be all over the place trying to help them live better. Churchill might freak out at first, but he will accept the change eventually. Cecile would be the first one to join you in exploring more about the habitants of the sewers.

She is always up for learning about new animals and how they live. It gives her a chance to improve her knowledge of healing and caring. I really think you should share this with them. You would get more help from all of them."

"You might be right, but I am not ready yet. I need to know more before I involve anyone else. Telling the others what I know might make it all more complicated, as they all want to be involved suddenly. I understand your concerns and appreciate you want to help, but this is my way of dealing with what we have found here. I want to make sure The Five Streets stay safe and believe me for the moment, the less they know about what is going on down here, the better."

"What are you saying, Azrael? Do you expect someone is playing against us from our own team? If this is the case, you need to make sure you have us all on your side as quick as possible. Let us not repeat what happened with Thumbs. You need to tell us if you know someone is betraying us."

Azrael regrets his words as soon as they leave his mouth. He knows Jack will not let this pass. The betrayal they all experienced is still too fresh. Thumbs is a very sore wound, even more than the leaders themselves. They all know they lost one of their own. Someone they might not have liked, but they trusted and worked hard with to make The Five Streets a better place. Azrael is not happy with what he just said to Jack, but it is too late to take it back. He seems to slip more often lately. Maybe he is just tired.

"Jack, believe me, if I knew, I would tell you all about it. Problem is, I do not know. I will find out eventually. What kind of master spy would I be if I don't." Azrael tries to play the situation down, but he can see Jack is already working on it. "Forget this for now. Let us focus on what we do today. You are the second one after me to meet a citizen of the sewers. Get yourself ready, as this will be something you won't forget for a while."

Jack accepts the diversion for now, but it is not out of his mind. If Azrael thinks there is a traitor in their midst, then it is most likely true. Azrael would not mention this light-heartedly and for no reason. Curiosity wins for the moment. Jack wants to meet Basil as quick as possible. Getting to talk to someone from down here might open a new lead on the case. This is a way better option than looking for traces in the dark sewers, hoping to find more blood drops on the ground or other hints to lead them to where the murder might have happened. Jack will take the change, even if it means he must stop bothering Azrael about the traitor. For now, Jack will stop talking, but not for long.

"Okay. Let's get this over with. Introduce me to your contact down here. I am curious to meet Basil and wonder what he has to say. I hope he is helpful, as we are running out of time to solve this murder. Don't ask me how I know we are running out of time. I agree with you, it is better to say less than too much if you do not have all the proof. For now, I want to talk to Basil and see what he knows about our dead cat and his potential killer. I hope this is not a waste of our time."

Azrael smiles at Jack. "You will see soon enough!" Then he jumps around the corner. Jack follows him quick. The last thing he wants is to be left alone in the dark sewers.

It is a good place to get lost forever. Jack keeps as close to Azrael as he can, his nose nearly touching Azrael's tail. It caught Jack by surprise at how fast Azrael suddenly moves in the darkness.

"At least it looks like you know where we are going this time!" Jack shouts at Azrael between quick breaths from running after him.

"Keep up, Jack, or get lost in the dark!" Azrael shouts back to Jack. Jack can feel the big smile on Azrael's face.

"He is really enjoying this," Jack thinks and tries to keep up with Azrael.

The cats whisk through the dark tunnel, Azrael in lead and Jack close behind. Jack has lost any sense of direction by now; all he focuses on is the tail in front of him. Azrael takes turn after turn and corner after corner. It is a never-ending maze for Jack. His mind is reeling from the idea of not knowing where he is. Jack trusts Azrael. Why else would the master of the spies tell him all about the sewers? It would be a big surprise if this turns out to be a trap.

Jack had played with the idea of Azrael being the killer. It made sense to a certain extent. Jack's suspicious mind sparked again when Azrael told him about Basil and how protective Azrael is about his knowledge of the sewers. It might still be a possibility, but not a big one. Jack disregards the idea again, but his mind is still checking the little details about the idea and running around in this maze with no idea where to is not helping to quiet his mind. His mind works on the idea of Azrael as a killer and his eyes work on keeping the bobbing tail in sight in order not to get lost. "Well, I asked for it, didn't I?" Jack whispers to himself in the dark.

Azrael stops so suddenly that Jack nearly crashes into him. Both cats sit down for a moment, breathing heavy.

Their little chests are heaving, and they try to catch their breath. Azrael has a big smile on his face. He enjoyed the race. Jack looks at him with a confused and worried expression.

"Well, that was a bit of a rush there, Azrael. How come you did not tell me we are racing around in the dark sewers first thing in the morning? I would gladly have skipped the exercise and used my energy on something more useful, like looking for food or catching the morning sun on my fur. Speaking of food, any chance for a snack down here? I am starving!"

Jack looks around him like he is searching for food. "You know I skipped my breakfast to be here with you this early? I hope someone down here has some food lined up. I am not the best companion when starving."

Azrael turns his head to look back at Jack. His eyes reflect the little light that is down in the sewers. They look like twinkling yellow stars to Jack. "You know, you are right. We should have some of the local cuisine while we are here. I am sure Basil will serve us the most delicious food, fresh from the sewers. Remind me to ask him when we meet him at his house in a few minutes. Not sure about his hospitality but let's find out, shall we?" Azrael points towards a little hole in the wall while he speaks. "Ready to meet the family, Jack?"

Azrael lowers himself as much to the wet ground as he can, avoiding his belly by touching the floor. He creeps through the hole and disappears into whatever lays behind that wall. Jack stares at the hole for a second longer, not sure if he should follow or turn around now. If it didn't look like a trap before, it certainly does now.

"Only one way to find out," Jack says and squeezes himself through the hole in the wall.

There is a moment of panic as Jack moves into the hole. The wall is much bigger than he thought, and he must squeeze his body through a tight tunnel. The edges of the tunnel scrape over his fur, and it is hard to move forward. His legs are all tucked in, and Jack can only move with little steps. The closeness of the space makes him feel trapped. He cannot see what is behind him. He cannot twist his head at all. He lays flat in the tunnel that is not much more the size of a tube, barely enough to fit his head in. It is dark and dusty in here; all light is finally gone, and Jack can smell the dust and dirt around him.

"My fur will be a big mess when I am out of here!" he thinks and continues to creep further. What took him only minutes felt like ages to him, but he finally sees some sort of light in front of him. He breathes in deeply as soon as his head pokes out of the tunnel. This is way worse than Gina's tunnel! Jack regrets the sucking in the air the moment the air hits his lungs and nose. There is a horrible smell around this place. The whole place smells pungent, a strange musky smell. Nothing Jack discovered before. Not in that kind of intense form. "That's how it smells to be in a rat's nest," Jack mutters to himself quietly, as he does not want to offend anyone.

"You are right, Jack. That's how it smells and that's what it is exactly. Welcome to Basil's home. Come on in, meet him and his family," Azrael says from somewhere further up the cave.

Jack cannot see him but is not surprised Azrael heard him. Jack finally pulls himself free of the tunnel and walks towards the voice. He enters the room behind the wall and is amazed how much bigger it is here. It looks like an actual room, not a dingy hole in the wall. Not at all what Jack was expecting.

He was not sure what to expect. The room even has some artificial light, an electric bulb hanging from the ceiling. Jack wonders how this got here. It must have been a place for humans once. Jack looks around him and absorbs everything in the room. His head stops moving when his eyes meet four rats staring back at him with little black eyes, whiskers twitching, and the little ones hiding behind the taller rats. Predator meets prey in a confined room. This can make none of them happy. Jack tries to put on a relaxed posture, trying to stop his tail from twitching with excitement. It is very hard to suppress your natural habits.

"Hello there! I am Jack! How are you all?" Jack asks in what he hopes sounds like a kind voice and not like a cat trapping its dinner in a dark corner.

The rats look at Jack with big, black eyes. The small one's hide behind the parents but keep on peeking at the two cats in front of them.

"Basil, nice to see you again. Been a while since I last required your services. How are things down here?" Azrael asks casually, trying to follow Jack's lead in pretending this is just a normal catch up between them all. He knows how stressful it is for Basil and his family to have contact with outsiders. "Anything to report? I have heard nothing from you for a while! Anyway, may I introduce my friend Jack to you all? Jack is a famous cat up there in our streets. He caught a fox once. A bad one, doing bad stuff. Have you ever seen a fox?" Azrael leans closer to address to the kids hiding. He tries to keep it calm, but it annoys him that Basil had not told him about the fox running around in the sewers. Azrael is sure Basil knew.

"Good day, Master Azrael! It is always a pleasure to welcome you to our humble home. Wish you could have sent a message prior to your arrival. We had no chance to ready ourselves. Nice to meet you too, Jack. Apologies for our behaviour, but we are not very used to having visitors here. Especially not unannounced and in the shape of cats. Makes us all very nervous as you probably can imagine. Welcome to our humble home. Please come in." Basil bows his little head and ushers his family back into the room.

Basil's reply amuses Jack. He totally ignored Azrael.

"Azrael, you never told me about your little friends down here. I never would have taken you for a family cat," Jack smirks at Azrael and follows Basil into the room. He is curious to see how someone lives down here. Hopefully, Basil can provide some new information about the murder.

Azrael does not waste any breath in replying to Jack or Basil. He just follows on silent paws behind Jack. This is how it works; he introduces his source and then steps back again into the shadows to observe. "Let's see how Jack handles himself as an interrogator," he thinks.

Jack enters the room the rats call home. There is a space between the walls. Humans have used it in some sort of function. It has electricity, an old, dirty bulb dangling from the ceiling, giving enough light to have a good look around. Jack can see a big metal door on the other side of the room. It looks like they have not opened it for years. Its metal looks rusty and dirty. The room itself is of a square shape, like the size of Gina's cave in the broken shed. The floor is hard, grey concrete covered with dust and dirt.

One thing Jack picks up straight away, it seems rats do not favour clean spaces. A few empty cardboard boxes are piling up in the corner next to the door. They look like beds for the rats. Right next to Jack at the entrance is another enormous pile of collected rubbish. Paper, various fabrics, strings of wool, plastic bottles, and caps, even a human glove.

Jack stops trying to identify what else might lie in that mountain of trash. It looks like the rats collect everything they find in the sewers and keep it here in the room. Jack wonders why.

"Kids, why don't you both go and take a nap? It is way beyond your nap time and the adults need to talk business. Martin, be a good boy and take your sister. Make sure she stays in bed and rests. You know how fragile she is," says Basil.

The boy rat drops his head in disappointment, but he does as he was told. He nudges his little sister to move into the cardboard boxes.

"Come on, Marcy, the grownups want us out of the way. Let's play along and pretend we go to sleep," Martin says and pushes Marcy towards the boxes. Both wiggle into one box and then the room is empty, apart from the two cats and Basil.

Jack understands what Basil is doing straight away. He clears the room of all ears, even the ones close to him. Whatever it is they are going to talk about is only for one rat and a pair of cats. His family has no dealings with him. Jack thinks it is Basil's way of making sure his family stays safe. Jack is not sure why Basil does this, but he will wait and listen to what Basil has to say. Azrael thinks it might be important for Jack and the case, so better pay attention to all the details. Jack sits down and waits for Basil to talk.

Basil walks to the farthest corner of the room, as far away as possible from his napping children and the hole in the wall his wife left through. He motions Azrael and Jack to follow him.

All three sit down in the small corner, heads stuck together closely, working on a conspiracy. Basil keeps his voice low so no one can hear what he will tell Jack.

"Listen Azrael, I do not appreciate you turning up here unannounced and with another stranger. You know this is not the deal. I told you I will help your spies to get along down here, and my only condition was to keep them all far away from my family. And now you turn up here and expect me to do what? I should kick you out of the sewers and make sure none of you ever come back."

The way Basil talks to Azrael surprises Jack. The little rat changed so much in its attitude and its voice is firm, not as feeble as before. It was all a show, another piece to keep his family away from whatever is going on here. Jack is more and more intrigued by the little rat. "This better be good," Jack thinks.

"Calm your horses, Basil! Do you think I would do this if it wasn't important for all of us, no matter if down here or up there? I understand you are upset, but I had no time to arrange this meeting properly. Time is of an urgent matter, believe me. I will make sure you and your family are safe. Trust me on that."

Basil looks at Azrael with his black, lifeless eyes. It's the eyes that get Jack the most. How come such a small animal has such disturbing eyes? Jack leans closer to get a proper look at those eyes. Normally, Jack is good at understanding and reading a character alone from the look of the eyes and how they move. But on this rat, all Jack sees is a dark pool. All Jack can read is nothing.

"Back off, mate! What do you think you are doing? I am not your dinner!" Basil pushes his whiskers right into Jack's face, making Jack flinch back. That caught Jack by surprise.

Basil is for sure not the whiny rat he likes to portray in front of his family.

"Tell you what, Jack, come that close again and you will regret it. We got taller ones down. You will not be the first to learn not to underestimate us. That's it, sit there and be a good kitten. Now, for you, Azrael, what do you need?"

Azrael takes a deep breath in and closes his eyes. Jack sees it takes a lot from Azrael to stay calm and tolerate Basil's behaviour. He is not sure why Basil behaves like he owns Azrael or Azrael works for Basil rather than the other way around. Jack admires how strong the little creature is, but he is not sure if Basil could back it up.

The two cats could take the little rat down in an instant. Azrael breathes out and stares at the rat.

"Tell him what you told me a few days ago. Tell him what happened down here and why you are so on edge. Stop playing the tough one. I know who you are, and you know who I am. Both of us have agreed to the truce, you and me under the same conditions. None of us want to go to war over the others. Tell Jack what you told me. That is all I am asking for now. Let me assure you, Jack needs to know so he can get on with a pressing issue from up there. I am not sure how much your problems relate to us in The Five Streets, but I am sure if someone can figure this out, it is Jack. Now get on with your story or let it be. It is up to you. I, for one, am sure we can help each other out, but it is up to you if you want Jack's help or not. For now, we are here, and it is your choice how this goes."

Basil nods his head multiple times, as if in agreement with Azrael's words. His little head bobs back and forth, his whiskers twitching with excitement.

He looks at Jack and gives a last nod to himself, as if saying to go ahead with Azrael's suggestion to talk to Jack. Basil steps closer and lowers his voice again to a faint whisper. Jack pricks up his ears to hear what Basil is about to tell him.

"Listen carefully, Jack. I am not repeating myself. All I am about to tell you must stay between you and me. I will be in deep trouble if someone hears what I am about to tell you. You know where you are. We do not need to waste time on that. But what you don't know is who I am or who we are. We are many, don't let our size deceived you. We might be small, but we are many. We have been here for a very long time, way before your streets have been built. We took over this place, down here to be alone, far away from humans and their pets. Life is good for us down here. It might not look like much to you, but that is what we want you to see. Azrael here already had a taste of who we are and what we can do. Believe me for now, you are only here because of us wanting you here. You would be just a floating body in the sewers if we decided you would not be welcome here. "

"I know, I know, you might not believe it right now, but you will soon if you do not follow our rules down here. For you only two rules apply, number one is, what happens down here, stays down here and number two is you do not talk about us up there on your streets." Basil takes a little break to give Jack the chance to hear what he just said. "When you leave here and go back into the bright world up here, make sure everything you see and hear down here stays here. No exceptions. This is all we are asking for. Tell me, Jack, are you able to accept these two rules?"

"Basil, what are you talking about? You sound worse than Azrael and he is from 3rd Street where all the crazy conspiracies come from," says Jack.

"I do not know who you are and what you are asking might compromise my case. How can I be sure what you are about to telling me will not put The Five Streets in danger? And if so, how can I make sure I can protect The Five Streets without exposing you? I am sorry, Basil, but I cannot agree to your terms, not without knowing more," answers Jack.

"No, No! This is not how it works. Look at Azrael. He gave the promise. He broke it today by bringing you here, and he will suffer the consequences. The only reason his little kitten heart is still beating is that he is here with me. I will still have to decide if he is about to leave and come back again or if he will stay forever with us down here. Agree or leave, Jack. This is not up for discussion. Your friend here took a gigantic risk. Will it be worth it for him? It is up to you."

Azrael looks a few shades paler right now. He just realized what he did by bringing Jack down here to meet Basil.

He broke rule number two, not exactly by talking about the rats in the sewers, but worse, by bringing an outsider down here to meet the rats. "Basil, hold on. You know who I am up there and what I am doing down here. We work together and bringing Jack will help us all. I had no option. Jack, tell him why we are here."

Jack follows Azrael's lead and starts explaining the reason Azrael came to see Basil and to make him meet Jack. "Azrael had no option, really. I do not know if you guys know what is going up there but we, Azrael and I, are investigating a murder case in the name of all the leaders of The Five Streets. A murder that has led us down here into your sewers. Azrael had no option in this matter, as I would have found you eventually anyway. All the traces of the murder lead down here. The cat we found dead in our car park had to be murdered down here and placed on purpose in our car park."

"All traces lead us here. Either to frame you or to frame us. I am not sure yet. But meeting now makes me think you could have set up this murder yourself. Oh, wait, the best is still to come. The cat that got killed down here was one of Azrael's spies. How about that for a motive?"

"It is true, Basil. Jack was on your trail already. He was about to find out. I had no option, and I decided it would be better the two of you meet now rather under other circumstances. Can't you see that this murder has the potential to blow up right into our faces? If Jack would have found out about you rats down here, you would have attacked him for the outsider he is. Jack would have had no option as to tell everyone what he or who he found in the sewers.

The other leaders would have called for war, for retaliation. Things are bad up in our world right now and the last thing we need is a war between your world and ours. Please trust Jack; he will make sure both the cats on the streets and the rats down here can continue to live as they know it, with no blood drawn from the other."

Basil looks from one cat to the other. His whiskers twitch like crazy. He does not like the openness the two cats just showed him. They would be better off leaving and forgetting they ever met. But Basil needs to protect his sewers now; it is not up to his opinion to risk the life of the others.

"A murder, you say? How interesting. And it is you two volunteering to solve the case? A cat spying on others and what are you, Jack? What makes you be involved in all this?"

"I am the leader of 1st Street. 1st Street is my territory, and I am the leader in The Five Streets that came to ask for your help.

The other leaders might not need to know about you or any other rats down here, but we need your help to avoid the worst." Jack waits for any reaction from the rats before he continues.

"Our streets went through this kind of threat. We know what it does to us and others. We lost one of our leaders back then, and we will not repeat the same mistakes. The murder is a setup. It has a purpose. Right now, I think it is to keep us out of the sewers. First, I thought it is, so we never met, but right now I am not so sure anymore. Tell me what you know, Basil, and I am promising I will respect your rules as best as I can if there is no harm to my streets or any of the cats living on them. Tell me if this cat got murdered by your rats or not. This is your only chance to get me on your side. I am here and I will listen to you!"

"Two leaders of the famous Five Streets in my room on the same day. What did I do to deserve this kind of honour? Excuse me, but I do not feel like bowing right now. I hope I have not offended your highness. Sorry, but I am not as impressed as you would like me to be. We do not accept the ranks and popularity of outsiders; down here, we are all the same. We care only about surviving and protecting our own."

"I understand that, believe me Basil, you are not that different from us on the streets. Every day is a fight for survival. We live off the scraps of the humans. It is not an easy life, but it is a living. The Five Streets provide all we need for all the cats living there, but we need to provide the protection ourselves. Might it be by laws and rules or by fighting outsiders that are not good for us? We are not that different at all. I am asking you once more, do you know anything about the cat and how it died? Why has it died? This is me asking one more time. Think good about your answer as it might decide the future of our two habitats. We might coexist without interfering with each other or we might fight each other over something we both think is right by our own standards. Don't let our egos make it worse for the many here in the streets and the sewers. It is your choice now, not mine."

Jack's tail slashes back and forth, betraying his attempt to show control. This entire conversation is rather fascinating, but it also hangs on the edge of creating a disaster. Azrael was right to introduce Jack to Basil and the ones who live in this underworld, but he also but the peace of both places at risk.

Azrael has nothing more to say. He sits on his paws and waits for Jack and Basil to work this one out. He works on a plan in his head in case this goes wrong, and they have to fight the rats.

The only thing that worries him is the number of rats that live in the sewers. Azrael is glad Jack doesn't know that little detail. They talk about the war between The Five Streets and the sewers, but Jack does not know how many rats they will have to face if it comes to that. The rats will flood the streets, biting and clawing at every cat they see. It will not be pleasant, not for anyone.

The only thing that will hold the rats back is the fear of the daylight and the open sky. But there is always a night following the bright day. A war will not help at all, but it might be unavoidable if Jack figures out that the rats killed the spy cat. Even he, Azrael, would call for retaliation. It would be his expectations and fit for this office. He would have no choice, the same as the other leaders.

The leaders of The Five Streets cannot leave an attack like this unanswered. It is all down to Basil's cooperation in this case. Azrael and Jack hope the rat agrees working together is better than fighting with each other. Only trouble is that the rats want to be left alone, that's why Azrael has told no one until now about the inhabitants of the sewers. He made all his spies swear not to tell any soul about what they or who they found down here.

The Five Streets is not ready for it yet and Azrael needs more knowledge about the peculiar creatures living in the constant dark.

Basil is still quiet. He walks around on his little legs, his ears and whiskers twitching like mad. It looks like he is debating hard with himself. It is a big decision to make. Basil wishes he could involve the other elders for advice, but the two cats have cornered him, and he is not willing to expose more of the way of how they live and function here. It is not the time to make hasty decisions. He stops pacing and checks the cats again.

Their faces, especially the eyes, tell him they spoke the truth. Both are worried about the world up there. That much is true. But can he trust them? After all these years, they built up a society and made a living for themselves. All is at risk now because of a cat and the new arrivals.

How could the elders agree to grant refuge to the other one? He is the one Basil knew from the first sight is trouble. But sadly, he got overruled by the other elders. He was a brilliant talker, same as this Jack fellow, the one waiting for Basil's answer.

Talk is what they can do, and talk is what will give them what they want. Basil wonders if Jack knows the other one who came down to hide here? Better not risk it all and tell them for now.

Basil stops, staring at Jack's face. He sits himself up and speaks clear and firm to both cats. "Okay, I get what you told me. It is a shame a cat died. It really is. We should cherish and honour every life. I can tell you with all the truth, it was not us who killed the cat. Believe me or not, but I can tell you, if it was us, the cat would have never made it back to the streets. It would still float in the sewers until it is gone. That's how it works down here. None of us would have dared to touch one of Azrael's spies. Azrael knows the deal we made. We stick to the deal, and we hope he does too. To break the fragile relationship, we just built would make no sense and only a very few know about it. Besides, it would take a few rats to kill a cat. You would notice this straight away from the way the cat died. Tell me, how did the body look?"

Jack explains the wounds and how they found the cat. He gave Basil all the little details, like the position of the cat and the mark underneath the body.

The sign of a 1 as if to tell them this is only the first one. Jack agrees with Basil that the wounds that killed the cat must have been from a bigger animal, but he tells Basil exactly how they, Azrael and him, could trace back the body to the sewers by following the drag marks and blood spots.

"Someone tried to vanish all the traces or tried to make them seem not too obvious, I am not sure yet. Anyway, they led us here. First, we thought they would lead us to the exit towards the woods, but we lost the trace. We checked on an old friend in the woods and he told us he had been in here as well. Maybe you know him? Reynard the fox?" Jack finishes his report, but Jack studies Basil's face closely throughout his report.

He looks for any sign of recognition for either mentioning the fox or telling the way they found out they killed the dead cat in the sewers and brought him back to the streets as a warning. Basil flinched slightly when Jack mentioned the fox. He must know Reynard. The rest of the time Basil was listening with his head tilted to the side, processing the details Jack shared, but as soon as Jack mentions Reynard, the rat looks up and his whiskers twitch. It was just a split second, but it was there, and Jack saw it.

"I see you know Reynard?" Jack asks.

"Reynard, the name sounds familiar," Basil replies slowly. He tries to win some time to sort his answer. "Yes, yes, he came into the sewers twice. He found us or better, we found him at the entrance one day. A broken, ill creature. We watched him and saw no threat to him. I talked to him and let him know that this area is off limits for any outsider. I remember, he laughed at me and told me to better be off. It took a lot of convincing to get him out. He was going on about how dangerous he once was and how life tricked him. Guess he was just looking for someone to talk to. I let him finish his complaints about life and politely told him again to leave. He did eventually, but it took more than just asking politely. Never saw him again after that day."

Jack can tell Basil is lying, but for now, Jack needs to know more about the sewers. Reynard and Basil are a matter for later. Fact is that both Reynard and Basil did not kill the poor cat, but Jack has the feeling that Basil knows a bit more about the potential killer. Jack changes his approach to get more out of the rat.

"Tell me, Basil. How is it you live down here? Why the sewers?" Jack asks to keep the rat talking.

Basil keeps looking back at the hole his wife vanished through. "She must be back by now," he thinks.

He hopes his wife made it back fast and brought the other elders to listen to this conversation. He needs the approval of all the elders before Basil can share any more details with Jack. Laws are laws. Basil was one of the six who crafted the laws back many moons, but it does not exclude him from obeying the laws. His head moves between Jack and the hole in the wall. "Where is she?" he thinks and his tail swooshes over the floor in a nervous twitch. Time is running out on him. Jack and Azrael want answers, answers Basil cannot give alone. He would lose everything in a blink of an eye.

Jack keeps staring at him, like he is trying to read his mind. "Maybe he can?" the rat thinks in a moment of panic. "Stupid outsiders, why do they need to meddle around in our homes?" Basil is just about to give a snappy remark about Jack's starring when Marta jumps through the hole. She runs over to Basil and sits next to him.

"I am so sorry; the well is dry. I could not fetch the water as promised, husband."

Marta is using the agreed words, telling Basil she got the Elders, and they are outside, listening in on the conversation with Jack. All Basil now needs is the approval to speak freely. He needs to send Marta back to get the approval.

"Thank you, Marta. You see, Jack, water is still a precious thing down here, even if we seem to be surrounded by it. Not all water is fit for drinking down here. In fact, it could kill you to drink the wrong kind. Full of humans' waste and chemicals. Better watch out before you try to quench your thirst. Marta, do me a favour and check the back room. We might still have some left from our daily allowance. Or just ask the neighbours if it is okay to use theirs for our guests."

Marta got the secret phrase to ask for approval, not for water, of course. She is not stupid. Marta nods and whisks out of the room again, through the same hole as before. Basil looks after her with a worried look. He does not like to leave it to Marta. She always gets very nervous when left alone with the Elders. Having two cats in her house doesn't help either. Jack is still staring at Basil.

Basil tries very hard not to jump on Jack. "What is that cat's problem?"

"Stop starring, Jack. It is not very polite," Azrael jumps in as he sees Basil getting close to losing his cool.

Jack is trying to intimidate the rat. A simple thing, staring at someone and pretending like you know everything about them. It can be effective, if done correctly, and Jack is good at it. Azrael must give him that, but it does not help the case right now.

Basil is on edge and if he snaps, he will throw them both out of the sewers for good. That can happen faster, as Jack can imagine.

Azrael worked hard to have some sort of agreement with the rats. He has seen the small army the rats raised when his spies tried to explore the dark tunnels. The moment Azrael turned around the corner and hundreds of tiny black eyes stared in his direction will always be a day to remember. It took a long talk to get out alive from the sewers that day. At the end of the talk, Azrael and the rats had a sort of fragile agreement. Azrael and his spies may use the tunnels, but only if they are kept away from the deeper levels. In exchange, the rats got maps and plans from the world above. It was a good deal for both sides and for Azrael; it seemed like the beginning of a co-existence with the newfound dwellers in the dark and the cats above. The murder put all his plans are in jeopardy, and he is happy to be here with Jack to avoid the worse.

Basil is still waiting for his wife to return with the update from the Elders. The silence in the room is as thick as fog on a London Street in Autumn. No one speaks. Everyone is dealing with their own thoughts. Jack waits for Basil to complete his story. Basil waits for his wife to let him know if the Elders agree to let him share info with Jack.

Azrael, well, Azrael has been holding his breath for a long time now. He has not said a word so far.

For him, all the work he and his team did in the past weeks hangs on a very thin thread. Azrael needs the access to the sewers. He moved his whole operation into the empty house in the city, using the abandoned junk yard as his base camp to explore the city. If

Basil kicks them out now, the entire operation will fail. No access to the city without being noticed. No extending The Five Streets territory into the city without fighting the leaders of the city openly. That would certainly not agree with the leaders of The Five Streets. A lot is at stake here, and that's why Azrael needs to find the killer. This all is too much of a coincidence in his opinion.

The room is still silent as Marta comes back the same way she left already twice to do her husband's biding. Not what she signed up for but who could imagine two cats turning up in their home unannounced? Basil turns around as soon as Marta enters the room; she is out of breath and looks with her big black eyes at Basil.

"The neighbours say it is alright to take some of their water for our guests. They agree to share, and we will pay them back later from our ration," Marta reports back.

"Thank you, Marta. You may start serving our guests. I am pleased our neighbours see the necessity to share the water with our guests; it certainly makes this meeting easier," Basil replies with a sigh of relief.

Jack smirks and he cannot hold back any longer. "Basil, why didn't you invite your neighbours to our little meeting? I am sure you will feel more comfortable if they all hear clearly what I said. We can talk in front of your neighbours just in case some of them might feel offended. It must be hard for them to listen to our whispering, bearing in mind they are sitting behind that wall over there and trying to catch our words through the little hole. I don't mind having them here in the same room with us. I am not the one who has anything to hide."

"How did you know?" asks Basil.

"I was not sure until your wife left us the second time. The first time Marta came back out of breath as if she had run around for a while. It seemed odd, as your water supply would be close by.

She took way too long to just fetch some water. But what gave it away was the second time she left. She came back faster from your so-called neighbours than the first time. I assumed first your neighbours must live close by, but to be honest, cats would have smelled any other rats in the area. I was not aware of you at the time I arrived here, but now I have caught your scent and will recognize it everywhere.

"The second time, Marta came back much faster than the first time. She smelled of other rats, not a surprise as she was supposed to get some water from the neighbours, but the smell she brought back was of fear and anxiety. Why would your neighbours be worried? Only because they are not your neighbours, and Marta went for the first time to bring them here so they can listen to us. Making sure you are not telling me anything without them knowing or even approving. That was the real reason for Marta to go back, wasn't it? Getting the approval from your leaders. I am sure they are behind that wall. To be perfectly honest, we in The Five Streets would have done the same. Why not get them into the same room and be open with each other? I am sure you agree, it will make your life much easier, and all your leaders can talk to us without one of you feeling the pressure of doing something wrong. Believe me, Basil, I am here to help. I need to solve this murder for the sake of The Five Streets, and now I believe in your sewers as well."

Jack could hear them whispering behind the wall from the moment they arrived. It surprised him they felt so safe, but they must be so unfamiliar with other animals that they thought they would be unseen, unheard. Jack is done with playing games.

All they are doing is wasting time. Time he could spend hunting the killer, protecting the cats in The Five Streets.

Getting the sewers and The Five Streets working on this together will cement the future relationship for both. Starting here with lies and in secret is wrong and will help no one. Jack looks towards the hole in the wall. He can hear scratching noises, little claws rustling over the hard floor, and then a grey rat appears in the hole and jumps into the room. Keeping a safe distance from the cats, the rat sits down and lifts his little head, sniffing the air. It squeaks back towards the wall and suddenly more and more rats enter the room. Suddenly Jack feels uncomfortable. He knew some rats were hiding behind the wall, but it surprises him how many rats flooding into the room. He hopes these are not all leaders. It would take weeks to make sure they are all on the same side. Jack knows how long it sometimes take to get the four or five leaders of The Five Streets to agree on something.

The rats stop spilling into the room. It must be hundreds of them in many colours and shapes. The floor was now a moving mass of bodies. Jack looks around and takes it all in. An unusual sight, for sure. Now the rats seem to separate, many moving back towards the wall, leaving only about nine of them sitting in the front row. Basil joins them, making it ten in total. Jack looks at each of the leaders. Ten leaders of the sewers have joined as requested but they each brought their own entourage. Only Basil faced the cats alone.

"Brave little rat," Jack thinks.

The grey rat steps forward and bows his little head towards Jack and Azrael. The other rats stay quiet as soon as the rat speaks. "Welcome to our humble home. We apologize for the way we treated you, but you must understand these are uncertain times and we do not know you. You could have come into our homes with worse intentions. We are glad you are here to talk but we would prefer you never came. This is a safe and quiet place. Well, it was, and we would like to have our place back as it was. I am sure you understand. You are a leader of a pack like us, you will understand. I am Elliot, and you will mainly speak to me. I am chosen to be your guide for this endeavour. Basil did a great job, but talking is not his strength. As you may have noticed, he is a kind of rough with strangers."

The little rat smiles and continues to talk. "Please, relax. As Basil said, if we wanted you dead, you would be already. We do not intend to harm you or any of the cats from above. Azrael, we still honour our agreement. We understood the urgency that made you bring Jack here. We agree, this needs to be addressed and sorted. No one wants a war between our clans!"

"Thank you, Elliot! Appreciate your open words and I agree it was unavoidable to bring Jack here. As I told Basil, he was about to find, anyway. I saw it as a good to gain his and your trust to bring him here," says Azrael. "We need to find a way out of this situation, and I am sure you know more about what happened to my spy. Am I right?"

Elliot and Basil exchange a quick look. Both rats know what Azrael is up to. Elliot moved back to the pack of rats in the background. He whispers with the other Elders. Jack cannot hear what they say, but it looks like a disagreement.

Two of the Elders shake their heads continuously, even stomping their little feet onto the ground. The rest seems to be inclined to listen to Elliot and agree with his idea. Jack watches the whole discussion while sitting quietly on his paws and pretending to clean his ears with his paw. The rat Elders get louder and more agitated. Basil has walked over to the pile of rats and gives support to Elliot, but the two other Elders seem to stand their ground.

"No real unison here as well," Jack whispers to Azrael.

"I know. I hoped Basil would skip protocol and help us out. Did not expect him to call the other Elders. All we can do now is wait and, in the meantime, the killer gets further away from us."

"Nothing we can do. Basil and the rats seem to be a good lead to me. I'd rather wait than wander around in the cold and dark sewers by myself. You have been right; it was or is a good idea. Let's hope they can agree soon on how to handle us. I am getting hungry."

Jack stretches his neck, twisting it to both sides. He tries to get closer to the rats without raising suspicion. He still cannot hear what the Elders are talking about, but the discussion is now a little heated. Elliot and Basil have the majority on their side. That is clear from what Jack can gather. Basil turns away from the group and looks straight at Jack. He winks and turns back to the discussion. Elliot suddenly raises his voice, clear to hear for everyone in the room. "That's it. You two are out of order. We are here to protect our homes, and all you care about is how to take advantage of your own good. I say we vote, right here and now. No need to postpone the vote. It will only give you the chance to draw others into your schemes. I say we vote now!"

The others nod in agreement. Many eyes move towards Jack and Azrael, the two intruders. "Everyone in favour of helping those two cats with our knowledge raise their hands right now. No worries, we will deal with any grumpy old fellows later. For now, let's make clear we will do what's best for us," Basil shouts out.

Five little claws shoot up in the air immediately. Basil, Elliot and three other rats. Five out of ten, not too bad but still no favourable vote or unfavourable. Jack looks at the remaining five rats.

The two Elders who argued the whole time turn their backs to the rest of the group. It looks like a fair gesture to assure they do not see who votes against them. Jack wonders how much more he could learn from the Elders. He feels like their way of ruling the sewers goes much deeper than the way of The Five Streets. They need disagreements in a group like this. You cannot always agree. As soon as the two rats turn, another three put their hands up. Eight in favour of helping the cats, which is more than enough. Jack wonders why the other three waited to vote in secret.

Elliot turns to the bigger group in the back of the room and announces the verdict. "Eight of our ten voted to help the cats. We all can agree this is the way for us to deal with the situation. You all have been a witness and you all will follow the rules. The vote is final. Basil and I will volunteer to deal as ambassadors between our pack and the cats. It has worked in past and shall work again. We both are best suited to protect the interest of our pack. Anyone against the vote shall raise his or her concern in the next chamber meeting." With that, Basil and Elliot turn away from the other rats and walk towards Jack and Azrael.

"You are lucky!" Basil whispers to Jack, "Most of the Elders are curious about the world above and they see it as a great opportunity to build on to the relationship we have with Azrael, but don't let them fool you. There are others who would gladly see you floating down the drain."

Elliot smiles at all of them. He looks pleased with the result of the vote. It gives him the chance to talk openly to two cats from the upper world.

He would not admit it in front of the others, but Elliot has a strong desire to see and explore the world above. This might be just the way to make his hidden desire come true. He continues to speak to Jack calmly, trying to hide his excitement. For now, there are many eyes on them, and he needs to control himself.

"I heard you are trying to solve a murder that seems somehow to be linked to our sewers. What brings you to that conclusion?"

Jack explains the story again, from how they found the dead cat in the morning in the car park and how he discovered the drag marks leading from the hole in the street to the sewers. He tells everything up to the point they met Basil and his family. Jack keeps it short and sweet as he does not want to lose more time. Jack wants answers to finding the killer, not to build a deep friendship with the rats. That's for later if the other leaders of The Five Streets agree. For now, he has other business to attend to.

"That's it. Nothing more to add. We are here now, and you are aware of the rest since we arrived and spied on us through the wall over there. Now, what can you tell me about our murderer? How are you guys are involved in all this?" Jack asks directly to Elliot.

Elliot contemplates his next answer. His eyes twitch while he thinks it over. He knows his answer will set things in motion with an unpredictable outcome, but Elliot knows they need help. Help to get their sewers back. Basil gives a comforting nod to Elliot, as if to say, "Go for it, nothing to lose."

"I know who killed your cat friend. We all know it. Many of us have seen it. It lives down here with us. We don't know when it arrived or from where it came, but it stayed here, and we are in fear of it.

It moves like a shadow but is big and dangerous. We have not seen someone like this for a long time. Some of our oldest rats remember the day a crocodile arrived in the sewers. If it is true or not is not relevant, but they say it is as dangerous as that. And to make matter worse, it speaks. It came with a warning to us on the first day. One warning was all we got. The second warning was no words; it was death."

"You, see? It looks like the same happened on your streets. Why do you think we are all here today? Normally we would live all over the sewers, but for now we feel safer in numbers, staying close together. It is a dangerous animal from the outside world that came and took over our territory, and now it is coming for yours." Elliot takes a breather.

Basil carries on where Elliot left, "Elliot is right. A few of us have seen the animal and survived. Many did not. We tried to fight it, but it seems always to know we are coming for it. I am not sure if it even knows you are here right now. We expect a punishment for talking to you any minute. One of ours will have to pay the price for asking you to help us. But helping you is helping us. We cannot continue to live like this. They confined us to live in between the walls, in small places where the beast can't go. This is not who we are!"

The other rats whisper in the background. They all agree with Basil. This is not who they are or who they want to be. The beast must go. The voices get louder, calling for the hiding to stop. The rats want to fight, but the Elders shush them quickly.

The tension in the room builds up quick, like the days in The Five Streets where food was not enough for everyone on the distribution days. Jack does not like it but understands now why they all are here. This is all fascinating for Jack, and he enjoys every second.

He cannot wait to find out more about the beast that lives in the sewers and how it relates to the murder in The Five Streets.

"Tell me more about that beast you mentioned. Where does it come from? Why is it here? Have any of you seen it for real?" Jack asks around openly. He wants to get the other rats involved, not just the chosen speakers. Jack knows that the word on the streets is worth more than what the leaders get to hear. The streets tell the truth, unbiased, as they do not care about politics or offending others. Jack hopes it is the same down here. Jack needs all the information about the so-called beast he can get his paws on. Jack checks on Azrael and he looks as eager as Jack to get started with the hunt for the beast.

"Is the beast the only reason you all are hiding here? Tell me all right now if you want the help of The Five Streets. Be honest, it is your only chance to get us on board," Jack tries to get more out of the rats.

"There is one more thing we need to consider. The voice. Sometimes the voice from above talks to the beast. The voice coming out of the darkness, from above or in between, from a space we cannot go to," Basil tells them with a hushed voice.

Jack's ears prick up. "A voice? What is it telling you?"

"It talks mainly to the beast. It gives orders or asks for things. The voice is always in the same place. We sometimes gather there when the beast is out and then the voice talks to us directly. It tells us not to worry, to follow his biding and it will reward us all. It is the same voice that orders the beast to kill us if we do not comply. For us, the voice is the terror. It is something we cannot get to, but it gets inside you. The beast we can see and avoid, but the voice is the worst of it all. We never know where it is. It might listen to us right now. We just don't know. If you could hear the voice, you would understand. It is a deceiving, evil snake that winds into your mind and makes you do things you normally don't want to do."

The other rats shuffle around, nervous about what Basil just said. They all know there is no way back now. This is it. They officially changed sides. They decided the rats will work with the cat from The Five Streets. The voice and the beast are the enemy now. It is for the greater good of the pack. Living in the sewers with the beast and under the control of the voice is no longer, and never really was, an option. Jack and Azrael are a welcome help, and having them here made it easier to make the final decision.

"All we ask from you is to have the cats help us against the beast and the voice. We will offer all the support you ask for, even beyond this incident. The sewers will be open for the cats of The Five Streets in friendship. Help us and we will be forever grateful," Elliot speaks officially for all the rats in the sewers. He offers the deal they all hope will help them get back to the safety of the sewers. Asking for help had never been an option until the cats arrived today. Now the rats have put it out, and it is down to the cats to accept helping or condemning the rats to their fate. A fate the voice has planned for them. The rats have taken control of their own fate again, the way they always did.

"Jack, Azrael? Are The Five Streets agreeing to our terms? Are you willing to help us, and we will share our knowledge and friendship with you? We have not much to offer, but we are giving what is ours. We need your help," Basil adds.

"Jack, a word, please?" Azrael whispers.

Both cats move away from the rats. They need to discuss the next steps first. This will have a big impact on The Five Streets. A decision needs to be made. Azrael tries to move as far away from the rats as possible in the small room. Basil and Elliot move back to the rest of the pack to give the two cats more space to talk.

Jack is not sure how good the rats can hear but the room is small, and the walls reflect every word anyway. It does not matter. Jack knows what he wants, and Azrael does not look too concerned, either. But can the two make a call on this alone? How will the other leaders feel if they find out? And they will, eventually.

"Okay, Jack, how do you want to play this? I will follow your lead on this. Right now, I know what I would do. I am sure you will do the same. We need a plan, not for the rats, but for forever frightened Gina, calm and controlled Cecile, and grumpy Churchill. What shall we do?"

Jack needs a second to think it through. His mind works in overdrive. His little synapses flash back and forth. Another big step is building up for him. Can he justify making this decision by himself? Will the other leaders agree? Can Jack trust the others to understand?

Hundreds of questions flash through his mind, overloading him with feelings of guilt, fear, anger, and mistrust. Jack closes his eyes. He tries to shut out his feelings, his emotions. He cannot make a decision lead by his emotions alone; he needs to be subjective. He needs to be logical and efficient for both him and The Five Streets. The danger is real, and the situation requires a quick reaction without delay. There is no time to call all the leaders for a vote. They will waste time with talks, finding proof for and against the decision. Jack has his conclusion.

"No, Azrael, we do not need the others. There is no time. We need to agree with the rats right here. We cannot afford to show weakness. The rats see us as strong and independent cats. We need to show them we are strong and in control. Otherwise, we will lose them to the voice. They will turn to whoever seems the stronger party. We will speak for all of us and agree to the terms and deal with Gina, Cecile, and Churchill later. They will understand, I am sure. They will complain and be upset, but they will understand. Do you agree? Are you with me on this?"

"I am with you, Jack! We know we need the rats, and the rats need us. Both sides will grow from this relationship. My spies have progressed too far to stop here. I am only worried that none of my spies have ever seen this beast or heard the voice. But the answers we need are with the rats. Let's make sure we get them. If we solve this mystery, we are the heroes down here and up there. If we fail, we better move to the woods and share the den with Reynard. And for me, losing is no option, I am not warming that foxes bum. Maybe we should involve the others after we talked to the rats. I do not want this to bite us back. Let's tell the rats we'll help them, check on this beast, and see if it links with our murder investigation. And even if not, I think it would be in our best interest to help them, anyway."

Jack agrees with Azrael again. It feels like the more time both cats spend together, the more they find they have in common. "It is a good thing," Jack thinks to himself while he tells Azrael to speak with Basil and Elliot. Both cats make their way back to the pack of rats. No need for more secrecy from either side. They can discuss the next steps openly for everyone to hear.

"Okay, here we go. Jack and I have decided it would be good for us to work with you on finding this beast. It might be part of our investigation or not, but it does not matter. We want to help you and in doing so we hope you can help us by letting us use your sewers as a passage to the city and other parts. Parts we have not yet discovered. We would be more than pleased if you'd share your knowledge with us and we will show you The Five Streets. You will be welcome above as we are welcome below." Azrael sums up the deal and hopes it fits the agreement.

Jack jumps in after Azrael and adds one more condition to the deal. "We would like to take the time to go back to our place and tell the other leaders about the deal we just made. It is only fair to involve all of us from above and let them know about the next steps. It is important that we are playing this open with everyone involved. You are more than welcome to join us on our trip back up. It might help to persuade the other leaders of our purpose. What do you think?"

The room is full of excited chatter after Jack and Azrael clarified that the cats of The Five Streets will help and work with the rats of the sewers. Many of the rats look at the cats with big, shiny eyes of hope. The Elders put their heads together to discuss what they just heard. There is still an animosity in the group from two the Elders. It would surprise Jack if not. It is an invasion of the private lives the rats lived for a long time.

Change is coming, and it is approaching fast, too fast for some of them. Elliot and Basil are trying hard to pull the others with them. All they need is most of the Elders and they have it already, but it would be good to have them all on board in unison. Jack and Azrael watch the scene in silence.

What they see is so similar they know from themselves and the meetings they attend as leaders of the streets. It is funny and interesting to see that others live the same way. It is a good way, the right way.

"Bringing these two cultures together will make both cats and rats stronger in the long run. The world up there is changing, and The Five Streets need to be open for others; it will help them grow into a new direction. It is part of survival," is all Jack can think of now.

This investigation shows him again how something bad can turn into something good, even if it is an unclear journey, but at the end, it will be good for all involved. Apart from the ones trying to stop them or the ones who committed the crimes against The Five Streets. For those, the journey ends here and now.

Basil and Elliot turn away from the other Elders. The discussions are still heated and ongoing between the other eight rats. But it seems to be clear that this will not stop any progress in the agreement.

"The rats of the sewers will accept as we offered, and we accept your additional terms in talking to your leaders first. It only seems fair you share what you have discovered here, and we are very pleased we met. We know the dangerous actions of a few overshadow our meeting, but regardless, it was good we met. Please return to your world and tell the others about us. Tell them we will help you with your investigation and, in doing so, you are helping us to find and chase the beast out of the sewers. This is what the

Elders have agreed, and this is the way forward. No Rat of the sewers will dare to ignore the agreement. You can move save and free in our tunnels from this day forward." Elliott made the announcement as official as he could. He spoke loud and clear for everyone to hear. This is a time of change. The rats have agreed to take the next step in their journey and the cats of The Five Streets are part of it.

Jack is pleased with the outcome; Azrael's smile says the same. Both cats look happy and ready to leave. Now it is up to them to make sure The Five Streets keep their part of the bargain. "Let's go, Azrael. No time to waste. A murderer is still running free, and we have a good lead, thanks to the rats. Let us get back and make sure the others are on board. We need all paws on deck to make this work."

"Agreed. Let's make a move. Basil, Elliot? Are you coming with us? It would help a great deal if one of you could speak for the rats of sewers in front of the other cats."

Basil and Elliot decline the invite to go with the cats. It is too early for them to face the outside world. "We have much to talk about among us. It would not be the best of ideas to leave right now. Basil and I need to be right here now to make sure none of the others take advantage of the already heated mood within the Elders. Let us meet again tomorrow and we can lie out our plan," Elliot says. "We will show you where we encountered the beast and where the voice comes from. It can wait another day I think. But we need to move fast. Word is traveling quick down here."

Jack and Azrael say goodbye to the rats in the room. Both cats squeeze themselves through the hole in the wall, back to the sewer tunnel. Jack shakes his head in disbelief at what he just witnessed. Amazing things happened in the last few hours. It all started with investigating a murder and now he found a whole new world. A world that exists right below his own paws. How peculiar life can be sometimes. Now he cannot wait to get back and tell Gina and Cecile all about it.

Churchill will throw a tantrum, but Azrael has to manage this part. Security and Spying are not Jack's world, and he will leave it gladly to Azrael and Churchill.

For Jack, it is more important to have Gina and Cecile backing up the next steps. Hopefully, they see the opportunity that lays ahead.

Jack is working on his speech while they walk back the same path they took earlier. Azrael leads the way in silence, working on his own tactic to win Churchill over. The day becomes more and more interesting. Jack nearly forgot about food; he looks up in surprise as he hears his stomach grumbling loud into the silence of the sewers.

"We might need to stop for some food, Azrael. We forgot about all that."

Azrael turns his head with a big smile. "Don't worry, I know just the right place for us to pick up a bite or two."

He climbs up into the sunlight, Jack following eagerly behind.

Chapter XI

A voice greets Azrael and Jack as soon as the little cat heads pop out of the sewers. "Bonne Journee messieurs!"

Both cats blink the bright sunlight away. It takes a couple of seconds for their eyes to adapt to the bright outside after being in the darkness of the sewers. "I hope your trip was successful. I felt a bit worried after the first hour after you stepped down into this dark hole, but I told myself, they know what they do, Ami, they know very well," says Lupine.

The French cat looks excitedly at the two appearing cats. It looks like he was waiting all day for them to come up again.

"Lupine! Good to have you on the watch again! Keeping us all safe? How has your day been?" Azrael asks.

"Nothing to report, monsieur! Just a normal day in a world that becomes more and more crazy by the day."

"I know what you mean. Well, we are off to share some of our crazy day with the rest. Thank you again for keeping watch!"

Jack nods towards Lupine as he walks past him.

"Funny," Jack thinks, "I was sure Lupine was not to be seen when we climbed down into the sewers. I wonder where he was hiding. But good to know that Azrael is taking his responsibilities serious, even if it does not always look like it."

Jack is pleased with this discovery as it means a lot to him to know that Lupine was indeed on watch this morning, maybe hiding somewhere to watch out of the shadows.

Jack can imagine Azrael instructing Lupine to do so. Trying to catch a sneaking individual off guard.

Azrael is already ahead of Jack, leading him to the place where they will find some food. Jack really hopes it is a good place. His stomach is rumbling louder. Lupine gives Jack a knowing look. His complaining stomach is clear to hear for everyone within miles.

Azrael runs down the street towards the allotment. Jack follows quick on his paws. His stomach keeps rumbling viciously. He really should have had breakfast before they left. It was a silly idea to skip breakfast, especially when going to a place you don't know. They could have been stuck in the sewers for the day. What would they have eaten down there? An interesting question forms in Jack's head: What do the rats eat down in the sewers? None of them looked like they were starving. Jack puts an earmark on that question. He wants to ask Basil about it later. For now, his mind paints him a wonderful picture full of exotic foods. Food is taking over his mind and Jack knows he is getting into the danger zone now. He follows Azrael and is glad he is not alone the moment he faces food. It would have the potential for disaster. For now, he will have to control himself or embarrass himself in front of Azrael.

Both cats slip into the Allotment managed by Cecile now after Nina left. It is a nice, relaxing place now.

Cecile and her helpers cleaned the place up and created a small sanctuary in the human world. They did it carefully to avoid the humans figuring out what happened with the abandoned site. For outsiders it still looks like a forgotten allotment, but for the cats it is a place of calm.

The fence and the bushes give protection from the rest of the street. You could stroll along the overgrowth and hunt or just sit on the pond and chill. If needed, you can see one of Cecile's healers to help with many illnesses or pains. And of course, where is food always available? First, for the ill and poor, but Jack is sure Cecile can make an exception for the two starving cats turning up at her doorstep. It is, somehow, a case of emergency. Two brave cats spent hours deep down in the sewers, starving!

Azrael scratches on the door to Cecile's home. The door, a flap of fabric, gets pulled to the site almost immediately and Cecile looks at two smelly cats with disgusting fur. First, Cecile thinks both are some poor beggars from the street asking for some food. It took her a little to realize it is Jack and Azrael in front of her. How poorly both look and how bad they smell!

"Where have you two been playing around?" Cecile asks. "And what is that smell?"

Azrael and Jack both smile stupidly at the master healer of The Five Streets. They look like kittens up to no go. "I am not letting you two in here like this. Go to the pond and clean yourselves up. Maybe after that I will see you two. Go now! Quick!"

"But I am hungry! Starving! Cecile, please, just a snack!" Jack pleads, but he stops as soon as he sees Cecile's amber eyes turn hard. No one messes around here. Cecile is the lady of the allotment, and everyone follows her orders, or you better leave.

Jack looks down and sighs, a bath it is then. His stomach grumbles in protest, but Cecile ignores it all the same. Both cats move over to the pond, feeling scolded like kittens. Cecile has her way with everyone, and there are few that would oppose her in her own house. This is a place of healing and mending, not the place for arguing. Jack smiles to himself and makes his way over to the pond.

It is just a short walk through the nice allotment full of nature. The pond feels a lot more different from the last time Jack has been here. Now it is a calm place, tidied up and made accessible for the cats to lie by and enjoy the cool breeze on hot summer days. The last time Jack saw the pond, lots of bushes that had overgrown enclosed it, blocking the sight of it. The perfect trap back then, now, the cats transformed it completely. It is a place of calm.

Jack likes it. He walks up to the edge of the pond and looks at his reflection. Cecile is right, he looks poorly. His fur is full of dust and dirt. Squeezing through the hole in the sewers really did not add to his appearance today. Jack's fur is all ruffled up, and it dearly needs straightening. Jack starts his cleaning routine, using his tongue to wet his paws and his paws to clean his ears, his forehead, and muzzle. All the while, he can smell the sewers on him. Not a pleasant smell at all. Jack lays down and rubs himself over the grass, trying to pick up a fresh smell. He will cover his fur with the grass, but Jack can clean that up later. For now, he wants to change his smell. He rubs over the grass, rolls from the left to the right and back. He stops and smells his fur. It smells like grass now. A more pleasant smell. Still not cat-like, but better. He hopes it will please Cecile. His natural smell will come back later, after Jack did his big evening cleaning. For now, he wants food.

He starts again, straightening his fur with his paws and tongue. He flicks up his tail and checks himself again on the pond surface. Now Jack looks more like Jack again. Jack is okay with what he sees in the reflection. He looks tidied up. Azrael stands behind Jack and looks better than well. A quick cleaning routine for both does wonders.

"Let's get back for a second check. Hopefully Cecile will approve now," says Jack, and both cats turn back to see Cecile.

"Much better! I can nearly recognize the two of you again. Wait out here. I will see what I can find for you both. Oh no, you are not getting in here! Not in my house and not like this!" Cecile says and closes the door in front of Jack and Azrael.

"Well, at least Cecile is checking for some food for us. Better than nothing." Azrael is all smiles, and Jack agrees. There will be food! Jack sits in front of the door, waiting patiently for Cecile to return with some food.

Jack and Azrael munch on the food Cecile found for the two of them. It was nothing amazing, but after skipping breakfast and all the excitement, it tastes like a feast to Jack. Some vegetables from the allotment, their very own first vegetables grown by the cats in The Five Streets. Jack is sure no one has ever heard of or seen something like this before, cats running an allotment. Things are really changing in the world. Humans locked up and cats growing vegetables. Old Boy and Nina would go out of their minds if they knew.

For now, the food is fine and fresh for a change. Azrael chats to Cecile. Both seem to like each other a bit more than the rest of the leaders. Jack doesn't mind. It works for Churchill and Gina. No harm in a bit of affection.

Seeing both cats chatting makes him think about Misty MooMoo. Jack wonders how she is doing. He really should check on her later today, regardless of the silly promise she made him make. Jack is sure she misses him, too. He would never tell, and she wouldn't either, but both know. MooMoo is Jack's affection, and he is hers. Both know it, but Jack is not sure if he is ready for the next step with MooMoo and besides, he is an outside cat, and she is an indoor cat.

Jack continues to munch on the food and let his thoughts flow freely when one question pops into his head. "Cecile? How do we get vegetables from the allotment? Cats are not gardeners? We cannot do that, can we?"

Azrael looks to Jack. "You are right, Jack. Never heard of cats doing stuff like that. We certainly cannot do this. Saying that, we also thought we could never heal each other until we discovered a long-forgotten technique. Tell us, Cecile, how do we maintain an allotment and grow vegetables?"

"Let me tell you the secret, then. We discovered an old encryption teaching us how to use our paws to plant things. The encryption also told us how to take care of the plants and crops. It was an amazing discovery, and we found it after we cleaned this place up. Some ancient cats left it. Can you believe we cannot grow our own food?"

Azrael and Jack look at each other. "That is amazing! I would never have guessed we can do that," Jack says.

Cecile bursts out laughing and rolls over the floor. Jack gets it, this was only a joke. She tricked them. "The master detective and the master spy really believe we could do such a thing. Ancient cats leaving messages for us. Really? The two of you are a treat! Honestly? We started cleaning this place up a while ago. We wanted to use it for the ill and old. A place to relax and heal. For whatever reason, as soon as we tidied up the place, the old came. Not cats, old humans. They started planting things on the ground and meeting for chats. We always stayed around, watching them. After a while, they accepted us around here and we let them stay. It works in both ways. They plant and we give them company. Not sure how it will be now with the virus, but we have dug out what we could find and store it in the back of the house. It will help us, but it will not last if the humans must stay away."

"Funny, no hilarious!" says Azrael.

It still fascinates Jack. Ancient cats would have worked for him and his curiosity the same way it does hearing about the relationship that has formed between some old humans and the cats living here in the allotments. It is worth investigating further. He tells Cecile the same and hopes she will continue to learn more about the humans. It can only help all the cats in The Five Streets.

Humans and cats are alike; there are bad ones and there are good ones. You only need to learn how to distinguish one from the other. And if it means the cats can get some fresh food rather living out of the bins, what do they have to lose? He turns back to his food and eats as much as he can. His stomach filling up with the food makes his mind fill with the feeling of happiness. Jack knows he is close to the danger zone and should stop, but the food tastes so good. It is fresh and crunchy, just vegetables. As unusual as they are for a cat to eat, he cannot stop.

"Come on, Jack. We said only a snack. We need to get moving. Lots to talk about with the others. Cecile, do you mind joining us in Gina's cave? We need to update all of you on our latest findings. I am sure you want to hear all about it first-hand," Azrael says.

Jack stops eating. Azrael is right. Stop now or regret it. "Alright, let's go!" says Jack.

Cecile agrees to walk with the others to Gina's house. She was due for a visit, anyway. Gina complains a lot about her anxiety lately, and Cecile is worried that her age makes the symptoms worse. Cecile is trying to check on Gina daily, not as a doctor but as a friend. Churchill is worried too.

All three cats walk along the streets like they own them. And for a fact, they do somehow. The humans must stay inside by law and fear, and the cats can walk freely around.

Jack wonders how the rest of the world looks. In his mind, he sees animals all over the world taking a deep breath and enjoying the new freedom. For now, the virus feels like a blessing, but for how much longer?

The walk only takes a few minutes, and the three cats jump over the hedge and into the tunnel that leads to Gina's little cave. Churchill meets them halfway through in the dark.

"Good afternoon! What brings you three here at this time of the day?" Churchill inquires, wasting no time. Jack can feel Churchill is not right. He feels how tense the old cat is. Much more than usual. Gina must be in awful shape today.

"Hello, Churchill. We are here to see Gina. We must share new discoveries from our investigation. Do you think it will be okay for us to see her?" Jack says.

"Hello, all. I was just about to go on my daily tour to check on the food storage. Looks like I may have to postpone that for now. Gina is alright, Jack. She just seems to get more tired by the day lately. I think it will be good if she sees you all. Keeping her involved helps a lot with her mind. Let's go. I cannot wait to hear what you found out."

Jack is a bit surprised by Churchill's unusual high spirits. Jack is sure the others picked that up, too. Churchill must be worried sick if he forgets to be grumpy. The cats follow Churchill through the tunnel and into Gina's home. The cats spread out to make the most of the room, each one choosing their favourite carpet on the floor to sit down. Gina lays in her spot and greets them with a long yawn.

"Oh, hello, dears! I was not expecting any visitors today. Churchill, no warning for her ladyship? Well, since you all are here. How is everyone? What brings you here?" Gina greets them with a big smile, but her voice sounds sleepy and tired. It is as Churchill said, Gina feels more and more tired. It worries all of them.

Cecile is the first one to reply, "Hello, Gina, I was about to come around and have a chat with you. Not sure if you forgot, but it is our catch-up day. Sadly, I found these two scoundrels on my way and had to bring them along to keep them out of trouble."

Jack stifles a laugh. He gets the idea of being careful with Gina. Cecile did well to jump in and make them all aware of her status. Jack and Azrael need to keep their report calm and short. They don't want to confuse Gina and make matters more complicated, but they also want to make sure all the leaders know about what needs to happen next. Jack looks over to Azrael and gives him a nod to go ahead if he wants to. Azrael shakes his head, telling Jack to tell what they found. Jack is not sure why but will do as Azrael asks.

"Gina, it is so good to see you. I am sorry we all arrived without notice, but Azrael and I have found something very exciting in the sewers and we thought you and Cecile might want to hear all about it. It is important for our murder investigation. We might have found another suspect, but that is still to be seen. I know it is not the best of times of the day. We all are tired and could do with a good rest, but we thought it would be best to discuss what needs to happen next with everyone. Let me know if this is okay for you. Cecile and Churchill are here as well, so it makes the perfect opportunity."

Gina looks at Jack. "Jacky, darling, you know I always have time for you! How are you? Tell me all about it, please. Laying here all day is not really my best contribution for The Five Streets. Don't look at me like that, Churchill. I know you keep everything running without troubling me. I might be old, but not stupid!" Gina's outburst makes them all laugh. Gina is still Gina, no matter how tired she might be.

Jack tells Gina, Churchill, and Cecile all about the sewers and how they found the rats.

He does not mention that Azrael already knew about the rats. That is for Azrael to sort out, and Jack does not feel like exposing Azrael for what he already knew. Jack gives a brief report about his second day in the sewers, but he stops when he describes the talk he and Azrael had with the rats of the sewers or, better, with the Elders. Jack wants to make sure the other three leaders understand the next steps clearly and what commitment comes with the steps they agree on. Jack hopes they all agree.

"All the Elders want is their sewers back as they were. Not so different from what we want from The Five Streets. They would like to try a treaty between us, the cats of The Five Streets, and rats of the sewers. I think it is a great opportunity for us to find out more about the rats and their culture. We might learn a thing or two, but we will have allies watching out for trouble for us in a place we cannot be present all the time.

"The rats can learn from us too. From what I have seen in the little time I spent with them; they are not so much different from us. Physically they are, of course, but their structure and way of living is close to ours. I thought it would be best to fill you all in before we make a final decision if we want to help the rats and they help us. Azrael and I gave an agreement in principle, but we really would like to have all the leaders on board. We have until tomorrow to give our yes or no, but please keep in mind that the rats are the best clue we have in the murder case, and they can guide us to our prime suspect. Please let me know what you all think."

Churchill grumbles in the corner, something about strangers in the streets. Jack cannot hear it clearly and ignores it. Cecile started wandering around the cave during Jack's report. Jack can see Cecile is already working on details and how to meet the rats. Cecile is the easier one to win over for this vote. The final vote needs to come from Gina, as Jack is not sure about Churchill. It can go both ways.

Jack would like a unanimous decision, as it would save time and energy for all the leaders.

The last thing Jack wants is an endlessly long night of arguing back and forth. Gina is as calm as usual. She lies on her cushion with her eyes half closed. Jack knows the appearance can be deceiving. Gina has a sharp mind and likes to hide it behind sleepy eyes. Azrael has not moved an inch the whole time. He sat on his hind paws and listened with no emotions.

Jack thinks Azrael was not sure if Jack would expose him for having known about the rats for a while. Now he seems to relax a bit, but he also knows he must tell the group the truth soon. Jack is not doing it for him, but he also has another reason to trust Jack a little more now. In the end, it is all a big game of charades and politics, not so much different from what Jack hears about the humans in the world.

"Shall we put this to a vote?" Jack asks, as no one makes the first step.

Azrael votes for it. The same goes for Cecile. No surprise there. Jack votes for it too. Three out of five is all they need to go ahead, but Jack still hopes Gina and Churchill will be on board. Churchill is still mumbling, not sure about what, as no one can hear him talking. Gina stretches and gets up from her pillow. She walks over to Churchill and whispers to him. Both talk in hushed voices.

The other cats cannot hear what they talk about. After a few minutes, Gina walks back to her pillow with a satisfied look on her face. "I agree, Jack," is all she says and Churchill hisses, "Me too."

Jack cannot believe his little ears. All the leaders have agreed to support the rats, and, in return, the rats will help with finding the beast that terrorizes the sewers and does as the mysterious voice commands. The hunt will begin tomorrow!

"Thank you all for making this a quick decision. I am sure the rats will be pleased, and I can't wait to arrange a meeting between us all and the Elders as soon as we solve the murder. I am sure it will be a significant benefit for both sides. Azrael, anything to add?"

Azrael has moved more and more into the shadows, watching them all with glowing eyes. A small part of him hoped this would take longer, giving him the same time to prepare. Now he must wing it. "I am okay. I agree with Jack. This is a great step forward for us all. The rats can teach us a thing or two about survival. The Elders are smart, and their knowledge is vast. We need to address the fact that the rest of our cats don't see them as a fresh food source. It will be tricky to break old habits. We might not hunt for rats openly, but some of us do. We should address this before we invite the Elders to our streets."

"A good point!" Jack agrees.

"I for myself find it very exciting. I cannot wait to exam a new species. There is so much we can learn from each other. I am curious how the rats survived in the sewers that long. Wonder what their healers are like. It is very exciting indeed and thank you for sharing this with us, Jack," Cecile says.

Churchill is still grumpy and silent. They all know he agreed because Gina ask him too. But that's how it works between the two of them. Gina leads and Churchill follows.

For the moment, Churchill is the knight in furry armour, but he will soon have to take over as the official leader of the streets. Gina is digressing, and it is only a matter of time. For now, Jack is happy that Gina is still here and can decide on her own. Without her, Churchill would never have agreed to let strangers into The Five Streets. It all worked out fine. Jack looks over to Gina. She is half asleep. Even that little of extra conversation took a lot from her.

Jack worries he is one of the main reasons for Gina's rapid aging. Jack remembers well the time and energy Gina spent to heal him after the fox attacked him. Jack feels guilty, and he wants to talk to Gina about it later.

For now, he has a more important matter at hand. Another day in the sewers is in front of him and Azrael.

Jack is just about to tell everyone that he is leaving, as it was a long day when Gina speaks up. "Jack? Azrael? Please do me a favour? Take Buddy with you tomorrow. He will protect you both from whatever is crawling around down there. I dislike the idea of you two darlings wandering around in that dark place alone, facing whatever it is you might discover tomorrow. Take him with you, promise me! It will give an old lady peace of mind."

"I am not sure, Gina. The Elders already had trouble accepting me and Azrael in the sewers. I know Buddy will be a great help, but we might stretch it to explain to the rats why we need another cat with us. Azrael, what do you think we should do?"

Azrael has been silent since they entered Gina's home to discuss with the others what they found. He sits in a dark corner and watches them all with his yellow eyes.

Now he moves forward back into the light and says, "I think we should take him, Jack. We do not know what we are hunting, and Buddy knows his way around. He helped with the fox. I trust him. His silence is golden, if you get my meaning."

In the end, Jack told Gina they would take him. Jack will see Buddy on his way back to his box and let him know about the plan. Jack is worried about what the rats might think, but personally, he will feel safer with Azrael and Buddy around.

"That's it then? We are all happy? Azrael, Buddy, and I will go back and speak to the rats tomorrow and hopefully by the end of tomorrow, we will know what we are up against and if the so-called beast is part of the murder. And let us not forget the voice the rats heard from above. I have the feeling this is a bigger conspiracy, and we are again being played by someone. You all can guess who I am referring to. I am more than convinced this is just another trick by the Grey to cause chaos in our streets. Be careful and watchful in the next days! The Grey will watch closely what we are doing next!" Jack says.

"We will continue to check up here for any signs of the virus. So far, no cat has been unusually ill. The virus seems to be only dangerous for the humans. Gina and I will make sure it stays this way," says Cecile.

Gina adds, "Churchill has increased the patrols we are running in the streets, making sure all cats stay put and do not wander around. The Humans are in their houses and do not move. Last thing we need is our cats playing up as they feel like they rule the world. Let's get this all done with so we all can go back to our little lives on the streets. I dislike that we are so often in the spotlight lately. I miss the old days where we would just lie around in the sun and let the days go by. All this hustle and bustle is not good for us. Jack, please make sure our streets are quiet again! Find the murderer and deal with it."

Jack gives a firm nod with his little head. His eyes sparkle with excitement. The hunt is on, and he now has more support than before. Whoever tries to play the cats of The Five Streets better watch out. Jack is coming for them!

The cats leave Gina's house quickly. Everyone is in their own thoughts and has tasks to do. Jack knows where to find Buddy at this time of the day. He walks straight to the storage bins, where he finds Buddy on guard.

"Hello, Buddy! How are things?" Jack asks casually.

Buddy looks at Jack and gives him a smile and a wink, his version of saying, "Everything is alright!"

"Listen Buddy. Gina asked me to take you with me into the sewers tomorrow. We are hunting the murderer and we have a good idea he or she might hide down there. I will explain more tomorrow with fewer ears around us. Be ready first thing in the morning and meet me at the sewer entrance. Churchill will send someone to swap guard with you so you can get some rest. Tomorrow will be exciting, and I need you fresh and strong for whatever might come."

Buddy confirms with a simple nod. His eyes have questions in them, but he will have to wait until tomorrow morning. For now, Jack knows Buddy will be there in the morning.

"See you in the morning, Buddy!"

Jack carries on with his walk back to his little box in 1st Street. It was a long day; he can feel it in his legs now. A lot is going on and he has the feeling this is only just the beginning. For now, all Jack wants is a bath and some rest.

His box is the right place for that, and Jack cannot wait to have some silent moments to digest all that has happened today.

He leaves the parking lot, still amazed how full of cars it is now since every human has to stay at home, and takes the shortcut through 3rd Street, now a big, abandoned building site. Jack sneak underneath the fence the builders put up at the beginning and the end of the street to keep people out.

They have ripped the streets open, but Jack hopes they will be put back to normal. Now The Five Streets are only four.

Jack makes his way through the rubble and machines. He jumps and crawls around a bit to get a better picture of what might happen on the street. For him, it all looks like a big mess. Cats are not a big fan of mess. The sight of 3rd Street disturbs Jack, and he rushes to get through to 1st Street. Better to leave the mystery of 3rd Street for another day. He has lots more to think about. But first he wants to get back to this box and maybe having a peek at MooMoo, just from the edge of the garden.

Chapter XII

MooMoo sits on her spot in the top window. She sighs out loud and rests her head on her paws. Life has changed again for her. From one extreme to the other. Until recently, she thought herself lucky to live inside a delightful house, but right now, the house feels like a trap. Her servants may not leave the house anymore, and MooMoo feels she is under constant supervision.

She would never admit it openly, but her servants pay her too much attention lately. MooMoo looks around the garden, but all she sees is the green grass, which needs cutting soon, and the empty patio area. The table and chairs are still inside. The garden looks empty and lonely. MooMoo feels the same way. She wishes Jack would ignore her warning and come to visit her. It has been two days since she chased him away. MooMoo knows it is for the best. She cannot imagine Jack being trapped in the house with all of them. Her female servant, The Gracious Lady, as Jack likes to call her, would have tried to catch Jack and bring him into the house. It would not have been for bad reasons. The female servant would have thought him safer inside the house rather than free outside with the virus.

The virus made it all extremely hard for everyone. MooMoo still has the latest pictures in her head of humans fighting for food and water. She hopes Jack is alright and safe.

They cannot trust humans under normal circumstances, but right now, it is even worse. All MooMoo wants is to see Jack, just to know he is alright.

"Why is he not even trying to sneak in?" MooMoo thinks.

She gets up and stretches her back into a massive arc. All the tension in the house is making her stiff and there is no way to get the energy out. The world is full of destructive energy now.

"Maybe, just maybe, I should go out and look for Jack? Maybe that would do me good?" MooMoo thinks further. The thought had occurred to her a few times already. It startled her at first. She would never have thought that she would give up the house and rather be on the street with Jack. It is still a strange thought, but one she cannot shake off.

"It might be the right way for both of us. I think I could do it. Living on the streets and solving mysteries and crimes with Jack. I am sure we would be a perfect team, not a sufficient team!"

MooMoo gets more and more excited about the idea, especially sitting on the window and watching the quiet world go by. It does not look so bad out there. They would have to stay away from the humans, of course, but that is normal for Jack and all the cats in The Five Streets. MooMoo is sure she can adapt to a new way of life, but will Jack take her with him?

Misty MooMoo jumps down from the windowsill onto the bed. She decided and no one will stop her from trying to break out of the house and join Jack and The Five Streets. She just needs to find the right way or, better, the right time to sneak out. The thought still makes her feel uneasy.

Getting back onto the streets after all that time in the house. Obviously, she blames Jack for all this. He put many thoughts in her head, thoughts she denied herself to follow for a long time.

But this new situation with the virus and all the mysteries Jack gets involved with makes her wonder if there should be more in her life than just hanging around and looking pretty in the house. She wants Jack in her life, and MooMoo has decided it is time to move on from being the docile house cat. She feels the pulling of the new calling. It is an intense pull in a certain direction, not so much physically, more mentally. She can feel the direction she needs to take to meet Jack. It is as clear in her head as the sun on a day with only blue sky. It is time and she will go.

MooMoo checks the downstairs. The humans are still more or less glued to the TV, following the news and latest announcements from the government. The humans think this virus will be gone and done by in a week or two; their leaders ask for the patience of everyone. Together, they will get through it.

MooMoo doubts the togetherness of the humans. The last few days showed the true meaning of many humans. Violence and fights have been everywhere. There is no togetherness. It is more like the jungle documentary she saw the other day. Everyone looks out for themselves and only the strongest survives or with the humans, only the most violent ones will eat and have what they need. The weak will hide and suffer. She is not sure if the humans can see this, but for now, the situation looks out of control. It will only get worse the longer the humans are in an imposed lockdown. MooMoo has had enough of watching her servants be glued to the screen and runs upstairs again. She jumps onto the windowsill and stares out into the open world.

"How will it be out there? Will Jack accept me with him?" MooMoo thinks. Lots of unanswered questions float through her head. Answers she only can find by trying something new. Sitting here will solve nothing.

MooMoo thinks about her escape plan when she spots a black cat sitting at the edge of the garden fence. Could it be Jack?

MooMoo sits straight up and tries to get a better look at the shape at the garden fence. It looks so much like Jack. MooMoo hopes it is Jack!

She lifts one paw onto the window, a slow gesture to make sure the other cat can see it. She leaves her paw lifted against the window and looks at the cat in the distance. The other cats tilt his head and lifts a paw in response to MooMoo. Jack has seen her! Little tittering noises coming out of MooMoo's mouth, telling him she is coming to be with him. All he can do is wait longer, but not much. Is he okay? Can she be with him? MooMoo lets it all out to the shape in the distance. The shape waves again and turns away from her. That is all he dares to do, honouring the promise he made her.

Jack sits at the edge of the garden. He can see the window upstairs. It is empty; MooMoo is not there. She might be downstairs with her servants. Jack's head drops. He had hoped to see her, at least from the distance. He does not dare to get any closer. He promised!

Jack is about to leave when he sees her. The small princess jumps onto the windowsill and looks straight at him. Can she see him, or is he too far away? The day's light is fading, and he is not sure. He looks up at her and sends her his thoughts. "I miss you, little princess. I miss our talks about the world and my latest cases. You are always willing to listen and help me when I am stuck. I wish you could go with me everywhere! We would be a good team!"

Jack let his thoughts say what he never would say aloud. It would upset MooMoo. For now, Jack is happy to see her in the distance, knowing she is safe.

Jack sees MooMoo lifts a paw and places it against the window. It looks like she is waving at him. Jack repeats the gesture. They connect with a simple gesture, and both feel happy.

Jack stretches his little leg higher and higher, telling her, "I am here!" Then the lights turn down downstairs in the house and Jack knows he has pushed his luck far enough.

He turns around and leaves the garden behind him. "MooMoo saw me!" he thinks happily and walks the small bit to his box, lightheaded and smiling. The walk is only a few minutes from the garden and Jack jumps into his little box and closes the door by pulling the fabric back into place. The inside of his little box is dark and comfortable. It gives him the perfect feeling of protection and cover from the weather. All he needs now is a good rest before the hunt tomorrow. Jack curls up into a small ball of fur and is fast asleep within minutes.

The sun is rising slowly over the sleepy Five Streets. It is silent as no one leaves for work anymore. All the humans stay inside their homes. The only movement so early are military trucks creeping through the streets with soldiers jumping in and out of the trucks to drop plastic crates full of food and water at each doorstep. The world is unaware of the dangers that lay underneath The Five Streets in these early morning hours. Humans are only concerned with their own crises.

The sun and the morning do not care about all this. The sun still rises and sets as if nothing has happened. Jack's ears twitch as they pick up the sounds of the trucks driving around in his street. His eyes are still closed; he only sees with his ears.

He tries to remember the last night, but nothing comes to mind. He has slept like a rock. Even his mind is too exhausted to keep him awake. Jack stretches his legs slowly away from him.

He lays silent, all stretched out for a minute, enjoying the comfort and safety of his home.

Suddenly, his little head shoots up. "Today is the day! We are going for a hunt!" The memory breaks in like the sunlight through a wide window. They flood his brain with what has happened yesterday and the agreement they made to hunt for the beast in the sewers. All the calmness is gone within a second from Jack and he sits up, cleaning his fur with his tongue and paws. He gets ready quickly to meet Azrael and Buddy. They said early morning, but how early is it or how late? Now Jack is worried that he overslept and let the others wait at the sewer's entrance.

He finally gets up and pushes the cloth that deals as a door aside from this box and steps out. The air is cool and fresh. It tells Jack it is indeed still early morning. "So far, so good!" he thinks and starts moving his sleepy legs. His paws touch the cold street; every step helps him to wake up more and more. Jack moves from a sloth-like walk into a light jog, enjoying the air around his muzzle. It is refreshing. His mind is already fully awake, and his body follows straight. Jack thinks about the adventure that lays before him today. Back into the sewers, meeting the rats, hunting for the beast. It sounds all too simple in his head. What else could happen?

Jack crosses by the garden but has no timed to stop like last night. Today, he needs to be focused. No distractions allowed. Well, so he thought, but his stomach has a different opinion. As soon as Jack passes by his favourite food place, his stomach rumbles.

A matter of habit, but it makes Jack aware of how hungry he is. Food has not been his priority the last few days and his stomach is not happy about it. Jack needs to find time for a snack. He is sure the others will not leave without a breakfast either.

"But where to go to?" Jack thinks. His favourite food place, the garden, is off limits and besides, The Gracious Lady has left no food outside since the virus started. Jack is sure they all are too scared to think about his empty stomach.

The only place Jack can think of is the bins. Not his favourite kind of food, but better than nothing. He needs to eat, and food is food in the end. Jack walks past the garden entrance and follows the street right up to the food storage bins.

The food distribution is not open yet, but he might get past the guards if he explains who he is.

Jack is deep in his thought and does not hear the military truck approaching from behind. He jumps up in surprise as the truck breaks next to him. A soldier jumps out with a crate in his hands and puts it down on one of the posh houses' doors steps. Jack stands frozen; there is no place to hide. The soldier turns around and is about to get into the truck again when he spots Jack sitting next to the truck.

"Hey, buddy! Who are you?" says the soldier and lowers himself down on his knee to look at Jack. "Come on over here, little fella, got something for you as well."

The soldier reaches into one of his many pockets on his uniform and shows Jack a rectangular bar. Jack is still doesn't move, watching the human in front of him, and gets ready to run away. Jack is just about to bounce away in the opposite direction of the soldier when he hears heavy boots behind him. "What you got there, Jack?" a voice says behind him.

Jack looks around, confused why the humans know his name. Jack looks behind him and see the other human is not even looking at Jack the cat. He talks to Jack the human. Jack shakes his head. That is way too much and well too close for his liking.

Jack makes a slow move to the side; he wants to sneak past the human Jack and be out of here.

"Hold on buddy, here, take some. Tough times for all of us!" Jack the soldier says and breaks some bits from the bar in his hand and throws them towards Jack. Jack jumps back and hisses at the soldier.

"Ha-ha, got a feisty one there! Get on with it. We must keep moving. These food parcels do not deliver themselves, and I want to be out of here before the neighbourhood wakes up. That's an order, Private Jack!" the second soldier talks while he goes back around the truck and into the driver's seat.

The soldier called Private Jack breaks another bit of something from the bar and drops it to the ground. "No worries. Take it when I am gone. It is not much but will help. Take care, little buddy, and stay safe!" The soldier waves at Jack and climbs into the truck. The engine roars up, and the truck moves away from Jack.

Jack still sits in the spot the soldiers caught him. How stupid of him to let his guard down. He was wandering the streets like a kitten; anyone could have jumped on to him. There he was thinking about focusing and not being distracted, where his thoughts have been the worst distraction of all. Keeping him stuck inside his head and ignoring the outside world.

"You are doing it again!" he says aloud to himself.

Jack stops his mind from distracting him and focuses on all his senses. He needs to be aware of what is going on around him. No time for thinking deep thoughts. This is not the right time for it. His nose picks up the smell of the stuff the soldier threw towards him. It does not smell bad at all. Jack gets his nose closer to inspect what it is the soldier left for him. It must be some sort of food; his nose is telling him that. But why would a stranger feed him?

Jack smells the food, and it smells good to him. He picks a piece and puts it into his mouth. It is food, and it tastes good.

Jack eats all the pieces around him and moves on to the bigger chunk the soldier left. Better than food out of the bins.

Jack's stomach stops complaining, and Jack enjoys the taste of something different and new. The food is all gone, and Jack's starving belly is full. Satisfied, he moves on, filing the strange meeting in the early morning into his achievements. Some memory to analyse later, but he has the feeling not all humans are bad. Jack walks on and falls back into his light jog. Time to meet the others. The sewers and some secrets are waiting for him.

Jack crossed the parking lot and heads straight to the sewer entrance. He can see a small group of cats has already gathered. Azrael and Buddy are standing next to Lupine. Churchill and Gina are there as well, chatting to Cecile. Jack wonders what Gina is doing here. She hardly ever leaves her house. Churchill looks up and nods over to Jack.

"You are late to the party, mate!" he shouts as soon as Jack is close.

"Hey, Jack!" Azrael greets him with a smile.

They all have been waiting for him to arrive. The small troop to explore the sewers is now complete, and the rest came by to send them off. Cecile and Gina look worried, and both give lots of advice to Buddy and Azrael to be careful not to do anything stupid. Buddy looks uncomfortable with all this attention about his persona. Azrael just nods and keeps on promising to take care of them all down there.

Gina calls Jack over, "Jacky? Come here, darling! Let me talk to you for a second."

Jack follows Gina to a spot away from the others. Gina leans her head too close to Jack's and says, "Listen Jack, I know you are eager to get down there and find that beast. But promise me one thing: do nothing silly. Promise me, Jacky. Remember the last time you followed someone evil around? I have no energy left to heal any of you, and I am not sure how far Cecile is if things get ugly for anyone of you down there. Promise me you will turn and run this time. Do not stay and do something silly. Please, Jack!"

Jack is taken aback by Gina's openness. He understands Gina is anxious about this trip into the sewers and trying to find the beast. Jack agrees to her bidding and promises he will run as fast as the wind if things get ugly. He learned his lesson the last time he followed the fox around the dark corner.

"Jack? Are you ready? Time to get moving if we want to make the most of the daylight. I do not want to be down there when it turns dark out here," Azrael shouts over to Jack and Gina.

"Ready when you are!" Jack shouts back and adds more quietly to Gina only, "No worries, Gina. I promised to be careful, and I will make sure we three will be back within a few hours with more knowledge about what is going on in the sewers and why it affects us up here."

Jack runs over to Azrael and Buddy; everyone seems to be ready to enter the darkness of the sewers to continue the search for the murderer.

Azrael is the first one to climb through the hole into the sewers. His tail vanishes into the darkness. Jack climbs after him and Buddy follows Jack. All three cats disappear from the sunny Five Streets within seconds, leaving behind a worried Gina and a grumpy Churchill. Cecile seems to take it easier than the other two cats.

Lupine sums it up for all of them. "Off they go into the dark to make sure we can stay in the light longer. Bon voyage, mes amis!"

Jack touches the ground inside the sewers. His paws feel the cold and wet concrete. His eyes adapt slowly to the absence of light. "It is a different world down here," Jack thinks.

He waits for Buddy and Azrael to adjust their senses to the new environment before they continue to walk deeper inside. Buddy walks back and forth in small circles. He does not look very impressed. Jack gets close to him and brushes his head against Buddy's shoulder.

"Everything alright, Buddy?"

Buddy stops pacing and looks at Jack, his mouth opens in silence, a petty attempt to complain from the normally silent cat.

"I know exactly what you mean!"

The three cats get their senses together and start walking down the path to the first crossroad. The rats have gathered at the crossroad, waiting for the cats to arrive. Elliot and Basil were at the front of the group of rats. There are many, but they all look frightened. The sheer amount of rats' scares Jack. This is a small army of crawlers that live hidden down here. He is glad that they are on the side of the cats from The Five Streets. Otherwise, this would be a hideous thing to deal with. This underground world never ceases to amaze Jack.

Buddy looks terrified. The big cat has shown no sign of fear in the world above. But here, facing the hundreds of rats in the dark, puts even him on edge. Azrael walks straight up to the leader pack to say his hello, unimpressed as usual. Jack and Buddy follow slower, observing the rats round them.

"Finally! We have been waiting for hours now. Never thought you will make it back," says Basil.

"Good to see you all back here! We thought waiting here for you would be better. This is as far as we go. We do not want to be seen from up there," says Elliot.

"Hello Basil! Hello Elliot! Thank you for meeting us here! We didn't fancy strolling through the whole sewers again to your lair. Makes it easier for us, very much appreciated!" says Azrael.

Buddy just sits down in silence. His big head moves around. He is trying to count the rats. He looks uncomfortable and tense. Jack sits next to him to give him as much comfort as he can.

Jack talks loud for all to hear, "This is Buddy. We took him with us for protection. Please don't feel offended, but he does not speak. Not since he fought another beast that took his voice. He was a great help in catching a fox in our world that caused us a great deal of trouble. Buddy has plenty of experience with troublemakers, and he knows how to fight. More than Azrael or me, to be honest."

Basil and Elliot come closer to Buddy. They sniff the air around Buddy, their little whiskers twitching excitingly in the air. Both rats nod in agreement after their inspection of the big, black cat.

"He is big and looks strong!" says Basil.

"Do you have more like him in your streets?" asks Elliot.

Jack knows what the two cats are after, checking out the potential danger of a cat like Buddy. He looks over to Azrael and the spy cat shakes his head ever so slightly, only for Jack to notice. Jack gets the message.

"Buddy is part of our guard team. We have a team of guards protecting our food and us from trouble. They also make sure all other cats follow the rules and laws of The Five Streets. All our guard cats are trained well; they are mostly calm and collected, but they know how to handle trouble," Jack explains.

The two rats nod again, taking the information as given. Jack thinks he gave the right amount of info to make them think there are more than Buddy up there on the streets. Never mind the fact that Buddy is a unique exemplar of a cat. The rats do not need to know that right now. The relationship between the rats and the cats is still fragile, and it is to be seen where it will lead after they have dealt with the common threat.

"Okay, I think we should make the most of the time we have down here. Shall we go for a hunt?" says Jack, eager to keep moving. The quicker they get away from the army of rats, the better for the mood of the three cats.

Basil and Elliot agree and start leading the way deeper into the sewers. The other rats staying behind and the three cats can feel the hundreds of black eyes following them as they leave the meeting point. The cats and rats walk in silence, everyone full of their own thoughts about the strange morning. For Jack, the most troubling thought is the vast number of rats they just saw. He thinks it over and it surprises him that the rats had to abandon their habitats. There are so many of them, they surely could have taken down the beast themselves. Why did they decide to run? Jack walks closer to Azrael. Maybe he knows more?

"Azrael? What do you make of all this? It makes me wonder why the rats did not fight the beast themselves. They are so many; I am sure they can fight anything that comes their way."

Azrael turns his head towards Jack and says, "You are right. I have not thought about that until now. It seems strange. There must be another reason they ran. Maybe the beast is more dangerous than we think? Thank you, Jack! I was already worried, but now I am getting terrified. What are we up against?"

"I know. I was thinking the same. This beast must be horrific if it scares away all the rats. Let me talk to Basil. Maybe he can explain a bit more. He must know more about the beast. They've lived here for ages."

Jack speeds up his walk to level with Basil and Elliot. Both rats lead the group into the sewers with confidence, never stopping at the many twists or turns of the path. Jack catches up with the rats as they stop at one junction to give the cats time to catch up. The little rats are much faster than the cats. Their little black eyes do not need to adapt to the dark. The cats are still struggling with the absence of any light.

It is pitch black where they are now. Jack nearly bumps into the two sitting rats in the middle of the path.

"Hey! Why did we stop?" Jack asks.

"Just giving you three a chance to catch up. Your long legs are made for running. Why are you slowing us down? We didn't know you cats move so slow," Basil replies with a sheepish smile on his rat face.

"It's not the legs, it is the darkness. A cat always needs at least a bit of light to see better in the dark. We are as blind in the dark as any other animal if there is no little light source close by. Now, we rely on our ears and whiskers to follow you guys, and the narrow walls do not help to get a clear signal all the time. Stop smiling, you. I will eat you up!" Jack replies.

Basil looks shocked and jumps a few steps away from Jack. The last thing he wants is to be eaten by a cat and squeaks, "Calm down, mate. Was only joking!"

Jack laughs out loud. He was not expecting Basil to take his last comment so serious. Jack sits down on his hind legs to show he has no intention of jumping after the rat.

Azrael and Buddy arrived in the meantime and sit next to Jack, taking the chance to rest and adjust their senses. Buddy looks totally horrified. Azrael looks more like he enjoys the trip a bit too much. Jack takes the chance of the break to continue his investigation.

"Say Basil, why did you guys leave your homes and run away from the beast? You are so many; I am sure you can take the beast out yourselves. What stops you from going back with all your little rat friends and chasing the beast out of the sewers?"

Basil looks at Elliot to see if he can tell Jack more about them. Elliot gives his agreement with a silent nod. "It is our way of living. We are here for many years, and we follow the rules strictly. Above all, the rules and laws we have is the one rule not to harm any other living being. I know we threatened you at the beginning and it worked, but we would do no harm to anyone. It is our way and for many years, it worked. We had no trouble, and it stopped our society from waging war against each other like in the old days. Now we are one collective, and we all work towards one goal. Life is good, well, it was until the beast turned up. The beast and that fox of yours. Both changed our way of living, but it does not make us break our rules."

Elliot adds a bit more context to the rule that Basil just explained to Jack and the others, "You need to understand where we came from and where we are right now. It took us years and years of war and suffering until the grand master rat appeared one day and united all the different rat clans. He changed our way of living together. Not to harm any other animal or human was the first law. It stopped us all from fighting for scraps. It made us all stronger and helped us to evolve in a way we never had thought of. Now we follow these rules and laws."

"The grand master is long gone, but we now have the council of elders to guide us. It works as long as we stay hidden with no influence from outsiders, and until now, only a few outsiders came down here but never bothered us. That was until now. Things have changed and we will need to adapt again, but this time we use our rules and laws, the teachings of the past and what we have learned to make sure we do not fall back into the old habits of violence. This is our way!"

Jack listens to the short story. He wants to know more about their way of living. Rules and Laws are not new for the cats. The Five Streets have them as well; otherwise, nothing would function. But living in a society with no violence or fights? That would be a whole different world for all the cats in The Five Streets. Jack doubts that would ever be possible, but he is sure the leaders of The Five Streets can learn a lot from the rats. Jack is sure the rats will be grateful if the three cats can help with the beast. It might be just the thing that had to happen to bring both societies together, to learn from each other and to grow.

Jack turns to Azrael and Buddy. Both cats have listened to the story as well. Buddy nods in agreement as if to say he is all for a life with no more fighting.

Azrael looks more calculating; he looks like he is working on steps to take advantage of what he just heard. It will make his spy work much easier now. Jack is sure Azrael is already working on a full infiltration plan for the sewers. Jack thinks it would be good to establish a kind of embassy down here, making sure the cats are always present and the door is open for the rats. Azrael will be more than happy to play the ambassador; it gives him plenty of options to sneak around. Jack files the idea for later to discuss with Gina, Churchill, Cecile, and Azrael.

Basil turns to the three cats and says, "Enough talking! Let's move on. From here on, we need to move carefully. We are in the old parts of the sewers now. The entrance to the woods is close by and the beast likes it there. Be as quiet as you can. It likes to hunt, and it is fast."

The rats continue to lead the cats deeper into the labyrinth of crossing and twisting paths. Jack hopes Azrael can keep up and map the way. Jack feels hopelessly lost already. His mind works on the case and how to approach the beast, putting no one at risk. It will not be easy, especially not knowing what they will have to face at the end of this hunt.

Now they entered some of the older parts of the sewers. Something darkened the bricks over time, making it even harder to see. It feels like the bricks absorb any light, sucking it right out of the air. The air feels humid and hot, making the cats feel more uncomfortable. Jack can feel the pressure in the air all around them. Everyone keeps close and they sneak along the way.

Jack sees the two rats in front of him. They slow down, stopping more often to check the air with their little noises and whiskers. Buddy does the same whenever the rats stop.

He sits down and sucks the air in, smelling what's around him. His eyes glowing in the dark, Buddy picks up the scent of something new. His fear turns into excitement, the thrill of hunting.

Azrael stays calm and watches them all, more observing and taking mental notes, like Jack, but with different notes. For Azrael, it is all about the rats and the environment they are in. How to use it later to make sure his spies can move freely down here. He looks for the weaknesses of the rats while spending time with them.

Jack, on the other paw, is looking for ways to solve the murder.

He is still not sure the rats are not part of all this. It is possible they killed the poor cat to protect their home. Jack buys the story Basil and Elliot told them earlier about the laws and rules, but Jack also knows what it means to be a leader of many and what you must do sometimes to protect the many. It might not always go along with the rules and laws.

His mind wanders back to Reynard and Thumbs, how that all escalated quickly. He could imagine the rats doing the same, but with a worse outcome. The dead cat was a spy, and he was mapping the sewers. It seems logical to make the rats one of the prime suspects. He even goes so far in his theory that the beast is a welcome alibi for the rats, or a scapegoat. Everything is possible. Even more so when you are wandering in this dark place. A place full of secrets hidden in the darkness.

The rats stop again. This time they turn to the cats and Basil points up a little outlet.

"This is where we heard the voice. My family was living right behind that wall. The little hole there? Behind it was our home. The voice started talking to us one day, asking questions about who we are and where we are. At the beginning, the voice was calm and kind, curious about us. Later, it became more forceful, trying to tell us what to do. That's when we stopped listening to it, tried to ignore it. The elders told everyone to stay away, but the voice was like a slow crawling poison. Once you heard it, it turned and twisted in your mind. It was evil. Someone dangerous was talking to us from the above. So, we closed this area off and for a while, it worked. We took care of the ones affected by the voice. Don't look so shocked! They all recovered, as we said, we do not kill our own or others!"

Elliot picks up where Basil stops, "After we isolated the voice, we felt okay. We went back to normal, continued with our lives. But then the murders happened. Rats vanished, found days later swimming half eaten in the water. Some were never found or seen again. We sent scouts out into the sewers. We discovered the fox entering our sewers a few times, but he only stayed close to the entrance in the woods, never made it far. But we found traces of something else. The paw prints we found were bigger, and the killings got more and more frequent. Fellow rats reported sightings of the beast. It became the horror for us here. All we could do in the end was move to the newer parts of the sewers where the light is more present, protecting us from this beast. We moved, and the killing stopped, but we lost our homes."

The three cats are moved by the second story of the rats. This time, they can relate even more to the loss. Losing The Five Streets has been a fear for all the leaders. For a long time, the biggest fear for the Five Street leaders was losing their streets because of evolution.

The city is growing day by day and it is only a matter of time until The Big City will absorb The Five Streets.

Jack also understands the threat outsiders pose for the streets; it is the same as with the sewers. Outsiders bring new rules and habits with them, making it hard to fall in line with the law and rules of The Five Streets. But Jack knows they also need the outsiders to keep the streets from falling apart. It is a narrow walk on the edge. But losing your home to a beast? The Five Streets were close with the fox and Thumbs. Jack sees now how much of a beast Thumbs was. Jack takes all the information about the rats and saves it for now. There is no time to dig deeper into it right now, but his feeling of the rats and cats being in the same boat becomes stronger and stronger.

Basil urges the group on to continue. He and Basil sneak on, deeper into the sewers.

Jack, Azrael, and Buddy follow close by. Jack sniffs the air and his nostrils pick up an unfamiliar smell. A faint, musky odour flows in the area. Not strong enough to be noticed straight away.

Jack has smelled nothing like this before and he ask aloud, "What is this smell?"

"It is the beast!" Elliot whispers back.

This is it; the hunt is in full swing. They have picked up the scent of the beast. Buddy and Azrael inhale the smell, too. It gives the cats a lead to follow. For now, the smell is overshadowed by others. It sits just underneath of the sewer smells. The beast cannot be close, but it was here. Maybe the beast was listening to the same voice as the rats. Jack has the idea that the voice and the beast have something in common. He wishes they could hear the voice themselves. But for now, they have the beast to investigate.

The group sneaks through the dark sewers for hours, but much easier now as they have picked up the scent of the beast. The cats and the rats can use their combined senses to follow the trail the beast left behind. The sewers change again from the dark, wet place into a lighter area. Basil mentions they are close now to the entrance into the woods—the preferred hunting ground of the beast.

They all can see clear traces now of the beast. It's fouled the area with its smells and droppings. It marked its territory. Jack can see some light at the end of the tunnel. This must be the exit or entrance to the woods Basil mentioned. It surprises Jack neither he nor Azrael picked up on the unusual smells when they passed by the same entrance the other day. He thinks about it and puts it down to being in the sewers the first time and everything smelled and felt unusual. How should they know this place does not look and smell like it should be? Jack feels lucky they did not meet the beast back then, unprepared, and alone.

Even now, with Buddy and the two rats, it seems like the beast is still at an advantage.

"Azrael, do you remember seeing any like this before? I mean, we must have passed by this the other day. I cannot remember any of it."

"Right, Jack. We have been here, I remember us leaving to the woods and talking to Reynard, but I do not recall the mess or the smell. It is strange."

"Not really, to be honest," says Elliot. "You might come in from the entrance to the woods, but I am sure it is not the same part we are in right now. The tunnels down here can be deceiving. This one, for example, might look like the only one leading to this entrance, but there are three more running parallel with this one. They merge into this main tunnel further down the path; you will see in a bit what I mean," Elliot explains while walking on.

"The darkness makes it hard to see the junctions from here. It is easy for you to follow one path and not see others coming off from it. I am sure you never have been in this part before."

"Interesting!" is all Jack says to Elliot's explanation. He cannot wait to see the other tunnels merging into this one. For now, he is not sure if this is possible and how it could have slipped his mind. The cats and rats walk on, eyes, ears, and noses open and checking the surrounding area for the beast. It could hide anywhere. Jack's tail is getting all bushy from the thought alone that the beast might watch them right now and they all do not know. Jack shakes the disturbing thought from his mind. He needs to be right here now, and all his senses need to be working. They are hunting for the unknown beast and every mistake could be fatal.

The rats continue to sneak at the front, followed by Buddy and Azrael. Jack takes the back of the group. They pass by the potential path Jack and Azrael took the other day.

Jack can now see what the rats meant. The path comes out of nowhere. Looking like a black hole in the wall of the main path, you could walk right into it without noticing you are leaving the path you are on. A perfect illusion and an easy trick on the eyes, especially when you walk and talk, not paying attention to anything around you, just like he and Azrael did.

They are now approaching the end of the tunnel; the light becoming more and more visible to everyone. No beast to be seen. Jack wonders if the beast has moved on. It might have done its purpose of moving the rats out of the area. As for why, Jack does not know, not yet. The group walks on and the rats stop right on the edge where the light tries to break the darkness.

"This is as far as we would like to go. We do not want to enter the woods. I am sorry, not sure why we did not encounter the beast here. It was always here!" Basil says.

"Maybe it moved on?" Jack asks.

"Possible, but our scouts saw it only last night here. It has not moved for days. Why now? Let us go back and try another tunnel. Maybe we can find another track," Elliot suggests.

"Good idea!" Jack turns around and follows the group back down the path.

The group is a bit more relaxed now. Azrael chats to Elliot about exploring more of the sewers with him soon. Basil walks next to Buddy, asking him lots of questions about the upper world.

Buddy looks over to Jack, with a plea for help in his little eyes. Jack closes in on the two and explains to Basil that Buddy cannot speak at all.

Jack and Basil chat away about the upper world as suddenly they pass the dark hole in the wall that leads into the other tunnel.

Just as they pass, a shadow jumps out of the darkness and crashes into Jack and Basil, throwing both to the ground. Jack's head rings from the collision. Basil squeaks in pain next to him. Jack hears Buddy hissing and Azrael shouting a warning to Elliot. The beast ambushed them in the least expected moment. Jack jumps to his paws, shaking off the dizziness. He looks around and faces something he has never seen in his whole life.

In between the rats and the cats stands a grey something. A stout body with small, black, furry legs and a head covered in white fur hisses and screeches at them. The beast looks dangerous. His head is low, and it plants its legs firm to the ground.

Jack just has time to shout a warning to everyone, "Watch out! It is getting ready for another attack!" and the beast jumps straight at Basil, targeting the smallest in the group first.

A fast blur of grey with sharp teeth tries to hit Basil. The little rat waits until the last second to move aside and lets the beast rush past him like a matador in the arena. The coolness of Basil surprises not only the beast but the group. The cats spread out and encircle the beast. All three cats try to keep the beast in the middle. Jack wants to have a better look at this new animal. Azrael's eyes flash with curiosity, too. Buddy's tail is all fluffed up, and he lies low to the floor, ready to jump and fight with the beast.

"Hold it, Buddy!" Jack screams. "Let us just hold it there for a second."

Jack checks the beast out. What a strange creature it is. Bigger than a cat, grey, white, and black fur flows over a muscular body. Its head is rather small, but its mouth is full of little sharp teeth. Jack looks at the legs and paws of the beast. They look like sturdy legs, legs used to fight. The paws end in sharp claws. Deadly weapons, Jack takes a note to stay away from these.

Jack meets the eyes of the beast. Dark eyes stare back at him, challenge him directly to make a move. It snarls rude words into the group, calling them cowards, losers, and worse. Jack ignores the cursing and swearing. He tries to see beyond all the threatening behaviour, looking for the true nature of the beast.

The beast charges again; this time it tries to attack Azrael. Buddy jumps in at the last second and crashed into the beast. Both cat and beast roll over the floor, slashing and biting at each other. Buddy fights silently, but the beast roars and hisses.

Buddy kicks the beast away from him with his muscular hind legs. He gets up, panting, but his eyes are full of determination to beat this animal before it hurts anyone else.

Jack and Azrael jump forward, claws flashing towards the beast from all sides. Jack can feel his claws bouncing off the thick fur of the beast. His claws leave no marks, no injuries at all. The beast snaps at both cats; it moves like a flash between Jack and Azrael. Jack checks on Azrael and he sees the spy master throwing viscous claw attack after claw attack, but nothing seems to affect the beast.

Buddy sneaks around in the fighting. He is looking to get behind the beast for an attack. The two rats cower in the furthest corner, frightened black eyes following the fight. All three cats are now at the beast, hissing and slashing from a safe distance, using the full lengths of their limbs and claws. The beast changes strategy and uses its thick, strong claws to hit back. The claws are much bigger and stronger than the cats.

The beast hits Azrael on his left leg and makes him retreat for a second, caught by the pain. The beast jumps after him and his teeth dig deep into the stretched paw. The beast shakes its head, tearing at Azrael's paw like a dog.

Jack and Buddy run over to help Azrael, slashing at the back of the strange animal but with no results.

Buddy takes a leap of faith and jumps onto the back of the beast, his four claws hitting the beast like a hurricane. The beast must release Azrael to take care of Buddy. Buddy tries to hang onto the back of the beast with all his strength. The beast is still bigger than Buddy. It does not hit at Buddy with his shorter legs or bite; it just lies on its side and rolls over Buddy, trying to squash him with its weight alone.

Azrael stumbles back from the fight. His paw is a bloody mess. Jack takes another go at the beast, trying to hit the underbelly while it tries to turn on its back with Buddy underneath it. Jack hits the beast and this time his claws draw blood from the soft belly. The beast roars in pain or anger. Jack is not sure. Buddy crawls out from underneath the hurt animal and drags himself away. He looks beaten up. Jack steps back as well and tries one more time to get through to the beast.

"Stop it! We are not here to hurt you! Stop!" Jack yells.

"It's pointless, Jack. Look at it; it's totally mad!" Azrael shouts from the other side.

The beast lowers itself to the ground, protecting his soft belly. It looks from one cat to the other.

"He said you would come for me! He told me all I had to do was get one of you. Make sure you find the tracks leading to me. He knew you would come!"

The beast talks with a low, deep voice. It sounds full of hate and terror. Its eyes are the same colour as the rats', just a black pit with no emotions in it. It looks like pure evil to Jack.

Regardless, Jack needs to try. The beast speaks and it might be the only chance to find out why it is here.

"He? Who is he and why are you here terrorizing the rats in the sewers?" Jack asks.

"He wants the sewers. He wants it all!" The beast whispers back.

"What does he want?" Jack tries again.

"All!" the beast shouts loud and jumps towards Jack.

Jack moves back, but the attack was just a fake. The beast turns last minute and charges towards the rats. "Traitors!" it yells and snaps at both rats, trying to bite the heads off them.

Buddy is again the saviour in the last minute. He uses his colossal body to push the beast away from the rats. Basil and Elliot take the chance and run behind Jack and Azrael. The rats whisper in panic with each other. It is too much for them. Buddy keeps the beast at a distance. The beast snarls at him but stays back, watching.

"Let it be! Why did you kill one of ours? Who sent you?" Jack tries again.

The beast looks directly at Jack this time, its black eyes full of hatred. "You know nothing, little cat. He is back, and he will take what he wants. He lost the city but now he will claim it all back. Little cats or rats do not matter to him. You better run, run as fast as you can. I will get you all!"

Jack cannot make any sense of what the beast is saying. It all sounds familiar, but the stress makes it hard for Jack to hear his own thoughts. He tries a different approach. "What are you anyway? I saw nothing like you here. What kind of animal are you?"

The beast snarls again and his deep voice whispers one word, "Badger!"

Badger? Jack is not sure what this means. Is it the beast's name or is it a badger? Jack has never heard of it. Either as a name or an animal. He wished MooMoo was here; she would know, Jack is sure of if it.

MooMoo knows more of the world than anyone else in The Five Streets. She loves watching this TV thing, telling her all about the world.

"Badger? What is that? Your name?" Jack asks, to keep the conversation going. It gives everyone a break to recover and maybe to calm down. This is going to be a long day, and Jack is not sure if everyone will make it to the end of the day alive.

"It's him. Badger is what he is," whispers a voice behind Jack. Basil got closer to listen in, his eyes still full of fear, but Jack can also see a curiosity in it. The little rat has a taste for the unknown and adventures.

"Step back, Basil!" Jack replies. "For whatever reason, it tries to get the two of you. The only thing that stops this Badger from killing you is Azrael, Buddy, and myself. Stay back!"

Basil moves back to the far wall, behind Azrael. He whispers to Elliot again. Jack wonders what the two are whisperers about. What are they not telling him? Something is not right at all. Jack feels more and more that they all got played. Not only the cats from The Five Streets but also the rats and the Badger.

It feels very familiar and now Jack knows why. He had the chance to sort his thoughts out while talking to the Badger. It calmed Jack down enough to make some quick assumptions and comparisons. This is well too familiar to the situation he had with Reynard back then. They all thought it was a one off and by banning Thumbs, all this would stop. They were wrong the whole time.

Thumbs and Reynard have again just been pawns of a bigger play. The mastermind is still out there and for whatever reason, it wants it all, but what is all and who is this mysterious "HE"?

The three cats build a furry barrier between the Badger and the rats. It seems all the Badger wants is to kill Elliot and Basil, but it also mentioned that it knew the cats would come down into the sewers as soon as they found the dead cat. It was all staged, and the plan was to lead them all here.

Jack growls and wanders around. He's annoyed with being played like this, even more annoyed that he did not see this coming. Someone is planning and scheming much better than him. It feels like Jack is working against his own evil mastermind.

"One more question, Badger, who are you working for? Why did you bring us all here?" Jack asks with steel in his voice.

The Badger just keeps staring at Jack with his dead eyes. "Nothing more to say, little kitty. You are here now and soon you are not. I will kill you all. He told me to do it, and I must obey."

The Badger doesn't wait until he finishes his last sentence and jumps at Jack. His mouth is wide open, showing the sabre-like teeth, lots of them flashing towards Jack. Buddy and Azrael have no chance to react or to interfere. The Badger flies at Jack and both cat and beast crashing into each other into a pile of fur and claws. Jack hisses and bites, clawing at everything. He tries to find the eyes of the beast, thrashing around with his front and hind legs.

The Badger holds Jack tight and tries to bite him. His head moves around quick, trying to catch Jack's paws or legs. Jack moves his head as far away as he can, but the teeth get closer and closer to this throat. Jack feels his legs getting weaker and weaker. He cannot keep up with the ferocity of the Badger. It is too much for the little cat.

Buddy runs around the two fighting animals, trying to find an opening to jump in and free Jack, but he cannot find an opening. Azrael stays behind, holding his bleeding paw close to his body and trying to shield the two rats.

Buddy tries a few attempts to distract the Badger. Quick hits with his paws, he hopes it will be enough to get Jack out of the deadly embrace.

Nothing seems to work; the Badger focuses in on Jack. He wants Jack to be the first one to die today. That little cat does not know who he is or why he is here. Trying to talk to him was a big mistake.

"Wait, please listen! We are not your enemies! Stay down and let us talk!" Jack tries one more time to get through to the badger.

"Stay away, little one. I warn you; these sewers are mine now and everyone trying to get passed me will die! He told me you would come and try. Go, RUN! I have no option. If you stay, I will kill you. He knows everything. He will hurt my family and I will kill everyone to avoid this. Go on and forget about this place. Let him have it!"

The badger jumps forward, unexpected, and vicious. Jack still tries to understand what the wild animal just told him about its family and why he is here. The badger gives them no chance to reply. Its attacks are fast and dangerous.

Jack tries to keep the Badger away from him. He has no strength for any attacks. He uses all that is left of his strength to defend himself. Jack feels panic welling up inside him, flashbacks crossing his mind from the night Reynard nearly killed him. This is much worse. This time, he will not make it out alive. He sees Buddy trying to help, but nothing pulls the attention of the Badger away from Jack.

Jack feels a big hit on his back; something hits him from behind and throws him out of the deadly embrace with the Badger.

All Jack sees is a flurry of grey and red attacking the Badger with no remorse.

A much bigger animal has joined the fight and rescued Jack in the last second. Jack shakes himself and gets onto his legs.

He knows these colours and especially the smell. Reynard came to the rescue. That old, sly fox must have heard the fight and decided the cats need some help.

Reynard bites and claws at the Badger. The Badger is now in retreat, looking for a way out and away from the new enemy. This was unexpected for the Badger, and he does not know how to deal with that old fox. The fox is much stronger than the cats, and he moves, intending to kill. This is no longer fun. The Badger turns around and runs for the tunnel. Reynard tries to follow, but all he manages is a limping stumble. The Badger hurt him badly.

Jack shouts after Reynard, "Stop Reynard! It is enough for now. Let him go!"

Reynard turns his head towards Jack and his eyes are full of murder. Like the night they met the first time. Jack tries to keep his cool. "It is okay, Reynard. Let him go. Thank you for rescuing me! It was close. Boy, he nearly got me. Where did you come from anyway?" Jack tries to keep the conversation casual, hoping to bring Reynard back from the dark place he is in now.

Reynard licks his bloody snout, savouring the blood of his nearly prey. It felt so good to let it all go. He could let it all go, all his anger and fear. All he wants is to run after that Badger and finish it. It doesn't matter to him anymore. The last few seconds he felt more alive than ever, something he had not felt in a long time. But Jack needs him. He owes Jack his life. Reynard stops running after the Badger. He sits down and licks his wounds. That nasty Badger got him well, too. Reynard hopes he dished out the same way.

"What, Jack? What do you want now?" Reynard snarls back at the cat. "Let me be. This is my time, my chance to make things good again."

"What are you talking about?" Jack asks and walks over to Reynard. The old fox looks awful. He bleeds out of various wounds, and his left eye swells up. "Why are you here, Reynard? How did you know?"

"Let's get out of here. I need fresh air. This place smells," Reynard says and gets up, walking towards the end of the tunnel.

Jack forgot that this is the entrance from the woods into the sewers. The fight must have been a big commotion. Jack is sure even the rats back in the newer parts of the sewers could hear them fighting the Badger.

"Very well. Let's get out into the light. I need to get some fresh air myself, and I am sure the rest of us agreed we need some time to mend our wounds, too. Lead on, Reynard."

Jack makes to follow the fox and motions Azrael, Buddy, Elliot, and Basil to follow. The two rats do not move, and Elliot calls out, "You guys go ahead. We do not leave the tunnel. We will go back and send out some scouts. We need to find that Badger before it finds us."

Basil looks undecided. He would join the group to get a peek of the outside, but he cannot disagree with Elliot in front of the outsiders. He nods to Jack and turns around to follow Basil back into the darkness of the sewers.

"Strange little things they are," Jack thinks and follows Reynard out of the darkness towards the light at the end of the tunnel.

Chapter XIII

The cats and the fox walk into the light of an ending day. It feels good to be outside again with the sky above their heads. The air is fresh and welcome after the stench of the dark sewers. Jack and the cats must wait a few seconds for their eyes to catch up with the brightness of the outside. All three cats look banged up and in need of medical attention, but for now all they can do is follow Reynard deeper into the woods.

Jack can feel a different darkness surrounding them as soon as they leave the small field behind that separates the sewer entrance from the woods. It is not as dark as in the sewers, but something seems to lurk in the shadows of the woods. Jack is very weary and follows Reynard slowly, blaming his eyes and injuries for the small trot.

"Where are we going, Reynard?"

"Back to my den. Where else would I go?"

The three cats follow the fox in silence, each one's head full of their own thoughts. Azrael limps on his blood-soaked paw while Buddy grumbles to himself, unhappy with the outcome of the fight. They look like an awful bunch. Jack cannot wait to hear Gina's comments later when she sees in what state they all are. It makes Jack smile, thinking of Gina telling them all off like little kittens.

"What are you smiling at?" Azrael asks.

"Just thinking about Gina's fit later when she sees us. We are about to get an earful of 'I told you so'. That's for sure, and probably the delicate version of it."

Azrael seems to think the same as a smile crosses his face. He regrets it straight away as pain flushes his face from a big cut. The face Azrael pulls into makes Jack laugh even harder. Buddy only shakes his head and walks along with the other two cats in silence.

The three cats follow Reynard through the woods until they reach his den. The enormous trees swallow the sunlight and make the day darker as it is, but Jack enjoys being back outside, even if this part of the world feels off, the same way it felt off in the sewers. Jack and Azrael exchange a look. Both feel the same. It is better to be out of the sewers, but the danger is not over yet. The beast, the Badger, escaped. The cats and rats survived the attack thanks to Reynard, but something tells Jack this is not the whole story. Jack speeds up and walks close to Reynard.

"Say, what made you go into the sewers this time?"

Reynard looks at Jack, his eyes swollen from the fight with the Badger. Jack sees that beyond the pain Reynard's true pain is much deeper than the injuries he sustained from the fight. "Reynard? Talk to me! Why did you turn up in time to save us? I do not believe this is a coincidence." Jack tries to get through to Reynard, but the old fox just keeps in walking, looking now and then with sad eyes at Jack. Jack's feeling is going from bad to worse. Reynard is hiding something, and it is nothing good.

They reached the den, and Reynard finally seems to relax. He lays down and tends to his wounds. The cats follow him, and everyone tries to clean and patch themselves up.

After a while, Jack tries again to reach Reynard for some answers.

"Thank you again for helping us out back there. I must confess, we were a bit in a tight spot with this wild animal. I am glad you came by to help."

Reynard looks at Jack as if he just realized the cats are here with him. He continues to lick his wounds and starts talking to Jack, "Jack, I am sorry. I am so terribly sorry!"

"Tell me, why are you sorry? You turned up at the right time to save me and the others. Without you, this could have been much worse." Jack tries to comfort the fox, albeit he has a bad feeling that Reynard had not been there by chance to help them out.

"Jack, she made me do it. She found me here, all alone and weak. She came and used my weakness again. I am so stupid. I told her about the sewers and how to get into them. All I thought was that she wanted to go home."

"What are you talking about?" All three cats are all ears now. Azrael and Buddy move closer to the old fox. No one wants to miss what the fox will confess.

"I found the sewers ages ago, but never paid a lot of attention to them. They are a dark and foul place, nothing I would step into by choice. The rats tracked me the first time I was in there, but they let me go, only because I promised to keep out of their home and never return. That was until today."

"What happened?" Jack asks again to keep Reynard talking.

"I told her about the place I found underground and that it would lead her under The Five Streets. She told me all she wanted was to go home and apologize to everyone. I trusted her. In the end, it was partially my fault that she had to leave her home. "

"I thought helping her would help me. But I was wrong, so very wrong. She made me show the entrance to the Badger. I knew him. I know him and his family. We are practically neighbours here in the woods. She got into his mind somehow, the same way she got into mine. She said all the Badger is doing is checking out a safe passage for her, but I heard him killing the small poor rats guarding the entrance. I ran and hid; it was too much for me."

"Who did you show the entrance, Reynard? Who made you do all this again?" Jack asks, but the answer is already on his mind.

"Who do you think, stupid?" a voice from behind the trees, a voice they all know and will never forget.

Thumbs walks out from behind the trees, all smiles. She walks down right into the middle of the cats as if nothing could harm her. "Who do you think?" Thumbs repeats and this time her voice drips of poison.

"Did you really think I was done with all of you? That sending me away would solve all your problems? I told you he is not done yet. He is still watching and waiting. His plan is in motion, and you all are just pawns in his game." Thumbs sits down and licks her left paw to clean behind her ears.

Jack is shocked but not surprised. He got the idea the moment Reynard mentioned she is using him again. Thumbs is back, and she looks more insane than ever.

Azrael is the first one to recover from the shock of seeing Thumbs again. He looks her dead in the eyes and asks, "Thumbs, what are you doing here? We have banned you from The Five Streets. You know the price for breaking the law. Why did you come back?"

"Shut up, you little son of a stray dog! You have no power over me. I am not finished with the tasks he gave me. You think you can scare me with your laws and rules? We are now in control. Look at the world. It is crumbling. Change is coming, and he is making sure the change is in our favour. The time of The Five Streets is over. Your time is over!" Thumbs spits her words towards them all.

She has enough of talking; now is a time for actions. Thumbs jumps up and runs back into the trees. The cats hear her insane laugh out of the trees. Buddy runs after her despite Jack and Azrael trying to stop him. Both Buddy and Thumbs vanish into the woods. The only sounds they hear is the mad laughter of Thumbs. It seems to stay around them, mocking and haunting them.

"Buddy! Come back! Buddy!" Jack shouts.

"Buddy! Stop! Do not run after her!" Azrael shouts over Jack.

Buddy ignores both cats, and Buddy is gone. He is after Thumbs.

Azrael shouts at Reynard, "You little sly fox, I am sure you couldn't wait to betray us again! What have you done, you stupid fox?" Azrael is moving slowly towards the fox, ready to attack. "Let me finish now what we should have done back then. It would have saved us all a lot of time and pain. Come here, let me put you out of your misery once and for all!"

Jack jumps between Azrael and Reynard. "Stop it, Azrael! This is not the time for it. We need to get back and warn the others. Thumbs is back and she will not stop. She is nuts. Have you seen her and listen to her? She totally lost it. We need to tell the others about her. Everyone is in danger."

Azrael hisses at Reynard, a final warning. He will be back and finish him. It is an unspoken promise. Reynard runs into his den to hide from the cats.

"I am sorry, Jack, very sorry!" Is all Jack can hear before Reynard vanishes in the dark hole underneath the woods.

"Let's get out of here. Nothing more to do for us. Churchill needs to know about all this. He needs to make sure we are ready for any attacks on The Five Streets. The humans are off the streets; anything can happen now!" Jack talks quick and tries to animate Azrael to follow him back to The Five Streets.

"Come on Azrael! Let's not waste more time! The Grey played us and now we need to make sure it does not happen again!"

Jack runs back out of the woods; he turns his little head to see if Azrael is following. Azrael limps behind Jack as fast as he can, his little face full of anger and pain. Reynard was lucky, but Jack is sure it is only for a short time. Azrael will get him when the time is right. All Jack hopes is that the old fox is ready for it. Next time, he will have to fight his way out or Azrael will kill him for the betrayal. It makes Jack sad, but he understands this is now beyond his capabilities.

Reynard signed his death sentence by betraying the streets again. Azrael will now be his judge. Jack is sure the shadow cats will find their way into the woods as soon as they are back from whatever mission it is they are on at the moment.

Jack and Azrael choose the way back over the field. It is much easier and safer. They do not want to go back into the sewers, not today, not after the encounter with the Badger and another potential trap through Thumbs. Jack wonders what the rats are playing in all this. They seem to be honest and scared. Jack does not believe they are part of Thumb's plan or his plan.

The field flies past the two cats, both running as fast as their little legs carry them. Time is important now; everything has changed from a simple murder to an all-out attack onto The Five Streets by an old enemy. Jack slips through the gap in the wall and his paws touch familiar ground. They are back home. Azrael squeezes through a second later.

"Jack, you tell everyone about Thumbs. I need to check on something else first. I will meet you at Gina's place later."

Azrael does not wait for Jack to confirm he runs away into the opposite direction of Gina's home. Jack wonders what he is up to but agrees wordlessly and continues to run to Gina's cave.

He must warn the rest of the leaders as quick as possible. Jack runs down the empty road. He cannot see any humans at all. Jack tries to remember the last time he saw the streets that were empty; he cannot remember. For now, it suits him as he can just run down the street without the need of being careful, no cars, no humans around to stop him.

Somehow Jack enjoys the new won freedom, but he knows The Five Streets will pay a high price for it, eventually. He crosses the big car park and jumps over the hedge to get to the small entrance to Gina's cave. The moment he jumps up onto the hedge, a familiar voice stops him from jumping down straight away.

"Jack! Stop!" A familiar voice shouts.

It is Churchill running over from the bin storage. He must have seen Jack jumping over the hedge. The old cat tries to run over to Jack, but it is a more awkward waddling. The old cat is not as fit anymore. Jack waits for Churchill to arrive at the hedge.

"Churchill! Good, you are here!" Jack greets him. "I must share something very important with the rest of the leaders. Is Gina in?"

"Jack, glad you are back! Where is Azrael? Never mind. You have not heard it yet, I guess. Gina is with Cecile, but they are not at home. There has been an incident! One family has fallen ill. Everyone is freaking out about it, as the cats think it is this human virus. They think the family is ill from it, that it finally got to us cats as well. I do not believe it, but Gina and Cecile had to check for themselves. The whole street followed them. It is a bit of a mess, to be honest. I was on the way to get there myself when I saw you. Best we make our way over as quick as possible. The girls will need all the support they can get."

Jack is not sure what to make of what Churchill just told him. A panic in The Five Streets right now is the worst thing that could have happened. Is Thumbs somehow involved? And why now? A weird and unexpected coincident, another one of those.

"Let's go! I must see them all for myself. I am sure it is not the virus. Just another distraction from what is really going on here."

"What do you mean, Jack?"

"Lead on, Churchill. I will explain later."

Chapter XIV

Churchill leads Jack through the streets to where the family lives. A bunch of cats have already gathered around the area and the air is full of whispers. Jack ignores the other cats and follows Churchill through the noisy cats. Churchill uses his voice and body to make a way for Jack. He growls and hisses at the other cats. They should go back to work or seek other places to gather.

One cat makes the mistake of talking back. Churchill stops and just stares the cat down with his one glowing eye. All the cats around him take a step back and they suddenly look very interested in their own paws.

"Get back, all of you! Last time I tell you. Get away and let us through!" Churchill yells.

The old cat's intensity impresses Jack. He can handle crowds with ease. Jack wishes he had the same confidence the old cats just displayed. For Jack, the entire crowd seems intimidating and dangerous. He never felt bad about being around other cats, but that many makes him feel uncomfortable.

He wishes himself back into his little box, where he can forget everything that had happened over the last few months. Sometimes he wonders if his life would be better off if he lived secluded, like Reynard. He has seen the worst of his fellow cats in the last months. They steal, lie, and hurt each other for their own advantage.

For Jack, working the streets rather than leading them has been a real eye opener. There is so much going on that the leaders do not know about. It is scary the longer Jack thinks about it; the leaders are supposed to know everything that goes on in the streets, but clearly, they do not.

Over the years, The Five Streets have built their own little society without the involvement of the leaders. Jack stays deep in his thoughts while crossing through the cats. He tries to ignore them and not to listen to the whispers. Many mention his name in connection with a crime that might have happened to the family. All the cats around him are suspicious and seeing him does not help their fantasy of running wild.

Jack and Churchill make it to the end of the crowd, and they stand in front of a house wall. The wall has a crack, and the family lives behind this crack. Jack knows the three living there, a young family, a kitten just born a couple of months ago. The parents were lucky to snatch up this place before the birth and now own it officially, a gift from Gina. Gina was over the moon when she heard of a new arrival, born on The Five Streets. It does not happen very often. But now this family is in danger of being exposed to this mystery illness? Jack doubts this is just a coincidence. Churchill squeezes through the crack in the wall and Jack follows.

Inside, they find a big open space. It looks like a house should be there, but somehow it is just an open space between the wall and the actual house. A funny contraption, but in this case, a welcome home for a family. Jack looks around while Churchill guards the entrance. He can see Cecile talking to a young female cat, the new mother, and Gina leaning over another cat, the father.

The father does not move; his breath is very shallow. In the corner, the kitten sleeps, unaware of all the trouble.

The female cat looks worried sick, and she hold her paws tight on the floor. Jack can hear Gina purring; she is in the middle of trying to heal the sick cat. It must be serious if Gina tries to heal the cat right here and now, with no preparation for either the other cat or herself. Cecile looks tired. Jack guesses she took a turn, already trying to heal the male cat. Cecile looks over to Jack and calls him over to join the conversation with the mother of the kitten.

"Welcome back, Jack! Looks like you came back from the sewers at the right time. Gina and I just arrived here to see after this little family. Rumours have spread like a wildfire of them all being sick. I tried to heal the mother and the kitten. So far both are on the way to getting better, but the father has been in the worst shape. I tried to heal him, but nothing worked. Gina had to take over. She is working on him for over 10 minutes now. I am getting worried about both. Not sure how long Gina can carry on."

Jack looks around the house. The air is tense, and he can smell the sickness. He thought outside was bad, feeling the mood and tension of the other cats waiting in front of the family home, but inside here it is nearly unbearable. He wonders how Cecile and Gina can stand it.

"What is going on here? Azrael and I just got back and wanted to share the latest from our hunt, but it looks like the whole Five Streets have gone crazy. How are these three poor cats and why is everyone so worried about them being sick? It surely cannot be the human virus!"

"We don't know yet. All we know is that the father went out to search for some food. The family starved for days. He left the house, regardless of the danger of the soldier and the virus. The little we could get out of him is that he found food in one garden, the large ones in the richer area, close to 1st Street. He said it did not smell bad, so he took it home to share with his family. The father ate last, but the mother and the kitten ate less, leaving the majority for the father, so he could gain his strength and protect the family. The mother and father argued about this but at the end he gave in and ate all the food after the kitten and the mother helped themselves to what they thought is enough to keep them going. Mother and kitten are out of the worse, but the father is not recovering or responding to the healing. The food got poisoned. He ate most of it and is close to dying. No human virus involved at all, but we are not sure if the idea of poisoned food lying around the streets is the lesser evil," explains Cecile.

Jack listens and thinks about what he just heard. Another hidden threat joining the already complicated scenario. The Five Streets seem to be surrounded by threats. Physical and non-physical. Human virus, poisoned food, the badger, and Thumbs' return. How much more can The Five Streets take until they collapse? And why is all this happening at the same time?

Jack is close to believing this is all not just coincidence. But it would go too far to think someone is staging all these events. Jack is not sure yet if the events have a connection. He only knows the real threat is still out there, planning and scheming the downfall of The Five Streets, using pawns and claws to do what he tells them to do. All of them are at risk of the Grey. The only threat Jack can lay his paws on and feel it. He does not deny that the virus and poison are threats, but he does not control them. Thumbs and The Grey need to be stopped. They are Jack's priority. Right now, he needs to step away from the other issues or he will get distracted, and nothing gets solved.

"Listen Cecile, I know this is bad, terrible indeed, but we have much bigger problems. Azrael and I had the chance to face the beast in the sewers. The one the rats talked about. We had a fight with a Badger. A fierce animal, trying to take control of the sewers, right underneath The Five Streets. This is real, and we fought the Badger off for now, but only with the help of Reynard."

"Reynard? The sly, old fox?" Cecile asks.

"Correct. He came to help us out. But there is more to the story. I need you, Gina, and Churchill to join us in Gina's home as quick as possible. I cannot say more here, too many ears around. We need to get together as quick as possible. I know this here looks bad and I understand you and Gina need to help. Believe me, what we have discovered will make this sickness and the virus seem like a child's illness. We have to deal with multiple threats here, but the one we discovered is the only real one we can fight right now. I will leave you and Gina. Do what you can to help, but please join me as quick as you can. Time is ticking and we still do not know the full scale of what might hit us in the next few hours." Jack stops himself from telling Cecile more. He does not want anyone else to hear more. "I am going now. Azrael will be back soon, and I hope we all can have a catch up sooner rather than later."

Jack stops talking and takes one last look at Gina. The old cat is still deep in meditation, trying to help the cat's father to heal.

Her little face wrinkled from the concentration and stress. Jack hopes Gina will be alright. He knows how much it takes from her to heal others. He nods to Cecile and turns around, making his way back to Gina's place, but he wants to stop at his place first to refresh and sort himself out a bit, and to be honest, maybe to get another peek at MooMoo. Jack wonders how MooMoo is doing.

He moves out of the crack in the wall and is back onto the street. The cats are still sitting and standing around, waiting for any sort of update. Jack ignores them all for now. There is nothing he can do for them and anything he might say will be like throwing oil into an already furious fire. It will just blow up and make the already tense atmosphere explode.

He sees Churchill amid the cats, telling this one off or scolding another one. He tells them all to go back home, nothing to see here. But they mostly ignored him. It seems to drive him crazy. Jack walks over to him and whispers, "Let's get out of here. The more we stay around, the more rumours will develop. Gina and Cecile will finish up soon and join us in Gina's place."

Churchill looks away from the cat he just tried to tell to go home. He hisses at the cat and looks at Jack.

"Listen, I am not moving if her Ladyship is still in there. You know how they all are now. She will come out and they will jump onto her for answers. I will stay and makes sure none of these scoundrels bother Gina and Cecile. They have gone too far already, all of them!" Churchill raises his voice so all around him can hear his last sentence.

Jack stares at the cats, doing his best to look angry and annoyed at the same time. He tries to show as much authority as he can, showing them his leader's face and attitude.

He calls out loud and clear, "I think it is enough for all of you! Go home! We will not give any updates until the situation is clear. Right now, some of us need all our help. Not just the help from us leaders, but from you all as well. Make some room; you all generate so much pressure it makes it hard to breathe and concentrate for the healing. Think about the poor family. This is not about you; it is about them. They need us right now, more than anyone else. Go home, rest, and let us do our job."

The surrounding cats do not move. They just look at Jack and Churchill with hostile, angry eyes. No one want to go home and wait. The cats demand answers right now. They all want to know if The Five Streets are still safe or if it would be better to move on.

Jack feels how his words rebound off the hostile cats. He could not reach them. He hoped he could scare some away, make them understand that this is nothing more than a sickness because of rotten food. He thinks about mentioning the food poisoning to explain the sickness of the little family. His mind tells him it would not be a good idea to mention it right now. It would create an even greater panic. His few words only helped to increase the already overpowering feeling of fear and anger.

Jack thinks it is better to stop talking and let Churchill watch the crowd. Gina will know better how to handle the situation when she comes out. Jack does not trust his own feelings in this situation. He cannot afford to be affected by his emotions right now. He takes one last look around the place and strolls through the cats, head high and tail up, like a leader should. He said what he had to and now he leaves the cats to their own fate.

You either follow and listen or you decide for yourself to deny the order and live with the consequences.

Jack takes one more mental note of the most hostile looking cats around him. These are the ones they need to deal with later. These are potential troublemakers, or worse, spies for The Grey. He scans the faces and details for each one individual, taking mental pictures for later. He walks on as nonchalant as he can, not giving away his doing. The cats stay behind him when he reaches the end of the space.

Jack picks up his pace now, jogging towards his home. The moment he is out of the sight of the rebellious cats he runs. His little heart pounds heavy in his chest. He hates being a leader. It takes so much from him. It was worse for him to face all these cats than face the fox or the badger. His mind can deal with the direct violence and attacks of one individual, but feeling the betrayal of his own kind is a different matter. He feels let down by the cats in his own streets.

His mind tries to reason with their behaviour, tries to find answers and solutions but does not come up with a conclusion. That scares Jack the most. Every scenario he plays through ends up in the same unpredictable way. He cannot predict how and what the cats of The Five Streets might do next. Their behaviour is not logical, only emotional. He continues his run to clear his mind from the fear of what might happen next to his streets.

For now, his priority is Thumbs, The Grey, and the Badger. These are the three he needs to stop first; they need to be stopped. One threat. The Grey seems to be the biggest threat to them all. Jack needs to know more about this illusive, mysterious character, but how?

Jack must work on a plan to catch one of The Grey's minions alive. He needs answers and either Thumbs or the Badger will know a bit more about The Grey. Jack sees his path clearly in front of him, the path to his home and the mental path his mind is drawing to show him how to make his plans real. Thumbs and the Badger, both connected, both work for the same, the one who threatens The Five Streets the most. The Grey has a keen interest in The Five Streets. He brings an unwelcome disturbance into the streets. Something that has not been on The Five Streets for a long time. He brings unrest, mistrust, and fear. All the things the leaders tried to keep out of the streets for a long time. What is The Grey after? What is his goal?

Jack's little paws hardly touch the street anymore. He runs now with full speed, the same speed with which his mind is working on the next steps of his plan. He arrives out of breath and refreshed at his little box.

The run helped to shake off the fear he felt from the mob in front of the house. It was clouding his mind. Now he feels clear, ready to work on more.

He stops in front of this box; a thought just came to him. What if all this is not just related to The Five Streets? How about The Big City? The Grey wants The Five Streets, his entry point to The Big City. Where is Azrael? Jack needs his shadow cats right now; they are lost in The Big City. Are the shadow cats still to be trusted?

Plenty of food for thought. Speaking of food, Jack thinks it is time to have some. His stomach rumbles in agreement. He looks at the little cloth that protects his box from the weather and turns around. "Not yet. First some good food," Jack thinks, and he has the right idea of where to check for some.

Jack walks over to the garden of The Gracious Lady. Jack thinks it is worth another go. Maybe the lady has left some food. She looked after Jack like forever, and it will surprise him if The Gracious Lady suddenly turns out to be ungracious. He must check to be sure. And he might also get another glimpse at MooMoo. Not that he would admit it openly, but he misses her. The talks, the banter, everything. The outside world is just not the same without MooMoo around. Besides, MooMoo always has some good ideas and has helped him in the past with her input to his cases. And this one could do with another pair of ears or paws. What often helped is that MooMoo stays disconnected from The Five Streets politics. For her, the politics and laws are irrelevant, which often leads her to different conclusions. Jack loves her out of the box, thinking. Jack cannot wait to tell her all about the Badger, Reynard, and Thumbs.

"MooMoo will freak out when she hears what we have discovered today!" Jack smiles at the thought and runs faster to the end of the street to sneak through the hole in the fence into the garden. His second favourite place in the all the streets.

Jack is so deep in his thoughts and enjoying the idea of reuniting with MooMoo that he does not see the hole in the fence. He hits his head against the fence and looks up, surprised. Jack walked this way a hundred times; he can walk it with his eyes closed.

He never missed the hole in the fence. But right now, his little head pumps right against the metal fence.

Jack shakes his head and looks closer; no this is the right spot. The humans have patched the hole up. The shiny new metal looks back at him. Jack feels a panic creeping up inside him. They locked the garden down.

They fix the hole with new metal wire. Strong, shiny wire. Jack lifts his left paw, touching the wire, checking if it is there.

"Who would do such a thing?" he thinks and touches the wire again with one of his paws just in case his mind is playing tricks on him. They used strong wire and layered it over the existing fence to stop anyone from coming into the garden. "That is impossible!" Jack thinks and continues to inspect the barrier.

Jack tries to push the wire apart. Maybe he can squeeze his little body through a small gap, but the wire does not move. Jack cannot believe The Gracious Lady agreed to this. Jack walks around the fence, looking for another entrance to the garden. He remembers the time he climbed up the shed, but he cannot find the part of the fence that was low enough to help him get all the way onto the roof. His little paws try to get some grip on the fence, and he tries to use his claws to pull himself up, but nothing works.

Jack stops and lets his frustration out with a deep growl. This was not his plan at all. Another mystery right in his own street. Jack is sure the soldiers are to blame for this.

"Who do they think they are? Fine enough that the soldiers keep the humans in check, but interfering with our lives goes too far!" Jack takes a mental note to discuss the soldiers with the other leaders. He is sure they all feel the same way.

For now, Jack needs to find a way into the garden. It drives him crazy that he cannot get into his favourite spot and can't see MooMoo. Jack feels rage boiling up inside him. The whole day feels like he is losing more and more control. Losing control of the streets, the case, and in the end, himself.

He lets his anger out on the fence, slashing and scratching on the metal like a lunatic, letting it all out. His claws hardly leave a mark on the metal wires, but it feels good to let it out. It makes Jack wild not to have control over what is going on now. It all breaks loose inside of him in that moment and he thrashes around him and growls loud.

His thrashing becomes less and less frantic, his paws growing tired and his mind exhausted from the outburst. He stops and looks around, tired and a bit embarrassed for letting himself go like this. Time to get real again and sort his case out. In the end, he should only focus on the case right now, the only thing he can influence. Solving the case around the Badger, Thumbs and The Grey might shine some light on all the other things that are going wrong in The Five Streets right now. Jack takes a last, longing look at the closed entrance to his favourite garden and turns his back. Another mystery that demands solving, but for now, it must wait until later. For now, Jack needs to put his personal feelings to the side and work for the greater good of The Five Streets.

Jack walks back to this little box. He needs to clean up and use some quiet time to think. This is all progressing too fast for his liking. The virus has more and more impact on the world he knows and likes.

Jack can see now why Gina and Cecile are so worried about this virus. Even if it only attacks the humans. The cats will feel the impact, not directly but in a bad way too. Food will be less, humans will be on edge, the streets will not be safe any longer.

Jack can think of nothing to avoid what might happen with this virus, but he can avoid the meddling of Thumbs and The Grey in his streets. He managed it once and he will do so again. Jack enters his little box and cleans himself up. He purrs while cleaning and calming his mind at the same time.

The cleaning ritual works like a meditation on this mind. His purring becomes deeper and smoother. His thoughts focus on the one case that matters and pushes all distractions away. He puts himself into a meditative state to sort out his thinking.

He visits the sewers again and reviews the conversation and fight with the Badger. Everything is clear in his mind; he can call it upfront and review it from different angles. Jack deducts the scene in front of him to the bare minimum. He removed the other cats and the rats, his focus alone on the Badger. The Badger is the key to getting more information about Thumbs and finally about The Grey.

It amazes Jack how similar this case is to the firsts attempt of The Grey. This time he uses someone to attack the Streets from underneath. Last time, he used an outsider to stir up trouble on the streets. Both follow a similar pattern. The Grey uses fear controlling others. The Grey must know the dark and dirty secrets of the ones he uses and if not, he will use others to pressure his victim to comply.

Reynard was lonely and full of hate; the Badger is not lonely but fears about his family. Thumbs is greedy and jealous. The Grey knows how to use someone's vices against themselves to help him get what he desires. What does The Grey want? Why is he so focused on The Five Streets?

Jack circles back to the same rudimentary questions. What is it The Grey desires the most? Jack does not know enough about The Grey but getting the Badger and Thumbs will help him understand this mysterious criminal being.

"The Badger? He looks terrified, scared to the bones." Jack zooms in on the Badger, trying to get as much detail as possible from his memory.

Jack sees clearly now that behind the viciousness hides fear. Fear for the Badger's family.

"If I could find the Badger's family, I could use them for leverage to get the Badger talking. We will keep them safe, of course, with no threats. But it might just work to get more knowledge about The Grey," Jack thinks loud, feeling safe and relaxed in his little box. His fur looks better by now, the cleaning nearly complete.

"Time to see the rest of the leaders. Time to talk and sort this mess out."

Jack gets up and leaves his box. He has a plan in his head how to progress further with his case, but he needs Azrael and the shadow cats to help him. Finding the Badger's family will be hard, but not impossible with the help of the spy network Azrael has at his disposal.

Jack walks down the empty streets. He still finds it weird to move so freely through the streets. No human in sight. In fact, he cannot even smell them anymore. No soldiers either.

Jack guesses they have strict timetables for feeding, same as the cats in The Five Streets. Jack sees other cats in the empty streets. But they move quick and silent, full of fear being caught.

Jack looks around. It is so quiet, so peaceful without the noise the humans normally make. Something the cats could get used to.

No cars trying to hit the cats by speeding up last minute, no humans shouting, trying to shoo them away. Jack knows this won't last and better not, as the cats still rely on the food the humans leave behind, but for now, it is just nice. He walks with confidence on the streets and nods to the chilling cats as he passes by. He crosses the road and jumps over the hedge into Gina's home.

Jack arrives as one of the first ones in Gina's home. He had hoped the others would be here already. He makes himself comfortable on one of the colourful rags spread out throughout the old collapsed shed and waits for the others to arrive.

The next one to arrive is Azrael. He looks more concerned now. His little face all scrunched up.

"Hi Jack! How is it going?"

"Not too bad! How about you? You look like bad news!"

"Time will tell, but for now, let's say yes. But let us wait for the others as I do not want to repeat myself. You look freshly groomed? What did you figure out? I can see it in your eyes. You have a plan. But let's wait for the others. No one wants to repeat himself, not after a day we all had." Azrael sighs and lays down on a green rag next to Jack, stretching himself out long and curling up after with a satisfied look on his face.

"Always gets you, this place. No matter what mood you are in, you arrive here, and you feel all your worries stay outside!"

Jack agrees with a long yawn and a smack of his lips. Both cats follow their own thoughts while they wait for the rest to arrive to discuss what to do next in this crazy time.

Both cats get up as soon as they hear someone approaching through the tunnel that connects Gina's home to the streets. It is the perfect warning system, as it is nearly impossible to enter the home without being heard or seen.

The cat that is coming through the tunnel right now clearly doesn't care about being heard. For Jack, it sounds more like the cat is in a rush.

"Strange! Sounds like someone is rather in a rush to come in. I wonder who it is?" Jack speaks out loud to Azrael.

Both cats are up and starring at the entrance, waiting for whoever it is rushing towards them.

The noise comes closer, and Jack hears the paws rushing over the floor. Someone is indeed running to get here. Just as he finished his thought, the cat bursts out of the dark from the tunnel. It is Cecile, all out of breath. She stops in front of Jack and Azrael and tries to catch her breath to speak.

"Jack! Azrael! Good, you are here! We were not sure. Churchill is looking for you two, too. Come quick, no time to lose. There has been another murder!"

Jack jumps up and shouts, "What are you saying? Another murder? Who?"

Azrael is already running past Jack and Cecile; he wastes no time. "Come on, Jack! I will explain on the way!" Cecile shouts and turns to follow Azrael.

Jack shakes his head in disbelief and runs after Cecile and Azrael. "What is going on now?" he thinks and focuses his energy on running behind the cats.

The three cats cross through the tunnel into the open. Cecile overtakes Azrael and takes the lead. "This way!" Cecile shouts and runs down the street towards the direction of the Sewer entrance.

Jack and Azrael follow. Jack has a terrible feeling as soon as he sees the direction they are running. They just turn around a corner and Jack can see Gina, Churchill, and Lupine.

All three look up from something out of sight. All three cats look grim and concerned. Jack breaks out into a sprint, leaving Azrael and Cecile behind.

He arrives first and tries to see what the others hide behind them. Gina and Churchill step aside and Jack sees two tiny black eyes staring at him. Basil the rat sits in the middle of the now four cats and stares up at them with his black unblinking eyes. He smiles a bit as he recognizes Jack.

"Jack! So, glad to see you! Was worried these three would have me as a snack. They do not look very pleased to meet me," squeaks the little rat.

"Basil! What in heaven's name are you doing here? You are out of the sewers! What happened?"

The little rat sits up on his hind legs to be closer to Jack and whispers, "We found him as you asked us to do. We tracked the Badger. We found him and they sent me to tell you we found him."

"That is great news! But Cecile said there was another murder? Do you know who the victim is?" Jack asks.

"That's just it, Jack. We found him and he was already dead. Full of cuts and bites. Someone got to him before us. The Badger is dead and will not hunt us anymore."

"Say again? The Badger is dead?" Jack cannot believe his ears. His sound plan is falling apart before he could even share it. The Badger dead means no chance to get to the Grey.

"You heard right. The Badger is dead! The sewers are safe again! Oh, and Elliot wants me to show you the Badger. He is waiting for us. He thought you'd want to see the dead beast for yourself."

"Let's go, Jack!" Azrael jumps in.

Jack agrees. It would be good to see the dead Badger for himself. This is a very unfortunate happening, but he hopes it will help clear the sewers and The Five Streets from another danger. It only surprises Jack that no one asks the obvious. Who did it? Another murder, but everyone seems rather happy about it. For Jack, this is a bigger concern, and he cannot join in the happiness Basil tries to share.

"Right, let me see the dead Badger. In the end, there is still a killer on the loose and we might have just discovered his second victim." Jack looks around and let his words sink into the minds of the other cats and the little rat.

"Well, didn't see that coming." Azrael scratches his head and nods at Basil to lead the way down into the sewers.

Jack follows Azrael down into the darkness again. Another trip into the sewers and this time Jack is worried that they will get stuck down here in the sewers after dark. It helps to get out of the sewers and enter the welcoming light of the outside world. But they have no choice. To wait would mean to lose valuable time and potential new clues.

Basil runs as quick as his little legs can manage; the two cats close behind him. Basil does not stop to think twice and leads them deeper into the maze of wet paths and stinking sewer outlets. Jack's head hurts from the foul smells around them. He gave up trying to keep track of the way. His mind will remember if he needs to. For now, he tries to follow the rat rushing around corners and jumping over leaks full of disgusting water. Azrael is right next to Jack; he keeps quiet and follows every movement of the rat.

Every few steps Azrael would stop and scratch a mark into the walls or the path, a clever way to make sure they can find a way back alone if needed.

"Not far now!" Basil squeaks and vanishes around another corner.

The darkness makes it hard for the cats to look further than the rat's tail. It is an all-consuming darkness. They follow the rat by following the noise its little claws make on the hard floor. Luckily, the rat is not running much faster than the cats. For Jack, it feels like a gentle jog, and he can continue like this for a good while.

Jack turns the corner Basil just vanished behind and stops. They arrived suddenly in a bright room. The light breaks through the ceiling and makes Jack disoriented for a second.

His eyes are caught by surprise and need time to adjust. Basil stops and waits for the cats to recover.

"Sorry, forgot about that," he admits and smiles at the cats. "This place always gets me. It is creepy having so much light down here. Not natural. The humans broke the ceiling once and never fixed it. Now the sun and the streetlights shine in whenever they feel like."

"Never mind," grumbles Azrael, not liking it being caught like this. "Lead on!"

Basil continues to lead the cats further into the sewers. The light diminishes step after step until they are back into the darkness.

The next time Basil stops, the two cats nearly crush him. Jack stops as he feels the tiny rat tail touch his whiskers. The rat has stopped and sits still in the middle of the path.

"That's it. The body is right over there, not much for you to see from here. Go closer, but I will stay there. Not a big fan of dead bodies." Basil points with his left claw for the cats to carry on. "Elliot will wait for you. He also made sure you can speak to the two scouts who found the body. He thought you might be interested in hearing their part. I will meet you later." Basil turns around and leaves the two cats alone in the dark.

"A strange fellow, this Basil!" Azrael says.

"I know, but what should we do? Let's see that body he is so excited about."

Jack goes on and sees some figures standing further down the path. The path looks like any other path in the sewers. Nothing points out why the Badger might have been here and why he got killed here.

The shapes of the three rats are in the middle of the path, but Jack cannot see the dead body. He walks closer, slowly and on silent paws. One rat looks up as soon as he approaches them. Jack hoped he could get closer to listen in on any conversations the rats have. But they felt his presence early enough to shut up. One rat walks towards him to meet him halfway. Jack can see now the shape belongs to Elliot.

"Hello again! We always seem to meet at the gravest moments. Did Basil lead you down here safely? He was all excited about the opportunity to go up."

"He did well, but he seems rather disturbed by the dead Badger. Thought he would be rather dancing around and celebrating," Jack replies.

"Well, it shows how little you know about us. We might live in the dark, but we cherish all living beings. The same way you do upstairs in the open world. Seeing a living being dead is a waste of energy and it always causes a disturbance that is not welcome. The only thing that is remotely satisfying is that this time, the dead is one who caused many deaths himself."

"Show me what you got!" Jack is not in the mood for a philosophical discussion with a rat in the middle of the dark sewers.

"Very well, follow me. Watch out. The path is rather slippery, and not all of it is water."

Jack picks his way carefully. The last thing he wants is to step into some of the blood splattered around the path. Jack keeps his head low to the ground. He can see lots of blood splatters mixed in the puddles of water. But no sign of the body itself.

"Over there!" Elliot says and points into the middle of the sewer's path.

The body of the Badger is floating in the shallow water of the sewer canal. The only way to identify the body is the bit of black and white fur that sticks out of the water.

"Azrael? Help me here. We need to get the body out of the water. I need to see how the Badger got killed."

Jack walks slowly into the water. He was expecting cold water to flush over his paws and up his legs, but what hit his paws and legs feels more like a sickly warm slush. The water floats around his legs, and it feels heavy and full of unpleasant additives. Something Jack tries not to think about.

He works his way into the water and tries to push the dead body with his paws. Azrael joins him and pushes with one of his paws, trying not to lose balance and splash into the water. Both cats try to move the heavy, soaked body towards the dry path. Jack refuses to use his teeth to drag the body and he can see Azrael has no ambition to do so either. It is a hard job using just one paw and pushing the body towards the other side of the path. They make slow progress and feel the dark eyes of the rats watching and judging them.

The cats managed after a bit and a lot of joined effort to move the dead body out of the water. Jack and Azrael can see the Badger laying in front of them. Jack walks around the body, looking it all over. The body has been beaten badly. From the wounds and bite marks, Jack can clearly see that the rats did not do this.

Not even an army of rats would cause the same wounds the body has sustained.

"Look at this one here," Jack says to Azrael. "It looks like a proper bite; you can clearly see teeth marks all around the skin. Pointy little teeth. Little but still bigger than rat teeth. I think the rats are out of the suspicion as killers. Would be possible at first thought, but why would they have called for us? They would make the body vanish. No, we are here because Elliot is still worried. Look at this scratch; it looks rather familiar, but I cannot get it right now." Jack concludes his investigation and makes room for Azrael.

"Right, right? I see the same. Much bigger, much deeper. For sure, no rats. A bigger animal, I would even say a cat. Maybe a dog as well. Also, a dog bite would be much deeper, and I see hardly any marks on the neck of the Badger. Believe me, dogs also go for the throat." Azrael leans closer to the body; he takes a sniff to see if the smells can tell him more. "Pah, nothing other than sewer smells on this poor guy. Laying in the water didn't help to preserve any other smells that could help us."

Jack admires Azrael's attention for detail. He is glad Azrael joined him on this case. For one, Azrael hardly ever loses his mind, and he also has lots of knowledge he is happy to share with Jack. They make a good team.

Jack turns away from the body. He thinks the dead Badger has told his story as far as it could. Now Jack wants to have a look at the surroundings. If possible, the ground will tell him his own story of what happened here. If you know how to listen, everything has a story to tell.

Jack walks through the water again, this time less concerned about it. There was blood all over the path as he reached the other side.

He lowers himself down until his belly touches the concrete and looks over the path. He can see the blood, the water, and the rats. They sit there quiet and not moving, only their little heads following every move he or Azrael make.

Jack looks back at the splatters of blood. One is rather large and calls his attention. He walks over to it, careful not to step on any other splatters. The splatter of blood is big enough for Jack to see a paw print in it.

"Azrael! Did you step into any of the blood over here?" Jack shouts over.

"Do you think me an amateur?" Azrael shouts back.

Jack expected the sharp response. "Okay, if this is not yours and it is surely not mine, then who left the paw print I am staring at?"

Azrael jumps over to Jack, and both cats look at the paw print.

"Bigger than mine," Azrael says and dips his paw into some water and places the wet paw next to the bloody one. Jack can see both paws on the floor and agrees with Azrael. It is an unexceptionally big cat or another animal.

"Do you think this was Buddy?" Jack asks.

"Not possible! How would he come in and kill the Badger himself? I mean, he is bigger and stronger than any cat I know, but no, I am sure this is not Buddy."

"I agree. The bite marks are not matching either. And the scratches look too harsh for cat ones. Look, there is another one." Jack jumps up in excitement as he spots another paw print on the dry path.

Still red, but more dried and hardly visible in the darkness. Jack leans close, laying his head on the cold stone to have a better look.

"Wish we had some more light. We could follow the trail if we could see better!"

Jack keeps his head very low and follows the path, trying to spot another paw print or blood splatter. It looks like the paw prints are full of the killer's own blood and not only from the victim. The killer must have taken a good beating from the Badger too. Jack sees another splatter here and there. He follows them down the path.

"Come on, Azrael. I think I have a trail here. Let's try."

Jack keeps walking slowly with his head and body low, nearly crouching along the path. Azrael follows him. Both cats try to find more traces as they move along. Jack finds another paw print; they seem to appear more frequently now.

The killer is badly wounded and losing a lot of blood. Jack is moving faster now; his excitement about the hunt is growing with every paw print they spot. The darkness seems to fade step by step and Jack can see some light at the end of the path. They must walk toward one exit of the sewers.

"Look, we are getting out of the sewers soon. Whoever killed the Badger must have left this way. We are close. I can feel it in my whiskers!" Jack whispers with excitement.

"Let's be careful," whispers Azrael back. "Still plenty of dark spots around here to jump on to us."

Jack slows himself down. The last thing he wants is being jumped on by a wounded animal in the dark. Desperate and deadly. Jack wants to find the killer, but he wants to be the first one and not the last one seeing the killer. It doesn't help anyone if both Azrael and he are floating in the sewer water like the Badger.

Jack stops his excitement and put himself into a cool, controlled state of mind. This is a hunt, not a race. Jack needs to be all alert and careful or he will miss some traces.

He stops himself from running towards the light at the end of the tunnel and puts his head down again, looking for more paw prints or other leads.

Azrael is paying attention to the surroundings, leaving Jack to find the next clue. Together, they make sure the other is safe.

The cats move through the darkness like shadows, stepping on silent paws from one bloody paw print to the next one. The prints are getting darker and bloodier the closer they get to the end of the tunnel. For Jack, it is clear the killer is severely injured. Good for Jack and Azrael to follow the bloody paw prints. It couldn't be any easier. Jack only hopes they will find the killer in time to get some answers. Jack continues to walk into the dark; he can spot paw prints more easily now as the light breaks into the darkness.

"The killer left the sewers through here, no doubt about it!" Jack says. "Let us pick up the pace and check the end of the tunnel for more tracks."

Jack jumps up and runs towards the end of the tunnel, very much ignoring Azrael's protests to be careful. Jack can see from the blood alone that the killer might not be alive for much longer. The paw prints are fresh, the blood not dried yet. "Come on Azrael! Time is of the essence. We do not have all day to catch the killer. Mother nature will get the killer before us if we do not hurry!"

Jack runs as fast as he can. He knows time is very short. Finding the killer alive is all that counts for him right now. To get answers, the killer needs to be alive. Jack lost his chance with the Badger; he cannot afford to lose this fresh lead. Azrael keeps up with Jack and both ignore any sense of danger. All that counts is finding the injured animal that killed the Badger.

Jack arrives at the end of the tunnel; the light welcomes him, and he feels instantly warmer. The sewers are just not his place. An interesting and exciting place to explore but nothing beats the open sky, sun, and fresh air.

He stops and looks around the exit for some more tracks. The hard concrete path gives way to soft soil, another part of the woods as it seems. They just found another entrance or exit that leads into the woods. Every time they follow a lead, it ends up in the woods. Jack is a little concerned about this as he knows Buddy, Thumbs, and Reynard are somewhere in those woods.

"Look, here!" Azrael shouts. "Another paw. Weaker, but it leads into the woods. I am sure of it. And here, more fresh blood drops. We are very close!"

Jack follows the tracks like a dog. His head is hanging low above the ground and his whiskers scan the air. The blood splatters are more visible and more frequent now. The wounds must be deep and still bleeding. Both cats enter the woods, following the blood trail. The trees and bushes give cover for anyone to be seen too quickly. A bonus for Jack and Azrael, but also for the killer.

Jack breaks through a thicket as quiet as he can, his paws hardly touching the branches and leaves on the floor. He stops in the middle of this movement. One of his paws just touched a big puddle of blood. More than they have discovered before. He signals Azrael to stop where he is and points towards his blood-soaked paw. The puddle of blood comes out from underneath another thicket. Jack holds his breaths, his whiskers twitching and his ears up in the air. He hears a slow breath; someone is hiding in the thicket in front of them.

Jack moves forward, slow and inch by inch. He stops at the thicket and listens again to the noises. The breathing is slow and shallow. Whoever is in the thicket does not hide it. Jack checks the air; it smells of blood and worse. The killer is dying, that is for sure.

Jack takes a brave step forward and divides the thicket with his front paws. Azrael joins him and both cats push the thicket out of the way. In front of them lays a creature all curled up. Reddish fur, red from blood and from his nature, lays in front of them.

"Oh Reynard, what have you done?" Jack asks and lays his paw on the poor fox's head.

Jack lays next to the fox, trying to get his attention.

"What have you done? Reynard? Can you hear me?"

Reynard lifts his head a little. His eyes are hazy, and Jack sees a big cut along his neck. The Badger got him bad. Reynard tries to speak, but his voice is little more than a whisper, "Jack? Is that you? I did it! I killed the Badger! Everyone is safe again."

"Reynard, why did you kill Badger?" Jack asks.

"I had to do it. I messed everything up again, didn't I? I wanted to help you all, finally do something good. Thumbs is back. She got the Badger because of me. I did it again and again. I thought killing the Badger for The Five Streets and the sewers would give me some peace. Is he dead?"

Jack tries to listen to Reynard without letting his emotions overwhelm him. Reynard did what he thought was right. How could he know Jack needs the Badger to find out more about what is going on?

"I understand, Reynard. You did well! The Badger is dead, and the sewers are safe again. Why didn't you wait for us? Look at you? All banged up and hurt. We could have helped!"

Azrael looks at the fox and shakes his head. There is nothing the cats can do for Reynard.

"Jack, I am sorry! Sorry for all I did to you and the others. Please forgive an old, stupid fox!" Reynard whispers with his last breaths. His head sinks down onto his paws and he falls asleep for the last and final time.

Jack pats Reynard's head gently with his paw and closes his eyes. "Sleep well, old friend! I hope you will find what you are looking for on the other side!" Jack's green eyes fill with tears, and he lets them flow freely down his furry face. He looks at Azrael, but the Master of the Spies is rock hard as usual, with no emotions showing on his face.

"Let's go, Jack! Nothing for us to do here. Nature will take care of Reynard now."

Jack takes one last look at the sleeping fox. Reynard looks peaceful, just asleep. Jack turns away and both cats walk back to the Sewer entrance. A bad day just got worse. The case nearly solved itself, and Jack feels upset about the loss of a friend and the potential of an unsolved mystery. Now all he has left is to find Thumbs to get some answers.

"Azrael? Buddy and Thumbs need to be found. We have no other options left. We need help to find them."

Azrael agrees with Jack's idea, but he is not sure how to make this happen. Azrael knows what kind Jack is asking for, but now Azrael does not know where his shadow cats are and how to get them back to The Five Streets. For him, this is the much bigger concerns and mystery right now. He lost contact with them. Something bad most have happened. Terrible.

The cats walk into the darkness again. Jack wants to have a word with Elliot. He hopes the rat is still there. Jack's idea is to involve the rats for some spy work. Maybe they can find out some secrets around the sewers and the Badger. So far, they have been helpful. Jack hopes this help is still available after the sewers are safe again. Jack is curious about the true nature of the rats. It will show how honest the offer for cooperation was back then when they needed help.

The walk is only a short one. They do not need to look for tracks. Jack flinches every time they pass by a bloody paw print on the concrete. He is angry at Reynard for getting himself killed. The fox did not deserve to go like this. Jack had hoped for a better ending for his old enemy. But Reynard chose for himself. As he always did.

Jack keeps his thoughts to himself, and Azrael walks by his sides in the same silence.

They turn around the corner and have only a little further to go to be back at the murder scene of the Badger. Jack can already see that the rats have left. The Badger floats alone in the dark. Jack is not really surprised to find no one here. It fits his expectation and confirms that the rats are content with the outcome.

"Do you think we will find them?" Jack asks Azrael.

Azrael shrugs his shoulders. "Not if they don't want to be found."

The cats take a last look at the Badger, hoping for new clues, but there is nothing more to see. The only marks are from Reynard. The Badger and Reynard are both gone and with it, Jack's hope to find the true evil behind all this mess.

"That's it! I think we are all done here. How about we go back and report to the others?" Jack suggests. Azrael agrees without saying and both cats follow Azrael's marks back to The Five Streets, a much quicker way through the sewers.

The other option would have been to move back to the woods and finding their way home through it. A much longer walk back.

Chapter XV

Jack and Azrael climb through the hole back into the last light of the day. The world seems so much brighter after the time they spend underground. Jack takes a deep breath in; he can smell The Five Streets. It smells right to him. He stretches his legs and neck, shaking off the stress from the last hours. It was not all for nothing. One threat eliminated and The Five Streets are safer. The rats had the better outcome, which is for sure. Jack does not blame them for retreating and hiding again. They must rebuild and move back to their homes. The Streets always come first. The same counts for the sewers.

Azrael takes a deep breath himself. Jack can feel even the Master of Spies had enough of the dark shadows down there.

"What's next, Jack?"

"I think we should give a full report to the others and then we need to talk about the rest that is going on in The Five Streets. You can feel it, can't you? The streets are changing. Different times lay ahead, and we need to be ready for whatever happens next!"

Jack just finished talking when a small voice squeaks out of the sewers. "Excuse me, coming through!" A small head appears out of the dark, peeking out of the sewers with whiskers twitching all over. Dark eyes squeeze shut against the daylight.

"Is it safe to come out?" asks Basil.

Jack and Azrael look puzzled at the rat. Where did he come from? And why does Basil want to come out?

"All clear. Come out," Azrael says, and makes some room for the rat to crawl out of the hole.

"Well, I am glad I caught the two of you. Elliot sent me to let you know he is sorry, but he couldn't wait any longer. The Elders heard about the Badger's passing and things moved rather quick as you can imagine. We are going home. We miss it a lot," Basil explains, and all the while his little head swooshes around, he tries to see as much as he can. "This is a strange world you live in. It smells funny. And look up! There is no end to it! How scary! How do you all manage with all this space?"

"Calm down!" Jack says with a big smile on his face. Seeing Basil so excited is fun, but also cheers Jack up. The rats have not forgotten about the cats in The Five Streets.

"What brings you up here? You should be with your kind. I am sure you have lots to do," Azrael points out the pressing question Jack wanted to ask at the same time.

"Oh, right! I am here as official ambassador for the rats of the sewers. I am tasked with meeting your leaders and discussing the next steps of how we can work more together. The Elders are still keen on growing this fragile friendship with your lot. I am here to help and to learn."

"How about that?" Jack smiles even bigger. "A little rat amid cats. Who would ever think we would talk about friendship rather than seeing you as another source of food? Don't get me wrong, lots of us will see you as food. It will take some time to change these thoughts, but I think the rats could not have sent a better ambassador. I am curious to see how the other leaders react. Come on, let us get you into the world of The Five Streets!"

Jack turns to lead the way, but he gets stopped by a flattering noise. Something flies over their heads and lands right in front of Jack. A grey, fat pigeon lands right on Jack's paws. It steps back and looks with two crazy eyes at Jack.

"Speaking of food. Who ordered food on the go?" Azrael shouts out and jumps towards the pigeon.

The pigeon flies up and lets Azrael jump into the empty place. It flaps its wings a few times and lands behind the cats and the rat.

"Stupid kitten! I am not your food! I am here to give you a message!" the pigeon croaks with a deep voice.

The eyes of the pigeon mesmerize Jack. They move in circles all the time, never staying still.

"A message?" Jack asks.

"A message!" the pigeon replies.

"Out with it then!" Jack shouts back.

"Well, out with it then!" the pigeon shouts back and flaps its wings again.

"Okay, funny! What is the message? Azrael, stop it!" Jack stops Azrael at the last second from jumping onto the pigeon again. He was sneaking up on the pigeon while Jack talked to it.

"Fine. Just thought it would be a nice snack." Azrael sits down behind the pigeon and sulks. In the end, they haven't eaten properly for some time now.

"I am here to give you a message from an old friend of yours. Who is Jack? Must be you! He told me you like to put yourself in front." The pigeon points with its beak towards Jack.

"I guessed right then." The pigeon did not wait for any confirmation. "The message is for you. He wants you to know that this is not over. We have warned you! All of you. The signs were a clear warning, but you all choose to ignore it. He wants The Five Streets, and they will be his. You better give up and agree or you will have to accept the consequences. This is the last warning. Take it or leave it. He is ready for you!" The pigeon throws itself into the air as soon as it speaks the last words. It knows better than to trust cats.

"What a strange bird!" Basil says and looks after the pigeon flying away.

"That was rather interesting." Jack follows the pigeon with his eyes. His eyes sparkling with curiosity and excitement. "It seems like we rattled the right cage this time. Finally, a sign directly from The Grey. Azrael, we did well, I guess! The game is afoot now! More than ever! The Grey challenged us directly. No more hiding. We need to prepare. Lots to prepare. Let's move and tell the others about it."

Jack is as excited as he could be. Finally, his mysterious enemy has revealed himself. After all that had happened, this is a good sign. Jack now knows The Grey is worried and worried enemies are the ones making mistakes. "I am coming for you!" whispers Jack while he runs through The Five Streets. Azrael and Basil try to keep up with Jack.

Chapter XVI

Jack cannot wait to get to bed. The day was full of excitement, sadness, and fear. He now needs some time for himself to come to terms with all that has happened and what will happen in the future. For Jack, it is clear The Five Streets are still in grave danger. The message the pigeon brought earlier made it perfectly clear. The Grey will not rest until he controls The Five Streets. All the previous attempts had been to tell Jack to stop trying to interfere. Jack does not agree with that.

He is not the cat that would roll over and expose its belly at the first sign of danger. The Grey challenged The Five Streets and Jack is the one who accepted the challenge openly. It brought him closer to the cat that he should be. The kitten that arrived in the middle of a rainy night is no longer the same cat that is now taking care of The Five Streets and all its members, no matter if above or below ground.

The rats are now part of The Five Streets and together they will fight The Grey. All the other leaders agree with this as well. Cecile and Gina will still work mainly on the mental and physical impact of the human virus on The Five Streets, but both are aware and keeping ears and eyes open for any unusual events.

Azrael will spend some time away from The Five Streets. He admitted the loss of contact with his shadow cats, and he must see for himself what happened to them. As Azrael mentioned, he sent the shadow cats to collect more information about

The Big City and The Grey. Somehow both are linked, the city and The Grey. Azrael believes the answers are in The Big City. He will go himself. A dangerous undertaking, but Jack knows, no one would suit the job better.

Azrael will spend some time with Tabs before he goes. Tabs is the latest member of The Five Streets joining from The Big City. Both Tabs and Azrael have already worked on infiltrating the city. Both are keen to take the next step in their plan.

As for Jack. Now, all he can think of is some rest to sort his feelings. Losing Reynard was or is very hard on him. He hoped Reynard would have found a better life after everything. But Jack understands the motive behind Reynard's doing. He just wished he could have helped the fox more. Nothing Jack can do now, but he wants to take some time to mourn his loss of a friend.

Jack walks the streets and plays the last few hours back in his head. The talk with the other leader went well. Everyone accepted Basil's presence and the offer of the rats of the sewers to share information and to help each other. It is a big step for both sides to open to the other, but it is the right way. The only way to fight the coming threat. It puts a smile on Jack's face when he remembers the excitement the little rat showed for being up here in The Five Streets. Everything was so new to him, and he asked thousands of questions. Jack cannot wait to go back into the sewers and see the world below with his own eyes, exploring and learning more. It is a shame that they all met under these dire circumstances, but they might have never met if not for The Grey.

Jack is deep in his thoughts about the event of the last few days. He walks past the garden of The Gracious Lady, straight up the little sidewalk where his box is, his home. He is so deep in his thoughts that he nearly misses the alarm signal his whiskers are sending to his brain. Jack feels he is not alone; someone has been here.

Someone has moved the cloth that covers the entrance of his box. His whiskers tell him something is in the air. Jack stops immediately and scans the area. He smells the air. He tries to pick up any sounds with his ears. So far, his two senses discover nothing unusual. His eyes wander over the box. It looks like always; it has moved only the cloth. Someone made it into his box. He lowers his body to the ground and sneaks closer. His paws make no noise, and he stops in front of the cloth. No signs of danger, but he can see someone went in. He lifts his left paw and pushes the clothes to the side.

"Hello, Jack!" whispers a familiar voice out of the darkness.

"Who is there?" Jack whispers back. He steps back from the box and gets himself ready to pounce as soon as the invader shows up.

"I was waiting for you. Didn't know where else to go. It has been a while for me. The outside is so different now."

Jack cannot believe his ears; the voice sounds like someone he knows better than anyone in The Five Streets. "Can it be?" Jack thinks and moves to push the cloth away again, but this time he puts his head through the hole to have a look at the mysterious voice.

"MooMoo?" Jack asks into the darkness of his own box.

"Yes, Jack?" MooMoo answers.

To be continued...

Acknowledgments

23. November 2022

This is my second book about the Adventures and Mysteries of Jack the Cat. The journey so far has been exciting and painstaking. What gets me going is the knowledge of all the Jack fans out there. I hope you enjoyed reading the second book as much as I enjoyed writing it.

It is thanks to all of you I can continue to write and make a childhood dream come true. At the end, I am getting closer to becoming a writer rather than an archaeologist. My second biggest dream after being a writer. You never know. So far, the journey has opened new doors and experiences I never thought possible.

It took me a little longer to complete the second book, but be assured the third one is already in progress. We need to find out about MooMoo, don't we?

I want to leave a few special thank you to the following people:

Rosa M. you have been my rock throughout the whole time.

Megan, my fantastic Editor. Your comments and ideas made this book even better, as it was in my head.

VIKnCharlie from Fiverr for creating the fantastic cover for the book.

Friends & Family who kept asking for the second book, you drove me further and motivated me when self-doubt rose.

Fans of Jack! What can I say? You are the core of all this! Writing this story was a great pleasure and I hope you enjoyed reading it!

If you liked The Adventures of Jack the Cat, then tell a friend about the books, spread the word on social media or leave a review on Amazon for me and Jack. It would help an independent author like me immensely.

Follow me on Goodreads, Facebook, Twitter, Instagram, or any other social network I cannot think of right now. Help Jack and myself to grow beyond our imagination.

www.SvenRodriguesWagner.com

Printed in Great Britain
by Amazon